Children of the Stars:
The Zodiac Modified

A novel by Herbert E. Menhennett

[redacted]

Green Ivy Publishing
1 Lincoln Centre
18W140 Butterfield Road
Suite 1500
Oakbrook Terrace IL 60181-4843
www.greenivybooks.com

ISBN: 978-1-945058-51-6

[redacted]

Preface

Thousands of years ago, the twelve signs of the zodiac were created, using a person's birth date as the basis of their calculations. However, the moment of conception and the initial combining of the DNA could help explain the cycle of differences among humans. The combination of DNA at the moment of conception could be influenced by very small amounts of energy, such as varying pulls of gravity, depending on where you are on Earth, the time of day, the phase and pull of the sun and moon, even the position and pull of the large planets. In addition, the sun creates varying amounts of radiant energy that strike Earth differently depending on your location during conception. These varying conditions could influence the combining of DNA as life is created.

What happens during conception in a zero or lower gravity and higher or lower radiation environment, as might be found in outer space or on other planets, is yet to be experienced; the resulting human physiology, personality, and intelligence could be very different. Yet we are counting on these differences being acceptable because the human race must leave Earth's influence and start to populate the Universe.

This story is about that first adventure into the possibilities for the human race to reproduce outside the friendly confines of Earth. The zodiac will need to be modified.

Sometime in the near future...

Foreword

Fresh out of the Navy's Top Gun program, Lieutenant Niels Borgue was very proud to be selected for the American space agency's latest astronaut team. It would be his first assignment into space. Okay, it was only a four-month mission to the International Space Station, and many had gone before him, but *space*—every young man's dream.

As the rocket plane, slung beneath the high lift–high altitude transport carrier, left the ground, Niels felt a sense of pride; he remembered the sendoff from his friends and family in his small hometown in Minnesota, a delight that he would never forget. Even pretty, young Nancy Ollofson came to see him off. Well, he might look her up the next time he was in town.

Irina Karpov had been on the ISS for three months when she saw Niels come through the port, and she knew immediately that he was the one for her. She had one month left to go on her assignment before she was to return to Russia for further assignment with the Russian Space Federation.

After an exciting trip into space, the rocket plane docked with the ISS, and as Niels entered through the port, the first thing he saw was Irina—her sparkling blue eyes, light blond hair floating in the weightless cabin. She was beautiful, and he was smitten.

The confines of the ISS left very little room for personal space, but the sleeping quarters and exercise area could leave a courting couple some privacy. Over the next month, Niels and Irina developed an intimate relationship; she was a science officer doing experiments, and his assignments as a junior officer were to assist the technical crew, including repair work outside of the ISS. They passed each other often in the narrow passageways, and gradually he got up enough nerve to speak to her. Their relationship slowly developed into something more than casual, but it wasn't until Irina's last night on board that she invited Niels into her sleeping quarters, and then into her bed.

Niels promised to take leave and travel to Russia after finishing his next three months on the ISS, and tears came to his eyes when she left through the port to return to Earth and Russia.

Acknowledgements

First I would like to acknowledge my editor at Green Ivy Publishing. This being my first book, I had no idea what was involved in bringing forth this attempt at writing. I could not have done this without her guidance and support.

I want to thank Chantal LaPointe, my granddaughter who helped design the book cover. She is a very gifted young lady. I would like to thank my other nine grandchildren for their patience in waiting a long time for this book. This story is for them and all the young people of future generations that may have to experience some of the things that occur in this story.

Lastly, I would like to thank my wife Jean who encouraged me to write this novel. She has been very supportive, extremely patient, and my toughest critique. Without her, this book would not exist.

Chapter 1

The President of the United States, Samantha Atwood, stood before the joint session of Congress to give her first State of the Union speech after her first year in office. She was very confident and commanding in her posture.

She was dressed to impress—not only as a leader of the free world, but also as a very attractive and alluring woman. Her husband, the first First Man, helped her choose her attire for this occasion. She was wearing black high heel pumps, and her long legs were accentuated by the short black skirt that hugged her slim frame. Her blouse was light blue with short but full sleeves, and modestly low in the front.

She looked out over her audience in the impressive old meeting room, the congressmen and senators seated together independently of their political affiliations, the justices of the Supreme Court, and the Joint Chiefs of Staff. But mostly she made eye contact with her husband, Ray, and their two children, Tony and Susan, who sat with him. Without these three and their never-ending love and support, she would not be here. This was their celebration.

"I will close with this: the economy is sound and growing, we do not have an army fighting a war in some foreign land, crime is down and our prisons are becoming emptier every day, our gross national product is growing, and unemployment is at four percent. It is time for us to take that first step off this planet.

"I have authorized the American Space Agency to plan and execute a mission to Ceres, the largest of the asteroids in the asteroid belt between Mars and Jupiter, to establish that there is usable water there and to establish the beginnings of a base that will be used for future exploration. This mission is fully funded from the current budget. All I request from you is your support and blessing to the mission and crew who will represent the United States in front of the whole world."

The standing ovation brought tears to her eyes, and she was overwhelmed with the support that she had received during her first year as president. She was determined, promising to herself that she would not let them down.

♈

Later, in the Oval Office, President Atwood challenged her chief science officer, Bill Worth, and the head of the American Space Agency, Dr. Charlie Gonzales. "You gentlemen have full authorization to go ahead with the Ceres mission. Get it right, on time and on budget. Charlie, have you chosen a crew?"

"Yes, we have, Madam President. The mission to Ceres will be led by Commander Niels Borgue. This will be his fourth and final mission into space. He is married and has two sons, Alan and Jon. He has earned the respect of all of his peers at the space agency. He will become the director of mission planning after this mission and will finalize a mission to Mars that has been in the works for ten years. Captain Scott Nettles will be the science officer. He has been married for one year, with no children.

"These two men will land on Ceres. Captain Nettles will be responsible for the water collection while Commander Borgue will set up the equipment for the automatic communication and science base operation. Captain Bill Lee of the US Air Force will be the space plane pilot and will orbit Ceres while Commander Borgue and Captain Nettles are on Ceres' surface. Captain Lee graduated from the Air Force Academy and is single."

It's still a man's world, President Atwood thought to herself; she was going to have to see why there were not more female astronauts and start to change policy to that effect.

She concluded by saying, "Fine, gentlemen. Make sure that we are on schedule. I understand that it will take not more than two years, and I am sure that the American public will be excited with this mission."

Chapter 2

Two years later, the high lift–high altitude carrier plane took off as planned. The event was televised around the world. The crew was in the cabin of the space plane, which was configured as a gliding plane, its wings swept back for travel through the upper atmosphere, as well as the trip to the Ceres Cruiser in orbit around Earth. The *Ceres Cruiser*, a ship built in orbit, was never intended to enter any atmosphere. Attached to the *Ceres Cruiser* was the *Ceres Lander* and all of the equipment that the men would need while on the Ceres.

The *Ceres Cruiser* would rendezvous with a special refueling station in orbit 22,500 miles above Earth, where it would take on the fuel required for the Ceres mission. From this refueling station the crew would leave and be on their way to Ceres. This was a very long trip, but the *Ceres Cruiser* had been configured such that the crew had Earth gravity by rotation of the spacecraft. The crew had not only quarters, but an area that would be for common use as well.

Eight months later, with Commander Borgue and Captain Nettles in the *Ceres Lander*, Captain Lee stopped the rotation of the *Ceres Cruiser* and fired the separation rockets, and the *Ceres Lander* was sent to its destiny with Ceres. The target was one of the two bright white reflecting areas that looked promising for water. The landing was successful, and both men started their separate activities.

The water sample vacuum collection bottles were made from glass that had been sterilized. The bottles were partially contained in metal canisters that protected the glass from breakage. Because the spacesuits the two men were wearing were very cumbersome, the process was slow. Commander Borgue finished with his task of setting up the functioning base camp for future use and asked Scott, "Can I help you finish? I'm anxious to get out of here. This is not a very appealing place, and the window for launch back to Earth is very small. Our return trip will be longer if we don't leave on time."

Scott replied, "I have six of the bottles finished and ready. I'll fill the other six, and you close them up."

They carried on, but Commander Borgue had trouble closing the final bottle and left it partially open, exposing the glass portion of the bottle. He thought that they could properly close it when they got back to the *Ceres Cruiser*. The twelve containers were loaded, and the two astronauts entered the lander and were happy to lift off for rendezvous with Capitan Lee and the space plane.

"Okay, let's transfer the water samples and stow them for return to Earth," said Scott. The lander had been docked with the *Ceres Cruiser* for transfer of the team and the samples. After all had been transferred, the *Ceres Lander* was jettisoned. The cruiser's rotation had been stopped for this portion of the mission and would be restarted after they left the asteroid's orbit.

"Damn," said Commander Borgue. The last containment bottle struck a bulkhead in the *Ceres Cruiser*. The lid that was partially attached opened. The glass broke. The water was floating in the weightless cabin, and the crew had to try to capture the small liquid globules, which was almost impossible to do. Commander Borgue made a decision. "Forget it. The water will not cause any problem, and we have to leave now!"

They blasted off and left Ceres for the return to Earth.

Later, once they were on their way, Commander Borgue made his report to mission control.

"Yes, the water is in all parts of the ship, and we cannot capture and contain all of it."

"Okay, the *Ceres Cruiser* is contaminated, but it will be sent into outer space after you transfer to the space plane for return to Earth. The space plane will also become contaminated when you enter it. It will also be secured into the quarantine facilities when you land," returned Mission Control.

The space center started to prepare a class-five quarantine facility sufficient for the crew and space plane. This facility also contained an adjacent lab set up to analyze the water samples that had been collected to ensure that the water was normal and not contaminated. All missions to land on extraterrestrial bodies must remain in at least three weeks quarantine. This was true of the first astronauts that landed on the moon in late 1969.

After the crew entered the space plane, the cruiser rockets fired, sending the *Ceres Cruiser* out into space, never to be seen again. The space plane entered stable Earth orbit and remained there until the facilities at the space center were ready; then it fired its retro-rockets to slow it down as it entered Earth's atmosphere. The space plane's wings folded out when the craft was slow enough and became a glider similar to the old shuttle. The space plane landed smoothly at the space center and taxied into the special quarantine facilities.

Addressing Scott and Bill, Commander Borgue said, "We are back from a successful mission, and I want to thank you both. However, our part of this mission is not over. Mission Control estimates that we will be in quarantine for at least three weeks, so settle down, get comfortable, and break out the cards."

Chapter 3

The quarantine facilities at the space center were old, the same ones that were used in the past. They had been designed for only three weeks of confinement and were not very comfortable. All three men had made phone calls to their families, telling them that they were safe and in quarantine. After being away for such a long time, all three men were looking forward to long vacations with their families.

From inside the quarantine facility, Commander Borgue spoke into the intercom a little bit testily, "We have already been in here three weeks now. Can't you speed things up a little?"

Dr. Tom Cuttle, the man in charge of the quarantine investigation team, replied over the intercom, "We are working twenty-four hours a day, but we have found something we cannot identify. It is in the water that you brought back, but it is also present in the blood samples we took, presumably from the water that spilled in the cabin. You all have ingested some of the Ceres water."

"Are we in danger?" asked Niels.

"So far we have not seen any adverse effects in your physiology," replied Dr. Cuttle. "It is just there in your blood and body fluids. By protocol, we must test this single-celled organism against any effects it may have on all other living things on Earth. This will take some time, so bear with us a little longer."

Niels turned to Scott and Bill. "You all heard what he said. We will be in here until they can clear up this mystery. You must tell your loved ones that this delay is normal, and do not reveal any specifics to anyone. That is an order. We cannot let this cat out of the bag until the science team figures this out." Niels was a natural leader, and his voice of command was smooth but forceful.

One week later, Dr. Cuttle contacted the crew on the intercom with an update. "The good news is that this organism does not harm humans, so you are safe. However, you are all carriers for what we are now calling the ARC1 bacteria. This organism thrives in water and grows very quickly, just like the bacteria that naturally grow in our bodies. The bad news is that ARC1 can destroy any grain plant it comes in contact with."

At this point, Niels realized that they were in for the long haul. He would not be released to see his wife and family any time soon.

He said to Scott and Bill, "It looks like I made a bad decision to bring that partially closed bottle of water with us. It would have been better to just leave it on Ceres."

Dr. Cuttle continued, "As you can imagine, this effect cannot be unleashed on Earth as it would decimate all grain crops. World starvation would occur. It is possible that we could genetically engineer strains of grain that would resist ARC1, but that would take years and we would have to replace the whole world's crops.

"I have informed Bill Worth, the president's chief science advisor, of our findings so far. He is meeting with President Atwood as we speak, and she will call you soon. I am sorry to be the bearer of this bad news, but you are safe and I'm sure we can come up with a satisfactory solution soon. In the meantime, you must stay where you are until further notice."

Niels looked at Scott and Bill while he replied, "Can you not destroy this thing in us?"

"Yes, we could incinerate you and this facility to destroy the ARC1 bacteria."

Holy shit, thought Niels, I hope no one else thinks that solution is the only one.

Dr. Cuttle continued, "I for one will not recommend that solution for you, but I am recommending that we burn the whole quarantine facility, including the space plane, and that we irradiate the water that you brought back in order to neutralize it. We are looking into chemical ways to attack the organisms in your bodies, but so far it is very resistant to any chemicals that are also safe for you. We will keep working and keep you informed."

The seriousness of Dr. Cuttle's voice and the worried look on both Scott and Bill's face gave Niels a fright, but he knew that he must remain firm in front of his crew and be the leader he knew was necessary to maintain some degree of sanity given the situation.

"We will do as you say and await a call from the president. Let me know if there is anything we can do from here to help the science team resolve this problem," replied Niels.

To Scott and Bill he said, "I'm very sorry that I have put you into this situation, but as you know, missions like these can be dangerous and have many surprises. I will be here with you, and we will get out of here together."

"Thanks for your support, but this is not your fault," said Scott. "We all made that decision, and we are all equally responsible for the current situation."

Chapter 4

In the Oval Office, Bill Worth was updating President Atwood concerning the situation with the crew and their plight.

The history between Bill Worth and President Atwood had not been good. After she won the election, she appointed Bill as her chief science adviser as a favor to Senator Jake and Vice President Conrad in return for their support in the national party conference. Since then, Bill had opposed everything she had tried to do in the area of environmental reform. She wanted long-term solutions to climate change, and he always supported big business and their interest in having cheap energy at the expense of Earth's environment.

Summing up their current problem, she said, "So the crew is infected with ARC1, as you call it, and if we let them out of quarantine, the ARC1 bacteria will spread around the world, destroying all grain plants. How in the hell did we get into this fix, and how do we get out without alarming the whole world?"

The president was exasperated, confused, and thoroughly perplexed at this dilemma.

"We have it contained," Bill Worth said. "I recommend that we burn the whole quarantine facility, including the crew, and call it an accident. Those few that know can be bribed and kept quiet."

Anger flashing in her eyes as she paced the floor, President Atwood replied, "I can't believe that you made that appalling suggestion! On the other hand, this sounds like a typical solution from you. I will hear no more suggestions like that, Mr. Worth. Those men are American heroes. You can leave now, and clear your desk. I never want you to show your face around here again. And remember your secrecy oath. You cannot talk to the press or anyone else about your work here."

Bill sputtered a protest, but one look from the president sent him heading for the door.

"Lori, call the vice president in here as soon as possible, and get me Charlie Gonzales on the phone," President Atwood asked her secretary.

"Dr. Gonzales on line one," said Lori shortly.

Samantha picked up the phone. "Dr. Gonzales, I have just been briefed concerning the situation at the space center. You must take personal charge of this situation immediately and ensure that no information is released. You will report directly to Vice President Conrad. Bill Worth has been relieved of his duty and no longer works for the White House. Remember, I want maximum security protecting those men at all times."

"I understand completely and agree. I will travel to the space center today and stay with the crew for the duration," Dr. Gonzales replied. After sorting out the details, they hung up.

Samantha was deep in thought when Lori announced that Vice President Conrad had arrived.

"Send him right in, and get me Diane right away," ordered Samantha. Diane Goldstein was the White House chief of staff and the president's right hand man when it came to the pressing needs of her office. She was the president's campaign manager during elections, and she was trusted to run the White House staff with a firm hand.

Samantha shook hands with Jim Conrad as he entered, taking a seat at her direction.

"Hello, Jim. We have a serious situation, and I need your help urgently. You are to drop all that you are doing or delegate where necessary and personally oversee this," informed Samantha.

"What is the problem?" asked Jim. During the last election, they were on opposite sides in a bitter run up to the Republican convention, where the ballot ran four times before Samantha made a deal to accept Jim as her vice presidential running mate. Together, they easily overcame all opposition, and Samantha was elected president. This was the first sensitive assignment she had asked him to do, and she was not sure of his total loyalty yet.

Samantha filled Jim in on the details and continued, "I don't have to tell you that if news of this gets out, the whole world will be up in arms, demanding that we destroy this organism completely, which means sacrificing the crew. That is unacceptable to me. We must find a better solution. Bill Worth recommended that we burn the entire quarantine facility, crew and all, and call it an accident. I have fired him, but he is a loose cannon. Watch him carefully. I don't imagine he will go quietly and is sure to stir up trouble."

There was a knock on the door. Diane entered the Oval Office, and President Atwood quickly filled her in on the situation. "While Jim oversees this issue, I want you to escort Bill Worth from the White House and see to it that he has no further access to this or any other issue. In addition, I am worried about what he will do concerning this potential disaster, especially if he goes to the press. Work with Press Secretary Filburn to discredit Mr. Worth and come up with a valid reason for his resignation. Also explore recommendations for his replacement. Thank you, Diane."

As Diane left the room, Jim sat, thoughtfully wondering if he was being set up for failure or if this was his opportunity to gain favor in the eyes of the media and the public. He decided on the latter and responded, "I understand, Samantha, and I will do everything possible to find a solution acceptable to you, the world, and, most importantly, the crew and their families. I recommend that we keep a lid on this for now. We must move the crew to a more secure facility and burn the space plane and the facilities at the space center as soon as possible. I suggest that we transfer the crew to the Center for Disease Control facilities in Atlanta. They are best suited to handle this sort of crisis. Can I ask your permission to talk to your husband? Dr. Atwood is family, and we can certainly trust him with this problem. My understanding is that he is familiar with the staff and facilities at the CDC, and I would like to put him in charge of the crew, if he is willing."

"Great idea. I will ask Ray to meet with you and take over responsibility for the crew. I will call the crew to let them know our thoughts and give them an open line to the White House. Get the ball rolling and report daily on your status. And thank you for your support. This will be a tricky problem to solve," President Atwood responded, warming a little to Vice President Conrad. As the vice president left, she called over the intercom for Lori to contact the crew via a secure phone.

♉

From the quarantine facility, Niels answered the phone. "Hello, this is Commander Borgue speaking."

"Commander Borgue, this is President Atwood. Please put me on speakerphone so the rest of the crew can hear."

Niels had some concerns that the easy solution for the president would be to sacrifice the crew in the interest of the rest of the world. He wasn't sure why he was talking to the president and not to Dr. Gonzales or someone else in the chain of command.

"Yes, Madam President." A few seconds later, he said, "We are now on speakerphone. Captain Nettles and Captain Lee are here."

The President began, "Gentlemen, please let me extend my concerns for your well-being and for placing you in this position. I have been fully apprised of the situation and have taken action to protect you and start the process of finding a suitable solution. Vice President Conrad will take the lead, and my husband, Dr. Ray Atwood, will be at your side as a direct liaison. Charlie Gonzales is on his way to the space center to help arrange your transfer to the CDC facilities in Atlanta, as well as start the process of destroying the space plane and the quarantine facilities. Ray will lead the team at the CDC in troubleshooting solutions to destroy that strange organism you have in your bodies.

"You have been in quarantine for three weeks, and it is my understanding that the plan was for you to be in quarantine for a max of three weeks. I realize that you must talk to your families. However, I request that you keep your conversations normal and do not talk about ARC1 until I tell you to. After you are moved to the CDC, I plan to address the United Nations. This could possibly concern the whole world, not just the United States, so I will tell them the whole story and show the space plane and facilities being burned."

"Thank you, Madam President, for your concern and support. We will talk again when we reach the CDC," replied Niels.

"Call me Samantha when we are having a private conversation and Madam President when others are present, okay? Goodbye and good luck," said Samantha.

Chapter 5

Bill Worth and Lori were cuddled up in bed in her apartment. A contented Lori moaned, "Oooh, Bill, that was wonderful." Lori knew in her mind that it was not professional to see Bill, but she rationalized that this casual relationship would not be a problem with Samantha. She had been friends with Samantha since their college days and been by her side as Samantha's personal secretary throughout the election. Besides, Bill was single, good looking, and very smart, and he had paid her a lot of attention. When he had asked her out on a date, she eagerly accepted.

As Bill got up to get a cigarette, she thought how lucky she was. Both Lori and Bill were single, but she didn't have any aspirations beyond this bed for them. Bill was brilliant—he had a doctorate in physics—but he also had a dark side. He was sometimes a little rough with her, but a girl has her needs and he was handsome, nearby, and great in bed. She knew a little about his family; they were from some remote area of Oregon and had a large ranch. He had three brothers that lived on the ranch, and Bill was the only one to go to university.

Bill came back to bed, and Lori snuggled up against him. They began to caress each other again.

Bill whispered in her ear, "You know that the witch and I had a final falling out, right? She actually had the gall to fire me. I knew that it would not work out between us. We just have two different outlooks on things. She is so rosy and naïve, and I am pragmatic and pessimistic. I don't know why I ever accepted this assignment with her. It's just that I owed a favor to Senator Jakes, and indirectly to Vice President Conrad. I know you and she are longtime friends, and I do not want to come between you two, so I think it best if we keep our relationship secret. I do want to keep seeing you though. You are lovely, fun, and great where it matters most."

And pigs fly, Bill thought, but he must continue with Lori because she was the only way that he could stay close to what was happening in the White House. During his usual phone call last night, his father was very clear that he and Bill's brothers wanted to muster the militia and take positive steps in eliminating the threat the astronauts were to the world.

"Even though Samantha and I don't see eye to eye on all things, it is possible that I can still help with this astronaut situation. I have many friends in the scientific community, and I can feed support through you. She won't know that it came from me and automatically rejected it," Bill continued to whisper.

Lori was torn between her loyalty to Samantha and her need to keep Bill near, but she made her decision.

"Yes, I can do that," Lori replied. "I have Samantha's ear and a longtime relationship with her, and she will listen to me. I know that this situation with the astronauts weighs heavily on her, but I know that she will protect them and provide for them and their families. They are going to the CDC in Atlanta soon, but I think another move will be necessary if they cannot find a cure at the lab there. I'm not sure when this will happen, but I will let you know as soon as I find out." Lori sighed and rolled over on top of him. "Now shut up, lie back, and enjoy this," she ordered as she started kissing him, working downward.

Later, after they both had dozed off, Lori woke up to the sound of Bill talking on the phone. "Yes, Dad, they are taking them to the CDC in Atlanta during the research phase and then somewhere else for long-term residence. I will keep you informed, but I do not recommend any action yet. The CDC is very secure, and we could not get near them there. Remember, they must be destroyed without releasing any of the organisms."

"Oh my," groaned Lori. "What have I gotten myself into?" She knew Bill was a radical, but she never thought he would take things into his own hands like this. He was dangerous. She had to be very careful from now around him, she realized. Should she tell Samantha? Lori was likely to lose her job over this as well. She would have to think very carefully about what she should do."

Chapter 6

Hazmat suits were placed in the sealed air chamber, and as the air was removed from the chamber, it was sterilized at a high temperature. Charlie Gonzales spoke into the intercom. "Once you put these suits on, we can then transfer you to the plane waiting to take you to the CDC in Atlanta. I understand that Dr. Atwood has been working to secure you much more comfortable accommodations than what you found here."

"Great. I have found bunks on board ships more comfortable than here!" Niels responded. "These suits look like they will be hot. Can we be cooled?" he asked.

"You will be connected to onboard liquid cooling systems so that no body fluids can be released. No body fluids can be expelled during the whole flight," Charlie emphasized.

"Right, I think we all need to take a final trip to the john before suiting up!" agreed Niels.

The three men helped each other into the hazmat suits. Niels said to the other two men, "We are all set for the trip to the plane, but I want you both to be very careful. We do not want to tear these suits and possibly unleash this organism on the world."

Charlie, listening in on the intercom, said, "You will be connected to onboard systems that will not only keep you cool but will also allow communications and ensure that all expelled air you breathe out is contained for final cleansing after you land."

Taking care to not damage the hazmat suits, they made a slow and careful trip out to the plane. Once on board, the crew was connected to the support system, and much to their surprise, they were prone and could sleep the whole trip if they wanted to.

The trip from the space center airstrip to the CDC in Atlanta occurred without mishap and out of the public's eye.

"Welcome to your new home," said Dr. Atwood. "Call me Ray. Look around after you get out of those suits and ask any questions you might have." He was speaking through a very high-resolution telecommunications system. It had full two-way visual and audio capabilities, and the crew could dial up family members, as well as the science team in the lab.

The crew found themselves in a sealed chamber with three bedrooms, a bathroom, and a living room, plus a small kitchen. The closets were filled with properly sized clothes and shoes. The décor was Spartan, masculine, and a little cramped. Each bedroom had a telecommunications terminal that allowed private conversations; the living room telecommunications terminal also functioned as a television for the crew.

Scott said, "Very comfortable, but it looks like they plan on us staying here for a long time."

Bill replied, "I like you guys, but I can think of better roommates." As soon as he said this, he felt bad. Both Niels and Scott were married, and he was sure that they would rather have their wives here with them instead of him.

Niels said, "Look, gentlemen, we have to make the best of a bad situation. I'm sure that this arrangement is only temporary and this problem will be solved quickly."

They soon settled into their new accommodations and met with Ray through a large plate glass window that looked into a conference room.

Niels said, "Ray, can you give us an update and an estimate on how long before we can leave and see our families?"

Ray responded, "First, I need you all to pee in a cup and pass it through the air chamber portal. We need samples twice a day to monitor the level of ARC1 in your bodies. I will have lunch passed through, and we can discuss the status and future while we eat."

Ray started the briefing, saying, "First of all, I want to personally assure you that all stops will be pulled out and the full resources of the United States will be at your disposal until we have a satisfactory solution to this problem. At the same time, we must ensure that this strange organism is not released on the world. We have found that ARC1 is easily destroyed by high heat, but the temperature required would also kill you. The burning of the space plane and the facilities at the space center was successful, and no trace of ARC1 was found, but heat is not the solution.

"ARC1 loves water, and as you know, a large portion of our bodies is water. The organism reproduces rapidly in water, and your bodies are full of ARC1. Once again, it does not attack the human body, so you are not at risk. I will be forming an international team of experts to discuss and research methods and procedures that will hopefully rid you of ARC1 completely."

"We must be able to give input to the research team, especially for the final solution," said Niels.

"You will be part of that team and be present for all of the meetings. You will have the final decision on implementation of the solution," said Ray.

"When will we be able to tell our families and friends?" asked Scott. "There must be a lot of speculation out there."

"At eighteen hundred hours, you can call your families and tell them what has happened. At nineteen hundred hours, Samantha will address the United Nations Security Council and inform them of your status and our intentions. She will not tell them your location. We do not expect trouble here, but you must understand that there will be many people that will want to see you destroyed. We will not let that happen."

Chapter 7

Nancy Borgue was waiting in her bedroom in Minnesota for the scheduled phone call from her husband. She looked worried; her instinct told her that something was wrong.

Nancy and Niels had been happily married for many years and had two teenage sons, Alan and Jon. Both boys were in the top of their class; Alan was athletic, and Jon had a beautiful singing voice. Nancy was very proud of them and of her husband, although she wished that he would take the mission planning directorship that the space agency had offered. No more flying missions to Ceres! Niels also had a beautiful singing voice, and he and Jon sang in the choir at the Episcopal Church where she had been minister for the last ten years. Nancy and Niels had discussed the new directorship for the Mars mission planning team at the space agency and how the family would have to move from their small farm in Minnesota to Houston; they discussed keeping the family farm and moving into rental housing while he worked at the American Space Agency too.

The phone rang, and Nancy answered, "Hello?"

"Hi, honey. I miss you and the boys. It sure is lonely here," Niels said wistfully.

"We miss you too. What is happening?" Nancy asked.

Niels explained, "We are still in quarantine, and I do not know when we will get out, but we are not in any danger. In an hour, President Atwood will address the United Nations Security Council and tell them of the problem that we brought back from Ceres. I cannot be specific with you until after her speech. I want you and the boys to watch the address, and then we will talk some more. Please have the boys available when we talk next. I love you and can't wait to be with you again. I am sure that this is my last mission, and I am giving serious thought to that mission planning position."

Nancy replied anxiously, "I understand. We will watch the president's speech and then call you right back. I love you too. Living in an apartment in Houston sounds very glamorous right now."

Niels gave her the number to reach him at before they said goodbye so Nancy could pick up the boys from school.

♊

In their new shared living room, Bill and Scott were trying to relax.

"Did you get a hold of your wife?" Bill asked.

"No, I don't know where she is. It's six thirty in Orlando, and you would think she would be back from work by now," Scott replied. "I bet she is out with her friends having drinks again. Too much partying and drinking... I think that our marriage is not going to work, especially with the situation the three of us are in now. Our marriage was rocky even before we left for Ceres, and I don't think anything has improved since we returned. I'm going to ask her for a divorce, and I'm sure she won't object."

"We might as well have another drink. What is your poison?" Bill asked. Bill's mother and father were killed in a car crash three years ago, and he and his younger sister Joy were the only family left. They maintained their parent's apartment in San Francisco's Chinatown; it had been in the family for three generations, and they still entertained friends and family from Hong Kong. There was a three-hour difference between Atlanta and San Francisco, so Bill didn't expect Joy to be back from school for at least four hours. His call had gone unanswered, at any rate.

Niels entered the living room and poured himself a double of single malt Scotch. "I wonder if I drink enough of this stuff if it will kill this damn bug inside," he grumbled.

"I don't know, but I'm willing to start trying," responded Scott. All three men were despondent after the calls to their families and in anticipation of their near-future prospects.

"Turn on the TV and let's see what President Atwood has to say to the world," said Niels. It was still fifteen minutes before the scheduled speech at the UN, and when they turned on the TV, they got the news.

"This is a major news flash. High-level White House sources say that the astronauts that returned from Ceres have brought back an organism that is a major threat. They were not specific as to the nature of that threat, but the three astronauts have been taken to special facilities for continued quarantine. President Atwood will address the UN Security Council in a few minutes. We will carry her address live on this network."

"Someone let the cat out of the bag. We are in for it now," said Niels as the intercom phone rang.

"Niels? Sorry about that," said Ray. "We think we know who leaked this, but the source of information has been cut off. This has been happening very quickly, and we have not been able to contain everything that we would like to. I have started action to step up the security here at the CDC, and specifically in near-proximity to your rooms and the lab doing research on the water."

"Is there anything we should be doing to help?" replied Niels.

"We need to start talking about how and where to

ensure the security of your families. We are open to any and all possibilities. Please discuss this among yourselves, and we will talk again after Samantha's speech." Ray hung up looking very worried.

Chapter 8

"Ladies and gentlemen, thank you for coming on such short notice. As you know, the United States has recently sent a team to Ceres to retrieve water samples. A spill of the Ceres water occurred on the space plane while transferring the samples from the *Ceres Lander* to the space plane, water that was breathed in by the crew during their trip back to Earth. This was reported back to the American Space Agency, and when the space plane landed at the space center, the plane and the crew were immediately put into secure quarantine pending analysis of the Ceres water. This quarantine is standard procedure for any extra-terrestrial return.

"The analysis has found that the Ceres water contains a single-celled organism not found on Earth. We have named it ARC1. ARC1 reproduces very rapidly in water and therefore permeates the bodies of the crew. This organism does not directly affect humans in any way, and although the crew is still in quarantine, they are safe and in no harm from ARC1.

"ARC1 can easily be destroyed by high temperatures, and we have destroyed the space plane and former quarantine facilities by fire. Subsequent tests for ARC1 found no evidence of the organism.

"However, our scientists have found that ARC1 attacks and destroys all grain crops that it comes in contact with.

"Vice President Conrad will take the lead to find a final resolution, and my husband, Dr. Ray Atwood, will lead the technical team to find a method to safely rid the crew of ARC1. Until then, let me assure you that ARC1 is contained without possibility of its release.

"Are there any questions?" Samantha asked.

Several hands were raised.

"The chair recognizes the representative from China."

"Madam President, we greatly appreciate your candid report to this august body, however, you may or may not know that a news report released these facts just minutes before your statement. That report said that the Ceres crew is located at a special facility. Can you confirm that report and tell us where they are located?"

"I have not seen that news broadcast, I do not know their source, and I will neither confirm nor deny their reporting," President Atwood replied. "Let me make it very clear—the location of the crew will not be released. The United States will protect our astronauts with all resources necessary. They are protected American citizens and will be treated accordingly."

Samantha responded to several additional enquiries and then brought the session to a close.

♋ ♋ ♋

Later, after a brief talk with Bill, Scott, and Ray, Niels was on the phone with his family. "Well you have heard the whole story now," he said. "We are okay, but we must stay in quarantine until a cure is found. Boys, I'm sure that you will be questioned by your friends at school. My recommendation is to plead ignorance and cut the questions short as much as you can. I hope that this does not become too awkward for you."

"Don't worry about it, Dad. We can handle them, and the teachers, if necessary. I find that people in general are courteous and respectful in these situations," said Alan.

Niels realized how mature his boys were. He could count on them to be responsible and take care of their mother in his absence.

"Let me talk with your mother now. I hope to see you boys soon," said Niels.

"Bye, Dad, love you," said both boys together.

After the boys had left the room, Nancy announced, "I am coming to Atlanta. I can't stand to be away from you any longer, and I'm worried about you." Her last few words came out in a sob.

"Don't cry," begged Niels. "It tears me up inside to see you this way. I want you to be there with the boys to help them through this and make sure that they do not have serious trouble at school or with their friends. I know that I have been gone for too long, and I promise that I will make this up to you as soon as I can. We have the best scientific team in the world here, and President Atwood has assigned her own husband to lead the team. We are safe, and I am sure that they will soon find a solution."

"Okay, honey, I understand, but you must keep me informed. I will be there as soon as you tell me to."

"I have been assured that the bacteria does not hurt us in any way, so we are not threatened by it directly, but it will destroy all of the grain crops in the world," reminded Niels. "We cannot let that happen."

"Well, I hope that they come up with an answer soon," she sighed. "I will try to be patient and hold it all together for the boys' sake."

"I know you will, Nancy. You are a strong woman, and I love that about you."

Chapter 9

Ivan looked in from the living room to the kitchen, where his mother was preparing dinner. She looked pale and listless—certainly not the lively, energetic woman he loved. He looked around the home where he had lived all his life. It was a small, cold place, although his mother had tried her best to make it as cheerful as possible with what resources were at hand. They lived in a small, backward-thinking town with dismal medical and educational facilities. It was no wonder that no intelligent person would want to come and be a doctor or teacher here, thought Ivan.

His mother had been a top cosmonaut twenty years ago and even spent six months on the International Space Station. Why she had come here was beyond him, although he had asked her many times. Each time, she was evasive and usually ended up changing the subject.

Ivan was not happy. Even though he was nineteen years old, he physically had the body of a twelve-year-old, and the other students in his school teased and embarrassed him constantly. He was the smartest student in his school, and the teachers could not keep up with him or challenge him intellectually. The library was small, and Ivan had read everything of interest to him. He was currently enrolled online at the University of Moscow, completing a degree in government, and still he felt something was missing with no interaction with professors and peers. Through online testing, he had been advised that his educational level was equivalent to a person thirty-two years old, and a very smart one at that. Over the years, he had tried to discuss his differences with his mother, but she was evasive on that topic as well. Ivan felt that she either did not know or did not want to tell him why he was different.

Ivan was nineteen, looked twelve, was as smart as a thirty-two-year-old, and he couldn't find out why—and he glowed light blue, especially when he was angry. He was stuck in Abakan, Siberia, and it had nothing to offer him or his mother. He once more vowed to find a way to get both of them out of the backwater, but it was difficult for Ivan to confront his mother while she was not feeling well.

Mother and son sat down to dinner, and Ivan took Irina's hand. "Mom, I'm worried about you. You don't look well, and you seem to be failing. What is wrong?"

"I'm just a little tired sometimes. It comes and goes," she answered dismissively. "I do have some news for you though. I have been asked to travel to Moscow to meet with the Russian Space Federation for follow-up medical exams." Irina hoped that this little white lie was okay. The Russian Space Federation had not asked her to Moscow, but she was going to present herself to them and demand a full physical. "I am going to ask them to find us a place in Moscow. I hope to be able to move in the next few months. This is not a promise, but I will try to make it happen."

Ivan was thrilled and wanted to ask his mother many questions, but he could see that she was tiring even as they ate.

Chapter 10

Two weeks later, around the dinner table in the White House residence, the entire Atwood family had one of those rare chances to be together. Even though Tony and Susan were young, seventeen and fourteen respectively, Ray and Samantha respected and trusted their children enough that they shared sensitive information with them, but as their parents, they still reminded them when their conversations should remain secret.

Ray said, "I don't think that the scientific team can find a solution. They have tried all possible combinations, and the crew has been very accommodating in drinking, injecting, and being exposed to all sorts of chemicals, drugs, light, and radiation. While some of these methods will destroy the organism in the lab in higher concentrations, if these are given to the crew, they will certainly kill them. They are becoming very frustrated with the lack of progress."

"You mean that the best scientific minds in the world cannot rid the crew of one small, single-celled creature without killing them? That is unbelievable!" Samantha exclaimed.

Tony said, "After your speech the other night, there has been some very negative talk on the internet recently calling for the destruction of the crew. Susan and I have been in touch with Alan and Jon Borgue, and we have started a youth campaign with a blog in support of the crew and the work you are doing to free them of this burden. We hope this will help give some hope that the youth of the world is behind them."

Susan said, "Mom, I like Alan and Jon. I think you should invite the boys and their mother here for dinner soon. It sounds to me that the families are feeling as much pressure as the crew."

Samantha exclaimed with a very proud, motherly look on her face, "Wow, I'm really impressed and proud of you two. I was hoping leadership would rub off, and it looks like we have a couple of leaders in the making. First thing tomorrow morning I will ask Lori to invite them to a private dinner with the whole family here, and I think it would be best if you could let Alan and Jon inform their father of the response of your campaign."

Ray said, "I think it would be nice if we invited Niels to the dinner also. I know he cannot actually be here, but I could set it up so that he can be here on screen and share in the occasion with his family."

"Great idea! See to it, and make sure you coordinate with Lori and Diane," Samantha replied. "In the meantime, I will call the crew and discuss the next step. What do you recommend Ray?"

"I think that the safety of the families becomes much more important now because they could become hostages. We should seek other, more-permanent facilities for the crew and their families. Charlie Gonzales, Vice President Conrad, and I have actually discussed the possibility of modifying the Utah Biosphere into private apartments and still maintaining full security and isolation for the crew and possibly their families. It hasn't been used since its original experiment in a fully contained and self-sufficient community, and that failed years ago. Should I pursue this?"

"Yes, the time is right. I am taking a lot of heat from the world leaders. So far we still have the full support of Congress, but I don't know how much longer they will be patient," replied Samantha.

"You could coordinate all family decisions with Nancy Borgue," suggested Ray. "She is very strong, a religious leader and mother of two boys, who happen to have their father locked away in confinement. From what I hear, Scott and his wife Georgia are having a difficult time of dealing with this situation. Their marriage is shaky at best, and they will probably seek divorce soon. Bill is not married, but he has his sister Joy. They are very close and worried about the future," Ray confided to the family.

"This is a huge dilemma for all of them," agreed Samantha. "I hope we can come up with a solution soon that will alleviate their situations."

Susan added, "We feel so sorry for the boys, and we will try to do anything we can to make things easier for them."

"Thanks, honey," Samantha said lovingly. "I knew I could count on all of you."

Chapter 11

The faces of Vice President Conrad, Charlie Gonzales, and Ray Atwood appeared on the screen of the teleconference system, and Niels, Scott, and Bill sat awaiting the final scientific briefing, although they already knew the answer before it came.

Ray started, "As you know, the lab team has not come up with any solution and is not likely to. They will, of course, keep working. The international scientific community still recommends destroying ARC1 by destroying you, though I assume that this is not acceptable to you. The other alternative that must be said is for you to commit suicide, but that conversation is very private and between yourselves. However, you must understand that it must be all of you to be sure that the entire organism is destroyed."

The vice president continued, "I have discussed with the building planners of the Utah Biosphere the possibility of its modification to accommodate three apartments that would be comfortable and still maintain isolation. Homeland Security has assured me that your safety can be maintained for as long as you wish to stay there. This construction could be finished in three weeks. We would like your input tomorrow morning."

"Thanks for your candid report, gentlemen. Scott, Bill, and I will discuss our future, and we will also talk to our families tonight. We'll meet with you in the morning and tell you our decision," replied Niels.

The men on the screen nodded, and the call ended.

"Well, not much of a chance, is there? I guess going to the Utah Biosphere will buy us some time, and hopefully someone will come up with a more acceptable solution for us. Call your families and let them know what is happening, and we will talk again at the meeting tomorrow," instructed Niels.

With some trepidation, Niels made a call to Nancy. "Hello, honey. The news is not good from the science team. I told you that if it came down to it I would like to introduce the crew to the Final Solution. I would like your blessing. I know that this is a very radical solution, and it leaves you with full family responsibility, but I don't know what else to do."

During their nightly phone calls, Niels and Nancy had gone over the options. No matter how distasteful, they discussed the pros and cons of each. They kept coming back to one, what they had begun to call the Final Solution.

Nancy replied, with tears in her eyes, "I support you in any decision you make. I know that you have the responsibility of the crew in your mind, as well as for our family. The boys are mature and very responsible, and I'm sure they will understand. As far as I am concerned, I would like to have as much time with you as possible. You know that I love you and I am very proud of you. Sleep on it, and let's talk early tomorrow morning, I will say a prayer for you and the team tonight."

They spoke a while longer, about the boys and the Minnesota weather, before saying goodnight again with another "I love you." Lying in his bed after, Niels recalled the moments and decisions he had made that had major influence in his life. His thoughts kept going back to his first flight into space and Irina Karpov.

The night before Irina was scheduled to return to Russia, she and Niels had met in her cubical and tried to talk about their future together, but the passion of the moment and their lovemaking in weightlessness stopped all conversation. Irina left the next day, and when Niels returned from his mission, she could not be found. The Russian Space Federation stopped all inquiries into Irina's whereabouts, and he was stymied at every turn in trying to find her. Frustrated at his lack of success, he went home to Minnesota, where he ran into Nancy and renewed their relationship; he gradually thought less of Irina, and he and Nancy were married several months later. Alan was born before Niels' second mission to the space station, and Jon was born between his second and third mission.

As Niels fell asleep, he thought that he had had a very full and happy life, but now it looked like it all might come to an end if Scott and Bill rejected his Final Solution.

Chapter 12

The next morning, the Ceres crew was sitting together in their shared living room. They needed to agree on what they wanted to do before the meeting with the science team.

Niels started, "In my phone call with Nancy last night, we talked about what I call the Final Solution—"

Scott interrupted Niels, saying, "Okay, but Bill and I want to tell you that suicide is out. We feel that we could still lead useful lives from inside the biosphere."

"Good. I feel the same way, but I don't feel that the world will let us live long enough to be useful," Niels responded. "As you both know, I have been working with the Mission Planning Department at the space agency in anticipation of my assignment to lead that department. I would like you to consider forming the advance team for a mission to Mars. By doing so, we remove ourselves as a threat to Earth and perform a valuable service to the American Space Agency and the United States. What do you think?"

Scott looked at Bill, and they both said at the same time, "We are in.

Scott added, "The other choices are unacceptable, and at least we have a chance to live a useful life by going to Mars."

Niels relaxed and said, "Understand that this must be a one-way mission. We will not be allowed to return to Earth."

"It is a sobering thought, but we do understand and agree. This contribution will be more than anything we could do from the biosphere. Thank you for your creativity and leadership, Niels. We will follow you anywhere, even to

Mars," Bill said.

"Okay, let's call the president together and get her permission to start this process," Niels said. "But first I feel that we should tell Ray and take some of the burden from his shoulders."

Chapter 13

Right at seven thirty, the four men were assembled, the Ceres crew in their quarantine living room and Ray in the conference room. Ray could see that the crew was looking much more enthusiastic than the night before.

"Ray, we have come up with the Final Solution, and before you get excited and try to talk us out of it, we are not talking of suicide. We have a plan that we hope you and Samantha will support," Niels said.

"Good. Samantha and I will support almost anything at this time, except suicide," Ray responded.

"Here's what we have in mind—Scott, Bill, and I will form an advance team to explore, set up the infrastructure, and form the basis for a colony on Mars. We realize that this is a one-way mission and that this is a very expensive solution. But we also feel that because the American Space Agency is close to finalizing the Mars mission that our skills can be put to good use there. A successful Mars mission would put the United States in a major international leadership position. Will you and Samantha support this idea? Will this idea take the pressure off of her?"

"I will certainly support you, but Samantha is the president and she has many more resources and responsibilities than I do, so you will have to ask her."

"Could you set up a call to Samantha as soon as possible?" asked Niels. "We can get the ball rolling, but I feel that Samantha's leadership in this adventure is paramount."

"Of course," said Ray. "Oh, this evening Samantha and I are inviting you and your family to the White House for dinner. I know that you can't actually be there, so I will set up the teleconference both here and there so that you can participate. Scott and Bill are included too, as they have an important stake in this also. I will instruct the chef here on our menu at the White House so that you can have the same as us."

There were excited murmurs all around from the crew.

♋

The call to President Atwood was set up for later that same day.

"Hello, Samantha. As you can see, Scott and Bill are here with me, and we have a special request of you," began Niels. "We feel that we can be useful to society and still not represent a threat to the world. The American Space Agency has had plans for some time now to send a mission to Mars. We would modify those plans so that Scott, Bill, and I would travel to Mars for the purpose of setting up an advance base for a future colony there. We realize that this would be a one-way mission and we would never be able to return to Earth. I think that with your support and the blessing of the other countries of the world we could send this mission off within two years. What do you think? Can the United States afford this kind of mission at this time?" asked Niels.

"I am very glad that you have ruled out suicide. I don't know what I would have said otherwise," replied Samantha. "Your proposal saddens me on the one hand, because it is a one-way mission. But you would be alive and doing important work for the whole world, and it would solve the problem of this organism without killing you, its host. I love the idea. Thank you for being the heroes that you are. I'm sure that we can find a way to accomplish this mission. You have my full support! I will talk to Charlie Gonzales as to feasibility, cost, and timing. Niels and Scott, have you discussed this concept with your wives yet, or Bill, your sister?" asked Samantha.

Bill shook his head, and Scott said, "I have not discussed this with anyone per Niels' orders, and I will not discuss this with my wife until we have a clear plan. All is not well with our marriage, and I am sure that she is going to file for divorce soon."

"I have discussed this with my wife," replied Niels. "She understands our motivation, and I believe she supports us, but I am worried. I think she is going to discuss this with you tonight at dinner. She needs a woman to talk to, not just a president. I hope you understand."

"I do understand, Niels. Leave it to me. I will put a call in to Charlie and let you know the results soon. See you all tonight," said Samantha.

Chapter 14

Nancy and the boys were escorted to the president's private quarters in the White House.

"Welcome to our home! After dinner, you all can have a tour of the White House," offered Ray. "Samantha will join us in a few moments. She is still on the phone working out some detail or other. Why don't you kids take Alan and Jon and show them your rooms and compare notes on your project before revealing the results to Niels and the team in Atlanta?" suggested Ray.

Nancy wandered around in awe. "This home is beautiful. Can you decorate it the way you want to?" she asked.

"Yes and no," said Ray. "We can have personal items that can be removed, but we cannot permanently modify anything—not that we would want to. There is history here, and the last thing we would want to do is lose that history. This decor is not necessarily our style, but it is very well done and very comfortable. The kids have made their rooms over, as you can imagine,"

"Nancy, how lovely you look! Welcome to our other home," said Samantha as she entered the living room. Nancy had not been sure what to wear to an informal dinner at the White House with the president and her family, so she decided to wear her normal Sunday morning attire. She was glad she did as both Samantha and Ray appeared very casual and comfortable in their own home. She felt welcome here.

The headwaiter entered and announced that dinner would be served in five minutes at both locations. Ray established the connection to the CDC teleconferencing screen, and the three men appeared over the dinner table.

"Ray, why don't you get the children and we can start dinner," said Samantha.

Ray quickly returned with all four children, and everyone sat themselves at the table.

"Hi, Dad! Man, this place is awesome. You should see all the neat stuff Susan and Tom have. Do you think we can move here someday?" joked Jon.

"I don't think you would like being away from your friends and Grandma and Grandpa," replied Niels.

"It would be okay, as long as we were with you and Mom. We would go anywhere with you," replied the more adult Alan.

"Thank you, son, for your love and support. Times are difficult for us, and I depend on your strength to help keep things stable. Now, mind your manners. And, Jon? I give Ray permission to thump you on the head with a spoon if you are rude," said Niels.

"Oh no! Dad is going to learn new tricks," joked Tom.

The conversation and jokes kept flying as everyone dug into their food.

"Boy, this grub is good. I knew I should have joined the Navy instead of the Air Force," said Bill. "Do you all eat like this all the time?" He knew that the chef at the White House was a Navy veteran.

"No, Mom and Dad have us on strict diets," replied Susan. "They say we have to set a good example for the other kids and stay slim. If we want junk food, we just go to the school cafeteria."

Once everyone had cleared their plates, Ray announced, "Gentlemen, the children have been working on something and would like to present it to you now."

Alan started out, "Dad, Scott, and Bill—Tom, Susan, Jon, and I wanted to find a way to show our support for your dedication and bravery. We have designed an online survey to try to gain input from the young people of the world about what they think of you and the situation we are all in."

"Here are the questions we asked in the survey," said Tom. "Do you approve of the mission to Ceres to collect water samples? Do you think that the astronauts are brave heroes and should be protected at all costs? If the Ceres organism cannot be destroyed in the astronauts bodies, should they choose to live in isolation the rest of their lives, and would you support them in that decision?"

"We have been overwhelmed by the response, and as a result, we are very proud of our generation," said Susan.

"We have had thirty-eight million hits," Tom reported, "and all but two hundred twenty-seven show support of the astronauts. Some have actually invited you to live with them, and many of them offer money and other services to support your cause. We will send some of the responses to you."

Alan continued, "Jon has come up with a money-raising idea that we think will help fund your support. Jon, why don't you tell us about your crazy idea?"

"Okay, here goes... It is a competition for a universal idol. All the nations of the world can compete, selecting their representative to a worldwide competition. The final competition could be held under the auspices of the United Nations, and the final judging could be by a series of judges similar to the rules for figure skating. All proceeds would go to a Ceres team fund to be used by you for the rest of your lives." Jon took a deep breath and sat down.

Niels smiled, amused at the idea and nodding in approval at their ingenuity.

"Scott, Bill, and I are overwhelmed with your effort and the response of the youth of the world. We can't thank you enough," said Niels, and Bill and Scott nodded next to him. "Jon, I like your idea for a universal idol fundraiser, but I will leave it to President Atwood to judge if it is necessary and feasible. We are going to sign off for now so that you all can enjoy the rest of your evening."

Bill, Scott, and Niels hung up to a chorus of goodbyes, and the dining room was quiet.

"Mom, Dad doesn't sound like himself. Is he going to be all right?" asked Jon.

Nancy was comforted by her son's sensitivity to his father's plight.

"He has a lot on his mind now, and he and the crew have to work out a lot of details," she answered. Then she asked, "Ray, could you and Susan and Tom take Alan and Jon on that tour of the White House and entertain them while Samantha and I talk for a while?"

As Ray and the children left, Nancy said to Samantha, "I need your understanding and advice as a wife and mother."

"What can I do for you? You know that I will do anything in my power for you and the boys," said Samantha.

"As you know, the crew is planning this mission to Mars. We know that this is a one-way mission, but as far as I am concerned, it is just a different form of suicide, and I won't let that happen!" Nancy said emotionally.

Samantha put her arm around her and said, "I know that this is a hard time for you, but understand that you have friends in Ray and me. We will help."

After she settled down, Nancy said, "I intend to join my husband on this mission. I want to help guide these men and represent religion and government in establishing this colony on Mars. I think that this colony should be a true colony with couples, similar to the Mayflower coming to America. Therefore, I would also like your help in finding the best match for Scott and Bill and see that romance takes its inevitable course. These two women must also possess skills that complement the mission requirements.

"I have not discussed this with Niels yet," she admitted. "I know he will try to talk me out of it, and I figured that together we could override any objection he may bring up. I believe a woman's touch and stability will ensure success in establishing a real, functioning colony and prepare for future travelers there. I believe that a six to ten-man mission can be supported with the technology we now have.

"Before you ask, the boys will stay with their grandparents. They stay with them a lot now, and they both are very mature and have their futures already mapped out. We can communicate with the space agency's help," she finished, hopeful.

"Oh, Nancy, what a brave thing to say. I would feel the same way if I were in your predicament. I just don't know if I can sell this to the powers that be... But, come to think of it, I am the highest power in this land, and I am sure that we can make this happen successfully. I will ask Ray to work with you to define the ideal requirements for the two other women and start the process of elimination immediately. But the final decision will have to be up to the two men, and Niels as their commander. Would you like to call Niels right now so that I can support you without delay?" asked

Samantha.

"Yes, but the first part of the call I would like to be private," said Nancy.

"Of course. Just dial the number on that screen and you will be in visual and audio contact. Good luck," said Samantha as she left the room.

Nancy sat quietly for a few minutes while she composed her thoughts. Then she dialed the number. Niels picked up quickly.

"Hello, honey. Are you by yourself right now?" asked Nancy.

"Yes. Scott and Bill are in their quarters for the rest of the evening. What is on your mind?"

"I'm not sure how to say this, so I will just come out with it—I love you and want to be with you forever. I have given this a lot of thought and soul searching and prayer. I have decided that I am coming with you to Mars to help start a real colony. We can leave the boys with their grandparents. Oh, Niels, please say that you will accept my decision and welcome me with you!" pleaded Nancy with tears in her eyes.

Niels was overwhelmed by her declaration.

"Wow, that is a lot to absorb. My decision is easy to understand, but your commitment is personal and I highly respect your decision. I love you too, and this separation is hard on both of us. The thought of us living apart for the rest of our lives is more than I can bear, but I didn't think it fair to ask you to come with me. I wanted to, believe me. I am so relieved and so happy at your decision, but what about Scott and Bill? It is hardly fair to them," he noted.

"I am working on that problem now," she answered.

"Have you told the boys? Where are they?" asked Niels.

"They are with Ray touring the White House. I have not said anything to them yet, but Jon did notice that you were down in the dumps this evening. I suggest that we wait to tell them until after we discuss this in more detail. We can tell them together in a few days, privately," replied Nancy. Then she asked, "Is it okay if I ask Samantha back into the room now that we have agreed that I will come with you to Mars?"

"Yes," he laughed. "I'm sure that you women have colluded on this decision."

Nancy stepped away from the screen, returning a moment later with Samantha.

"Hello again, Niels. Why are you grinning like that?" asked Samantha.

"It's just that I have been blessed with the most wonderful woman in this and any world, and she has agreed to join us in forming the new colony on Mars. I could not be happier. I hope you support us in this decision, but I am worried how this will affect Scott and Bill. What should I say to them?" asked Niels.

"Nancy has suggested that we find two women who would be willing to join you on this mission. The intention would be that they are suitable as partners for Scott and Bill and also experienced in disciplines that fill mission needs. I will ask Nancy, Ray, and you to recommend to Scott and Bill your short list of choices before they make their own final decision in this very private matter," Samantha instructed.

The three of them talked over various possibilities and options until Ray and the children returned. Jon, always the perceptive one, looking back and forth between Niels and Nancy, observed, "Mom, why do you and Dad look so happy? I haven't seen you beam so radiantly in a long time."

"Thank you, son. I haven't had such a lovely evening in quite some time. Being with you boys and your father is just what I needed—and, of course, having such wonderful hosts made the evening even better." Turning to Ray and Samantha, she said, "Thank you both for having us to your lovely home. Wouldn't it be nice if Niels and I could invite you to our home in the stars someday?" said Nancy cryptically.

Chapter 15

Lori woke up for the second time Sunday morning and rolled over as she remembered the first time. A girl should be woken up like that every morning. She sighed as she remembered Bill beside her, half asleep in slumber, and then being very awake as he made love to her.

She sat up in bed, looking around for Bill, and heard him on the phone through the partially closed bedroom door.

"Yes, Dad, I know it is the middle of the night for you, but I wanted to make this call from this phone just in case there are repercussions in the future. The crew will be moved to the Utah Biosphere, and that is where we should make our move to eliminate them from the face of the Earth. Make some plans with the militia leaders. Remember, we must kill them without destroying the biosphere. We do not want to release this organism. Once dead, the military will see to it that their bodies are properly destroyed by intense heat with incendiary bombs. I will leave today for Oregon. Have someone pick me up in Portland and drive me to the ranch."

After a moment of silence, Lori heard, "Thanks, Dad. See you soon."

She slipped back under the covers and pretended to be asleep as Bill entered the bedroom.

"I'm going to be out of town for a few days," Bill said as he gathered up his clothes. "I will call you and let you know when we can do this again." He gave her a quick kiss on the cheek.

Lori shuddered under the covers and did not reply as Bill took his suitcase, leaving her apartment. She replayed in her mind what she had just heard. Man, I have really screwed up this time, she thought. Bill's call had creeped her out, and she wondered what he was up to. After some thought, Lori realized she had to tell Samantha and take the chance on getting fired.

Without a second more of delay, she picked up the phone and dialed Samantha's private number.

"Samantha, this is Lori. I'm afraid I'm in trouble. I really messed up. I'm so sorry," said Lori through her tears.

"What is it, Lori? I am your friend, and I'm here for you anytime. Tell me what is wrong," urged Samantha.

"Is this line secure?" asked Lori.

"Yes, it is, but what are you worried about that you need this line to be secure?" asked a concerned Samantha.

"I have been seeing Bill Worth for the past four months. He is great in bed, but I don't believe he is trustworthy. I just overheard a phone call to his father, and I believe they are plotting something against the crew," explained Lori.

"That's very disturbing, but I'm not surprised that he would retaliate after I fired him. I should have had him watched more closely," Samantha noted. "Lori, don't worry. We will see this through together. If Bill gets in touch with you, don't let him suspect that you feel differently towards him. First thing tomorrow morning, get the director of the FBI over to my office and the three of us will discuss your information and make a plan. Don't worry. You have not done anything really wrong, and you know that I will support you. Love you, see you tomorrow," said Samantha with some emotion in her voice, knowing that it was necessary to get Lori to reveal everything to her.

Boy, I really do hope that line was secure or they will

be lined up three deep tomorrow thinking that I am an easy touch, thought Lori.

Chapter 16

"Commander Borgue, we have uncovered a plot to attack the biosphere and kill you, Bill, and Scott. I know that you have not yet decided to move to the biosphere, but I'm worried that we cannot protect you while there," said Samantha the next morning.

"We have been discussing just that, Samantha, and we feel that we would like to have secured quarters at the space agency complex in Houston, rather than move to the biosphere. I would like to be near the team planning the mission, and we feel that it will be easier and cheaper while still keeping us safe since the agency already has top security. What do you think?" asked Niels.

"Great idea, but do not talk to anyone else about this until I get back to you later today. I will call you with our plan," replied Samantha. After they hung up, she called Lori.

"When Director Nelson arrives, escort him in and remain with us," instructed Samantha.

"He is here now, and we will be right in," replied a very nervous Lori. It was not every day the president's secretary made a mistake that warranted a meeting with the director of the FBI.

As they entered, Samantha sat behind her desk with a serious look on her face that caused Lori some concern. Samantha always took the bright side and greeted everyone with a smile.

"Director Nelson, thank you for coming on such short notice," started Samantha. "Lori has committed a transgression that could be very serious to the office of the president. It requires the understanding and deep resources of the FBI."

Lori cringed in a corner chair as both Samantha and Director Nelson looked at her.

"Lori, please tell Director Nelson what has transpired between you and Bill Worth," President Atwood requested.

Although Tom Nelson held a very high and tough position in the government, he looked like a kind, old grandpa, and he could use that appearance when necessary. Knowing that Lori was a personal friend of President Atwood and in a special position when it came to access to the president, he let his kind grandfather personality take over. "Don't worry," he said with a wink, "I assure you that this will not leave this room without your permission. Now tell me everything that has happened to you."

Lori was nervous, but she told them about her relationship with Bill Worth and the conversation she had overheard between Bill and his father about the possible attack on the crew at the biosphere.

"When did this last phone call happen?" asked Director Nelson.

"Yesterday morning at about seven. He left soon after for his home in Oregon, and he said he would call me from there," replied Lori.

"Lori, please excuse us for a while," instructed Director Nelson. "We will call you at your desk if we need any more from you."

After Lori left the Oval Office, Director Nelson said, "I'm sorry this had to happen, but there is something to be gained by this unfortunate episode. The FBI and ATF have been after Bill Worth's father and family for some time now, but they are very careful in their planning and execution. The militia that they operate is anti-government, which is not illegal. However, we know that they have collected a large amount of illegal weapons and the materials necessary to make bombs. So far, they have not used them, but ATF would like to recover those weapons and destroy them. As far as we know, Bill Worth has not been part of their operation, but blood is thicker than water so we have been watching him."

"Commander Borgue and the crew have asked to be transferred to the space agency's offices in Houston and not to the biosphere as previously planned. In anticipation of your needs, we have not told anyone of this decision," said Samantha.

"I would like to use Lori as a conduit of false information, with your permission, and see if we can trap this group once and for all," said Director Nelson.

"Okay, but I do not want the Oval Office involved, and I want to ensure that Lori is not hurt by this. After all, she came to me with this information voluntarily."

"I agree. Can we call Lori back in now?"

Over the intercom, Samantha asked, "Lori, please come back in now."

Once Lori was back in the oval office, Tom began, "Okay, Lori, we want you to help us catch this family of anti-government people. I will go over the details with you later, but you must understand that you will be in no danger. The astronaut crew will not be in any danger either."

"Tom has promised that the office of the president, including you, will not be exposed during this operation," explained Samantha. "Your job here is secure. However, next time you want to meet a young man, let your friends know and we can help," she said, smiling.

Lori looked relieved. "Thank you, Madam President. I will definitely be more careful before I become involved with someone again."

Chapter 17

A few days later, Irina flew to Moscow; her thoughts were full of worry because she instinctively knew that something was very wrong with her.

Irina's meeting with her oncologist had been arranged by the Russian Space Federation's medical department at her insistence. This department was responsible for keeping track of the health of all cosmonauts that had spent time in space. This was as much for research as it was concern for the health of the cosmonauts. They wanted to see if there were any long-term effects of weightlessness and radiation from spending many months in space.

After two days of tests, the doctor entered the private consultation room where Irina was awaiting her results. "I'm sorry to tell you that you have a very rare form of cancer. It is very advanced and not operable. You have about six months to live, and for the last two months, you will need medical support. In our opinion, your cancer was not caused by your time in space. However, the Russian Space Federation will assist you and your son any way we can during this difficult time in your life. You will be sent back to Siberia, and we will give you contact information for end-of-life support there."

Irina was visibly shaken by the news but quickly pulled herself together as she replied, "Thank you, doctor. I will be staying in Moscow for the next two days and will plan the near future for myself and my son. I will let you know what we are going to do before I leave Moscow."

Irina had no intention of leaving her and her son's future to the unfriendly hands of the Russian Space Federation; she had made up her mind and decided on a drastic course of action.

Released from her appointment, Irina found the nearest cellphone store and bought a burner phone for her next call.

She dialed, and the instant someone picked up, she said, "Dr. Charlie Gonzales please."

"Can I tell him who is calling?" asked the person on the other end.

"This is Cosmonaut Irina Karpov."

After some time on hold, she heard the line pick up again. "Hello, Irina. It has been a long time. Where are you?" said Charlie, surprised.

"I am in some trouble, and I need your help. You are the only one that can help us," replied Irina.

"I will do what I can. How can I help you?" said Charlie, wondering why she was contacting him after all these years. He didn't need this old acquaintance putting more of a burden on him now that he was dealing with the results of the Ceres mission and planning for the Mars mission.

"When I came back from the Space Station, the Russian Space Federation found out I was pregnant. I had conceived during my time in space. You can imagine the furor this caused. I was an embarrassment to the Russian space program, and they were anxious to keep it quiet. I was banished to this little outpost in Siberia where my son Ivan was born, and we have lived there ever since. I recently returned to Moscow to undergo some exams, and the doctors discovered that I have a rare form of cancer. They denied that it had anything to do with the experiments that I did while on the space station. They thanked me for my time and sent me back home to Siberia.

"You have my deepest sympathy, Irina. What would you like me to do?" asked a very troubled Charlie.

"I would like you to send plane tickets for myself and my son to fly from Abakan, Siberia, to Houston, and I would like accommodations for us until I die. I am told that I have about six months to live. I am asking this of you not only to help me through my remaining days, but to help my son also. You will understand when you meet him, but he is very special and has been from the moment he was conceived in the space station. I'm sure that the American Space Agency will take great interest in him and that he will contribute to their projects. I have not told Ivan about my condition yet, but he is very observant and suspects that something is wrong. Please say yes. You will not be disappointed," pleaded Irina.

"I cannot tell you how sorry I am, Irina. I cannot believe how the Russian Space Federation has treated you over the years, and now in your time of need they have written you off and sent you back to Siberia to die. I cannot accept responsibility on the space agency's behalf. However, I promise that I will help with your request. Please call me back in three hours and we can discuss this further," replied Charlie.

♌

Charlie was head of Mission Control during some of those space station missions and knew all of the members of the crew on board at the same time as Irina. One of them was the father of Irina's son. He wrote down a list of crewmembers that overlapped Irina's time at the space station. When he was finished, he realized there were twelve men on that list!

What did she mean about her son being "special" from the instant of his conception in the space station? As far as he knew, no child had been conceived in the weightless environment of space. Perhaps her son was special.

Charlie's curiosity was piqued, and when Irina called back he said, "Give me your email address and I will send you the tickets you requested. Please be assured that the American Space Agency and the United States will do anything possible for your medical situation and make you and your son comfortable here in Houston."

"Thank you very much. I am so grateful and relieved to have you help us, you will not be sorry. I should have done this earlier, but I did not want to compromise Ivan's father's career," she explained. Then she added, "I have not told Ivan about his father or the circumstances of his conception yet, but I will do so prior to him meeting his father, if that can be arranged."

"If you can tell me who the father is, I can prepare better for your meeting here," he commented.

"I understand why you need to ask, but I would rather discuss this after I arrive and make a personal approach to Ivan's father," she replied. "Thanks for your help, and I will see you soon."

Chapter 18

"Mother, why are we waiting in the international terminal? We are in Moscow. You are not telling me everything," Ivan said.

On the flight from Siberia to Moscow, Irina had been thinking about how much she should tell Ivan about their situation and her plans for them. She decided that she must tell him something, even though it was only partially complete.

"Ivan, we are not going to live in Moscow," she confessed. "You know that I was a member of the Russian Space Federation. That austere body of people is the reason that we had to live in Siberia for the last nineteen years. They want us buried and gone out of sight, partially because I was an unwed mother and they felt that I had dishonored the space program. Up to now, I have followed their requests, but now the circumstances are different for both you and me. We are going to leave Russia and live in the USA, at the American Space Agency facilities in Houston. They are paying for our tickets and will provide living accommodations. In return, I will become a member of the agency team and you will be able to participate in higher education and meet many new friends."

Ivan was totally shocked at his mother's words.

"Wow, Mom that is a lot to take in, but I'm still worried about you. Promise me that you will see a doctor when we get to Houston." Irina nodded, and Ivan continued excitedly, "I can't wait! When does our plane leave? When will we arrive? Who will meet us? Mom, you are wonderful!"

Irina was happy to see that Ivan was thrilled at this turn of events, but she was saddened by the knowledge that in a few short months she would no longer be around to see all the changes that would occur in his life.

♍

After many hours in flight and two stops, Irina was still trying to calm a very hyper Ivan, but they arrived in Houston and prepared for immigration. They were escorted to a special desk where Charlie Gonzales was waiting to help them through the paper work and also ensure that their arrival was without incident. When Charlie saw Irina and her son walking towards him, he immediately recognized Irina, but he wondered who the young boy was. He looked too young to be the son she mentioned. Irina noticed his look and whispered that they would discuss Ivan's appearance later.

Irina introduced Charlie to Ivan. Ivan was looking all around and was very quiet.

"I will be taking you to my home, and Martha and I will help you get settled. We have a large home with only Martha and myself, and we have plenty of room for you as long as you like," Charlie told Ivan and Irina.

Charlie and Martha had been married for forty-five years, but they had been unsuccessful in having children of their own. They owned a very nice, up-scale home in the suburbs of Houston. Prior to the arrival of Irina and Ivan, Charlie had asked Martha if they could have houseguests, explaining the situation surrounding Irina and Ivan. Martha agreed to give it a try; she was a very caring person and had volunteered in a hospice program in the past.

On the trip to the Gonzales home, both Ivan and Irina were quiet and deep in thought, somewhat overwhelmed by what was happening to them. They had lived a simple life in Siberia for the last nineteen years, and the United States, Houston, and the Gonzales family were stranger and more different than anything they had ever experienced.

"Welcome to the USA and our home!" said Martha as she opened the door to greet her visitors. Martha was a large woman who reminded Irina of the matronly image of a Russian mother. She had a friendly face and a mild, pleasant voice. Both Ivan and Irina spoke very good English, but it was Ivan who stepped forward and offered his hand, saying, "My mother and I want to thank you and Dr. Gonzales for the help you are giving us. We promise to try not to interfere with your normal lives." Martha ignored the offered hand and gave Ivan a very large Russian-bear hug.

"I'm not sure what normal is around here, but I will do whatever I can to help you to make this transition a happy one," said Martha, still smiling, as she showed Irina and Ivan around the house and helped them settle into the rooms that she had prepared for them.

Chapter 19

Press Secretary Filburn entered the Oval Office and handed a press release to President Atwood.

> The FBI and ATF have announced the capture of a militant family in Oregon and Utah. The Worth family has been under observation for many years. The family, under the leadership of George Worth, recently attempted a raid near the Utah Biosphere. The FBI had inside information that this raid was to be carried out and set up a trap. Mr. Worth and three of his sons were arrested, and a very large cache of weapons was secured. Mr. Bill Worth, previous science advisor to President Atwood, and was not present during the raid and was not arrested.

"Please remove the last sentence. I would rather be left out of this story and let this sad episode end," said Samantha.

Chapter 20

"Samantha, I have a very sensitive subject I have to talk to you about, and I hope you will be open-minded about it," Ray said. They were in their own quarters in the White House; they both had a drink and were relaxing for the evening.

"Per your direction," he continued, "Charlie and I have been working on the Mars colony mission, and I emphasize *colony* because it is a one-way mission and the result will be a permanent colony on Mars. As you suspect, that is not possible with the skillset we have in the current crew, and unless we complement the crew with different skillsets, the mission will fail. Of course we will cross-train the current members of the crew, but that will not be enough. I have not discussed this with anyone else yet because there is another problem with the limitations of the current crew that I need your help with.

"We will be sending Scott and Bill to live a lonely life on Mars without a partner to build a family with. Nancy will be traveling with Niels, but Scott and Bill are on their own. We will be condemning them to a lonely existence for the rest of their lives. I think you agree this will not work. So Charlie and I recommend that we kill two birds with one stone by recommending that two additional crew members be selected based on the skillsets needed for the mission and that they have one special feature—they must be female and of a similar age to Scott and Bill, and as compatible romantically and professionally as possible. Can you help us please?" pleaded Ray.

"Nancy and I have already discussed this and agreed that we will interview the team's final selection. I assume the mission can handle two additional people on board, correct?" asked Samantha.

"Yes, we can, but there is something else you need to know. For a very small colony to survive, the gene pool must be large enough to ensure the health of the children born there. Even with three couples, this gene pool would not be big enough for more than one generation, even with cross insemination, if you know what I mean. One of the new crew members must be a medical doctor, but must also be a specialist on reproduction who is up-to-date on all of the latest technologies. Even with all of this 'help' to ensure the ongoing success of the colony, we would recommend a second manned mission in the future," Ray explained.

"I am sure glad I asked you to oversee this project and that you brought this to me. This requires a women's touch. If you and Charlie will prepare the technical requirements for these two women and a short list of ten of each of those that you think meet those requirements, Nancy and I will consider the more feminine aspects of this selection. Arranged marriages have been around for a long time, and, if done right, can be lasting and successful.

"I really have not considered the need for a second mission or the cost of it, but I can now see your point in planning for it. Please keep this aspect of our conversation private for now. Fortunately, we have technologies in the reproductive area now that will help with the starting of a colony. I'm sure the Pilgrims considered this when they planned their trip to form a new colony in America," said Samantha.

Being hopefully prepared, Ray handed over the technical specifications of the two new crew members.

Crew Member #1: 26 to 32 years of age Medical doctor, general practice & surgery training

PhD in genetics

Good health & athletic

No family ties

Willingness to partake in a one-way mission

Willingness to marry with the intention of having children on Mars

Crew Member #2: 24 to 28 years of age

PhD in civil engineering, habitats for harsh environments

Good health & athletic

No family ties

Willingness to partake in a one-way mission

Willingness to marry with the intention of having children on Mars

"I will work on this with you and Nancy, and I would

like to have Niels, Scott, and Bill be part of this selection, but I feel that Niels and Nancy must have the final decision. Do you agree?" asked Samantha.

"Okay, but I would like to have a private discussion with Niels before we get Scott and Bill involved," offered Ray.

Chapter 21

The sprawling campus that was the Monsanto Company included open spaces and park areas that the employees could use for lunch and just to clear their minds prior to returning to their work area. Dr. Ronda Polanski used these areas every day, sometimes with a friend, but usually alone. Today, she was with her workmate from the next cubical. She had known Dr. Eileen Ortiz for only a few months but found that she could trust her and open up to her without fear of retribution or scandal.

"I have spent the last eight years of my life going to school and getting my doctorate in genetics and my medical degree. There was not much time for a love life, and no real fun. Now I find myself in a small cubical genetically designing seeds that will make tomatoes taste like pomegranates. As you can tell, I'm not a happy camper today. I wish I could find something more interesting to be part of. Don't get me wrong, Eileen, I like you and this environment, it's just... *seeds*! Ugh!"

"Ronda, you are much too talented for this job. I know how you feel, but my situation is different. I haven't told you yet, but I am pregnant. Carlos and I will have our first baby in about seven months, so this job is just perfect for us. We need this income, and Monsanto has a very generous policy for maternity leave.

"You know, I want to introduce you to a friend of ours. Carlos and I have known him for years, and I think you will like him. His name is Juan Pedro, and he is just here from Columbia to play baseball."

"Well, congratulations to you and Carlos. I know you will make a great mother. I don't think it would be right for me to strike up a relationship just now though. Don't tell anyone, but I am thinking of seeking a new position that has more responsibility and excitement."

Ronda did not need or want a blind date; it was not that she didn't have plenty of offers, but even short-term relationships did not interest her at this time.

"Well, in that case, I should give you the job offer that came across my desk yesterday," laughed Eileen. "I almost threw it away because I can't see myself working for the American Space Agency. Do you want to read it?"

"Sure. You never know what may come of it. Thanks."

When they got back to their cubicles, Eileen gave Ronda the job description, and she read it with keen interest. I can't imagine what the space agency needs with a genetics specialist, especially if that person must be a medical doctor as well, thought Ronda as she started typing a response to the job offer.

♎

The sands on Venice Beach were hot, and the beach was full of beautiful people—at least they all thought they were beautiful, thought Linda with a smile. Linda White lived in a small apartment nearby and was seen on the beach every day. She had resigned from her job a few months ago, and she had no desire to go anywhere but the beach. She had experienced a tragedy on her last job, and the beach—and many gin and tonics—were helping her forget.

Linda was young and very attractive; she looked great in her small, pink string bikini, and the beach boys were always approaching her to try to gain her attention. She wasn't interested in the muscles or tans or thongs, but it amused her, so she went every day. Her mother lived across the country in Florida with her second husband, and they didn't have much to say to each other. Linda knew she had to break the mold and start a new life, even if it meant leaving the beach behind.

The next day, instead of laying out in the sand once again, she had an appointment at a headhunter's office to meet with the engineering representative there.

After shaking hands, the representative said, "I have reviewed your resume and am very impressed with your credentials. You have a master's degree in civil engineering specializing in habitat structures, and your last job was direct experience in that field. Before you came in today, I called a friend of mine in the human resources office at the American Space Agency, and she has authorized me to give you a job description that has not been released to the general public yet. Please take this home with you and review it carefully. If you think you might be interested, contact her directly. Good luck to you."

That night, Linda did not have another drink. She curled up on the couch and read the requirements and description of the job of her dreams.

Chapter 22

"It is important that this conversation is just between the two of us for now. Are you sure that Scott and Bill cannot hear this?" asked Ray.

"No problem. I have asked them to review part of the mission planning. What is this all about?" asked Niels.

Ray outlined the two issues they faced, the technical skills needed for the mission and the colony to succeed and the fact that Scott and Bill would live forever alone. He also reviewed his meeting with Samantha and explained that Samantha and Nancy were meeting on the second aspect of this issue. Niels printed out the technical requirements for the two new crew members and read them over as they discussed the problems.

"Ray, this short list is interesting... They are all women!" observed Niels.

"I know," said Ray. "Based on one-on-one interviews, do you think Scott could reduce list one down to five people for us while Bill reduces list two to five, both considering only the technical needs of the mission? After that, Nancy and Samantha will vet the ten people, and then Scott and Bill will make their final decision based on their reaction to the women on a personal level. You and Nancy would have final approval after your interview the two women. They will then meet with Nancy and Samantha, who will explain to them the mission with all the hopes, drawbacks, and personal commitments it entails. I would like to be a fly on the wall for that meeting."

"I know Scott and Bill," said Niels. "They are very loyal and will follow orders all the way, but this is different. This is personal, and they are not stupid. They will see through this for what it is. However, the need for additional complementary skills will be obvious, and they will support the selection process with that in mind. They are both vigorous young men and have all the needs that young men need. I'm sure that they will be very serious in this endeavor to satisfy both needs for the mission," he finished rather seriously.

"By the way, the coast is clear. The divorce between Scott and his wife is complete with no difficulties," said Ray.

Chapter 23

In their common room, Niels, Scott, and Bill were meeting to review the plans for the mission and so Niels could outline the additional skills needed to ensure its success.

Niels said, "Scott, I would like you to review this list of ten medical candidates and their CVs and reduce the list to five for me. Also, Bill, here is a list of ten for the engineering candidates. Please review and reduce to your top five."

Quickly, Scott and Bill reviewed the lists and then compared them. They looked up to Niels with smiles on their faces. "All of the candidates are women," noted Scott.

"Okay, that's true. Our president is a woman. Do you have a problem?" Niels responded.

"No problem, but are there any other expectations for us?" asked Bill.

"For now, consider the mission first. These skills may save your lives and will ensure mission success. If something else falls out from these selections, so be it. Nancy and I will make the final selections based on your recommendations. That's all for now. Good hunting," Niels instructed.

♏

Later, Bill and Scott sat together, discussing the lists in Scott's room. "Do your resumes have pictures?" asked Scott. "Mine do, and it's not surprising. I think there is a dual purpose for these selections."

"Yeah, mine have pictures. I feel that cupid is at work here. But I don't mind. My prospects do not look good from inside here, at least not without some help, so I will work hard at this and be serious about both aspects of this selection," Bill remarked seriously. Then, pointing at a CV, he exclaimed, "Man, look at this one! She is hot!"

"Do you think nationality is important in these selections?" asked Scott.

"I don't think race is important, but I for one will choose an American. The colony should have only one allegiance," stated Bill. "Did I hear Niels right that the Mars colony will initially have six members?"

"Yeah, I think that he is going to tell us that Nancy will join the mission, but he will wait for us to go through with this selection process and accept the fact that we need partners to make it a true colony and ensure its future. I'm all for that. Let's get to work," said Scott.

Chapter 24

Martha and Irina sat in Martha's cozy kitchen, enjoying a cup of coffee. Charlie had taken Ivan with him to work, so they were alone. Irina looked less tired than when she had first arrived yesterday, and she was in good spirits. Martha reached across the table and took Irina's hand.

"I have taken the liberty of contacting an oncologist and making an appointment for you. We will leave in an hour. I know that this is short notice, but I feel that we should take action as soon as possible. I understand that you have not told Ivan of your condition yet, and I would recommend that you wait until you have met with the oncologist before you do. I will of course drive you to your appointment and be with you during this time, if you want me to," Martha explained to Irina.

"Thank you, Martha, for all of your help and understanding, but I do have a problem," confessed Irina. "I do not have enough money to pay for a doctor and all of the follow-up needs."

"Charlie and I have discussed this, and we recommend the following—Charlie is offering Ivan a job today at the space agency. He will have full benefits, including health insurance. You can be listed as his dependent and be covered by Ivan's insurance. His salary will be enough to cover all of your needs as long as you both stay here with Charlie and me," suggested Martha.

"That is a great relief and peace of mind, knowing that my son will be looked after by friendly people that care about him and his future. That makes my future much easier to endure," replied Irina.

♐

Later that afternoon, before dinner, Irina came into the den. "Charlie, may I have a private word with you?" she asked.

"What can I do for you?" asked Charlie as he fixed Irina a drink.

"If you have not already guessed, Ivan's father is Niels Borgue. I would like you to arrange for me to have a private conversation with him before introducing him to Ivan. I will tell Ivan at dinner tonight about my illness and prognosis," expressed Irina.

"I am not surprised. Ivan looks just like his father," said Charlie with a smile. "As you know, Niels is in a very special situation, but I cannot refuse to let you see him. There is much you do not know about Niels' future, but I will let him explain things to you. I will set up a private call to Niels tonight after dinner, and I will keep Ivan busy with a game of chess while you are on the phone, though I have no doubt that he will beat the socks off me." Charlie grinned.

"Thank you. When I returned from my space station assignment, I did not know that our moment of love in the weightless environment would have such dramatic results. We were both irresponsible, to say the least, and we let our emotions get in the way of common sense. The Russian Space Federation was very angry with me, and I was banished to Siberia within weeks of landing. What is strange is that they just left me there with no follow up after Ivan was born. I think over the years and with changing management that they forgot why I was sent there. They just kept on sending my salary. I did not require much, but what little I have left

I have set to be transferred to the account that you helped me open," Irina explained. She sighed. "Now I must face the most difficult time in my life and tell Ivan what was confirmed today. Let's go into dinner and take it from there."

Together, they walked to the dining room. The conversation at dinner was lively, though Irina still struggled to portray a happy face for Ivan some moments.

"Martha, that was a lovely dinner," said Irina as she looked up from her empty plate. "Ivan, I see that you have eaten all of your food again. Martha's cooking is going to put some meat on your bones."

Martha laughed, beaming at the compliment.

"Ivan," Irina continued, "I know you have been worried about my health lately, so I took your advice and went to a doctor today. The results are not good. I have cancer. I only found out about it just before we left Russia, and the American doctors say that it is inoperable. I have at best six months to live." She tried to keep her voice steady. "I am so happy that we came to America because your future is much better than it would be in Russia, and we have good friends here in Charlie and Martha."

Ivan jumped up and ran sobbing into his mother's arms. "I knew that there was something wrong with you, but not this!" cried Ivan. "What will we do? I can't bear it!"

Irina tried to comfort him. "Martha is trained in the care of cancer patients and wants us to stay here until I have to go to a hospice facility, where I will be made as comfortable as possible. I'm so sorry, son, that our last days together must be like this, but rest assured I will be at peace here with you and this wonderful family." Irina cried and continued to hug Ivan.

When Ivan's sobs subsided, he asked his mother if

there was anything he could do.

"If you will be patient with me, I will tell you everything about your father and how you came to be so special," said Irina. "I know you have had many questions about him and how you came to be the way you are."

"You are the one that is special," said Ivan. "We must plan the next few months. There must be something you have always wanted to do."

"I want to go to Disney World with you," shouted Irina, spinning out of Ivan's arms and dancing across the floor. "It is time that we had some fun, don't you agree?"

"Oh yes, Mom, anything to put a smile on your face. I want to fill our remaining time together with lots of happy memories."

Chapter 25

"Ivan, get the chess set out, will you? We have a challenge match to start!" said Charlie. "Your mom and I will be in my office for a few minutes, and then we will begin."

Niels was ready to retire for the evening when the call came through.

"Niels, this is Charlie. This is a special call, and a very private one, so please make sure that you are alone," said Charlie.

"Hi, Charlie," answered Niels, a little surprised at a private call from Charlie this time of evening. "I am alone in my room, and the door is closed. What's up?"

"I have someone here that wants to talk to you. I will leave you alone, and we can talk tomorrow," said Charlie, and he mouthed "Good luck!" to Irina as he left the room.

Niels watched as a woman came into view and looked carefully at her in puzzlement until it slowly dawned on him who stood before him on the screen.

"Irina, is that you? I can't believe my eyes."

A flood of memories swept over him as he took in her appearance. She had always been a pretty little thing, back then, with blonde curly hair framing her oval-shaped face; he could understand how easily they had been drawn together. They had shared one night of passion before coming to their senses, realizing that such behavior could jeopardize both of their careers.

Irina had matured into a beautiful woman, and a feeling of longing overcame him. Niels shook his head to clear it. He was happily married with two great kids, and he wouldn't change that for the world. It was just the shock of seeing Irina again.

Irina, a beautiful mature woman, was looking at Niels expectantly, trying to judge what his reaction would be. She thought him to be as good looking as she remembered him, although over the years she had seen news reports of him...

"Hello, Niels. I'm sure this is quite a surprise for you," she said.

"That's putting it mildly, Irina. What happened to you?" asked Niels. "I tried to get in touch with you a hundred times but came up against brick wall after brick wall. Where were you? Where have you been? Did you try to contact me or just forgot about me once you got back to Russia? Was there someone else?"

"There has never been anyone else in my life before or after you," replied Irina wistfully.

"But why?" began Niels.

On the screen, Irina put up her hand to stop him.

"There are many things we need to talk about, but there is only one thing that is more important than anything else. When I returned to Russia from the space station, the medical team found out I was pregnant. Yes, you have a son." She paused, looking at the stunned expression on Niels' face, then continued, "Ivan was born in a remote village in Siberia where they sent me after they found out I was pregnant. I also tried to get in touch with you but was blocked at every turn. I was afraid to draw too much attention to myself for reasons that will become apparent to you when you meet your son.

"After Ivan was born I did some research and found

out that you had married. I did not want to spoil that for you, but things have changed now. I felt you had a right to know, and, more importantly, I want Ivan to know his father. Charlie has explained to me the situation you are in now, and I don't want to add to your stress or put pressure on you, but my circumstances are special also and I feel that Ivan has a right to know you. I have put off answering his questions so many times that he doesn't even ask any more, and that's sad," she finished.

"I have another family!" exclaimed Niels. "I need some time to digest all of this, but tell me about Ivan. Tell me about your last nineteen years. How wonderful to see you again! Wait, what do you mean 'while you still have a chance'? Where are you and Ivan staying? How long will you be staying? Can I meet Ivan?" pleaded a very excited Niels.

"Niels, unfortunately I have some bad news, and this will help answer many of your questions as to why I am here and why I want you to meet your son so you both can get to know each other. A short while ago I found out that I have a very rare form of cancer, and, as you know, usually by the time you have any symptoms it has advanced to where there is no hope of remission. I have been told that at best I have about six months to live."

At this, Niels looked stricken and held up his hand to say something, but Irina stopped him. "Please let me continue. This is hard enough as it is. Once I knew I was dying, I had to make plans for Ivan. I wanted him to know you and if possible for him to stay in this country and be near you, but at that time I did not know about your difficult situation. Ivan will need someone when I am gone, and I have no family in Russia. I remembered Charlie Gonzales was very much a part of the planning for missions to the space station, and so I contacted him to see if he could help me get here and arrange for us to meet.

"Charlie and Martha have been wonderful and have welcomed us into their home, and I don't know what we would do without them. We will stay with them while I am still well, and then I will enter a hospice for a few more months, so we have plenty of time to catch up. I am happy you want to meet Ivan. I will sit down with him tomorrow, explain to him about you, and see what he wants to do. Ivan was conceived under special circumstances and therefore is a very special young man to me and the rest of the world. When you meet him, you can judge for yourself. I am very proud of the man he has become. I see so much of you in him," Irina explained.

Niels and Irina talked well into the night, catching up on their lives until Niels saw that Irina was exhausted and told her to go to bed and rest. He also needed some time to absorb everything and to think about what he was going to say to Nancy and the boys.

♑

At breakfast the next day Irina explained, "Ivan, you are going to go to work with Charlie, but you will both be late today. I have asked Charlie and Martha to be part of our conversation this morning. I am going to tell you about your father and the special circumstances of our meeting and falling in love."

Ivan sat there with his breakfast untouched and his mouth open. He had noticed his mother's long phone conversation the night before, despite beating Charlie at chess three games in a row. When he tried asking Charlie about it, he was sent to bed. Ivan never would have guessed it would lead to this conversation.

"Mom, I have wondered for many years if you would tell me about my father. Please carry on. I can't wait to hear all about him," said Ivan as he held his mother's hand.

Irina took a deep breath and began, "We met on the space station. I had been on board for three months when your father came on board. He was tall and blond and young, very handsome, and I was attracted to him immediately. I had only one more month left on my assignment, and he said that he would find me after he landed. Our romance was somewhat limited by the tight confines of the space station, but we managed to have some time alone. That last night was too much for me, and I invited your father to my sleeping quarters.

"Ivan, you are the first human to be conceived in the weightless environment of space. It is my theory that this is why you have the special characteristics that you have. When I landed, the Russian Space Federation and I found out that I was pregnant, and they sent me to Siberia with very stern orders to remain there or both you and I would suffer serious repercussions. They provided us with housing in Siberia, and I received an allowance each month to support us, but other than that, there was no other contact. It was almost if we never existed. They forgot about us for nineteen years. And when your father came looking for me, he was blocked by the Russian Space Federation and forced to leave Russia," explained Irina.

"But, Mom, who is my father?" asked Ivan.

"Your father is Commander Niels Borgue," replied Irina.

Ivan sat back and looked at Charlie. "You mean the Commander Niels Borgue that is in quarantine and cannot come out? That Niels Borgue?" asked Ivan.

"Yes. Niels and I talked a long time last night, and I explained our whole situation. He is now married and has two sons—the eldest, Alan, is near your age. Your father would like to meet and get to know you. Charlie says we can go together today, if you feel comfortable with that. I'm sure you need time to process this information. Everything has happened so quickly since we came to America. Are you okay with meeting your father today?" asked Irina.

"Yes, Mom, I am, and I can't wait to meet him. I wonder what he will think of me," said Ivan.

Charlie spoke up then. "I have arranged for you to take placement exams next week in hopes that you will be accepted into the University of Houston to round out your education and get a degree. With your high IQ, it shouldn't take much time at all. In anticipation of your interest in the Mars mission, I am arranging for you to assist with the Mars team so you can become an active member of the team during the next couple of years and therefore have plenty of time to get to know your father. You may stay on campus at the university if you wish or continue to stay with Martha and me."

"Oh no, I want to stay as close to my mother as possible! I would prefer to stay with you and Martha. In that case, I will need to learn to drive and get my own car!" said Ivan with a smile.

"Martha and I couldn't have children of our own, and we are delighted to have a youngster in the house. Besides, one of these evenings I will beat you at chess. Considering that you look like a ten year old, I think taking the bus to school is the best plan for now," replied Charlie.

Chapter 26

Charlie arranged for the meeting between Niels and Ivan to take place the next morning. Neither of them got much sleep that night, thinking of the amazing events that had led up to this moment. In spite of his excitement and curiosity at meeting his father for the first time, Ivan was also sad as he realized none of this would be happening if his mother wasn't dying. He was quite somber as Charlie led him and his mother into the conference room attached to the quarantine area.

They could see Niels through the glass. Ivan was drawn to Niels, and they both reached out and touched the glass separating them. Niels had no doubt that Ivan was his as he looked at the extraordinary young man before him, and his heart filled with pride. Ivan just stood in awe for a few moments, words deserting him. Irina's eyes filled with tears of happiness as she witnessed the reunion of the two most important people in her life. Then pandemonium erupted as all three of them started talking at once, firing questions at each other, laughing, hardly taking time to breathe.

A short time later, it became apparent to Irina that Niels was looking at Ivan in a strange way, and she decided that she must tell Niels about Ivan's unique characteristics.

"Niels, you must be wondering why Ivan looks only ten years old when you know that he is actually nineteen. My theory is that when Ivan was conceived that wonderful night on the space station, the DNA that came together did so in a unique way that has never happened before on Earth. Ivan ages at one-half the normal rate, and he has been blessed with very high intelligence. We still have not explored all of the unique characteristics that he may have. I hope that you will explore these differences with him in the days to come," explained Irina.

"Thank you for that explanation. I'm sure as his mother that you have the best understanding of Ivan's situation," replied Niels. To Ivan, he said, "As far as you are concerned, young man, I will treat you as the nineteen-year-old son that you are."

It was clear that Irina was getting tired, and they decided to part for now. Ivan would visit again the next day. There was not a dry eye amongst the three of them as they said goodbye, but all were full of joy at the thought of being able to see more of each other in the days to come.

Niels was on the video phone with Nancy later that day. "How is the move going? I understand that Charlie has found you and the boys a home here near him and Martha."

"Yes, Charlie sent me a video of the home, and it looks fine for us. Actually, it is much too large for just the three of us. I'm looking forward to seeing it for real. It is furnished, and Martha has taken care of stocking us up with food and supplies. Charlie and Martha are so helpful. They have made the move so much easier. We are all packed and ready to come to Texas. Today is the last day for school, and we will fly down tomorrow. Charlie is going to meet us and take us straight to our new home, and I will leave the boys there and come to have dinner with you. The farm is for sale, and the real estate agent said we will not have any trouble selling. We should get full price for it, so the college money for the boys should be secure," said Nancy.

"Okay, I can't wait to see you and the boys again. The video phone is great but no substitute for seeing you up close, even though there will be glass between us. Have a safe flight and see you tomorrow."

♈

After they arrived in Texas, Nancy fixed dinner for the boys and left them to settle in while she went to have dinner with Niels.

When Nancy walked into the conference room, she saw a worried look on Niels' face. "Why the long face? Aren't you happy to see me?" she asked.

"Of course I am happy to see you and have you here with me, but I have something to tell you and I wish I could be out there with you and hold you to make this a little easier. This is going to be a bit of a shock," Niels started.

"What is it, Niels?" Nancy asked, alarmed at his somber voice. "Tell me, please."

Niels told her of his meeting with Irina on the space station and the fact that they had become intimate. He explained how he had tried to find Irina once his assignment on the ISS was over but to no avail, and then how he had met Nancy and fell in love. He told her how happy he was.

He went on, "Irina is here in Houston with Ivan, her son—my son." Niels became emotional as he said those words. "Charlie brought them here today to meet me. I was shocked, as I'm sure you are now.

"They are here in Houston, staying with Charlie and Martha for very special reasons. I would like to introduce you to them and let them tell you their story. You have a lot of compassion, and I am sure you will sympathize with their situation. Oh, Nancy, I know this must be stressful for you on top of our situation, and I'm sorry if this causes you any pain, but be assured this in no way changes the way I feel about you and the boys. I love you all very much."

After taking a deep breath, Niels continued, "You will be surprised when you meet Ivan. Even though he is actually nineteen years old, he looks like he is only twelve. Irina told me that he ages at half the rate of you and me. She also believes that Ivan's conception in weightlessness is the cause of this and other phenomenon."

After a short pause to collect her thoughts, Nancy said, "Niels, you are a man of many surprises. There is never a boring moment with you. This all occurred before we were married, and knowing you, your intentions were honorable. Some time you will have to tell me the whole story with all the details. Meanwhile, I look forward to meeting Irina and Ivan."

Relieved, Niels commented, "There are a couple of things I need to tell you before the meeting. Irina is dying of cancer. She has about six months to live. As I have explained, Ivan is unique and special in many ways, and this uniqueness is the reason they are here in Houston. I will let you form your own opinions, and then we can discuss the future together later."

"I love you, Niels, and nothing you have revealed today or done in the past will ever change that. I will be here tomorrow morning without the boys. We still need to tell them about our decision for me to join you in the mission to Mars and leave them here with their grandparents. That is going to be very difficult and emotional for all of us. I hope we can explain things to the boys in such a way that will cause them as little pain as possible."

"We cannot tell the boys anything until the real colony members are selected and agree to form the six members that we need," he reminded her. "At that time, Samantha will make the announcement, and then at the same time we can tell the boys."

Niels continued, "I will have Charlie bring Irina and Ivan here so that you can meet them, and we will have lunch tomorrow together. Goodnight, Nancy. I can't wait until we no longer have this glass between us. I do so want to hold you in my arms and make love to you. It has been too long."

"I want that too, Niels," said Nancy passionately.

Chapter 27

Scott and Bill met privately once more in Scott's room to discuss their lists of resumes.

"I am already leaning towards one, Linda White. She is the only one I am interested in. She is very qualified and certainly attractive. I think we could make something exciting and lasting from this relationship," commented a very animated Bill.

"I have the same situation. Her name is Ronda Polanski. Let's exchange the resumes and personal profiles, and if you have any problem with my selection or I yours, we will be honest with each other. A lot of our future success and happiness is at stake," replied a mature and serious Scott.

They exchanged papers, and after reading the respective resumes, Scott said, "You are right, she is very attractive, and I feel that her technical specifications meet our needs. In your interview, you need to question her about the collapse of the underwater habitat and her responsibility in the design and result. Lives were lost, and I'm sure it affected her."

"Agreed. I like Ronda. As a medical doctor she is well qualified, but I don't understand the need for a genetic specialist in our colony. I'm sure we can figure out how to have babies on our own. Oh, by the way, she is very beautiful, but with darker complexion than I would expect a Polish woman to have," replied Bill.

"The need for a genetic specialist probably has to do with the small gene pool and the future growth of the colony. I agree that Ronda's complexion is a little dark, but there could be many reasons for this. I really don't care, and I hope we don't bring this up again. I say we hand these two names over to Niels and tell him that these are the only two we want to interview. We can have him and Nancy see to it that they are convinced to join us, but we should still have the final right to refuse them after our face-to-face interviews," offered Scott.

"Let's do it, but first I think we should meet with Niels and explain why we are giving him only one choice apiece. I can't wait for the first interview," said Bill.

Scott agreed, and they went out to join Niels. They sat around the kitchen table with coffee, and Scott started, "We realize that we were supposed to give you five people to select from, but we feel strongly that these two are the only ones that we want to recommend at this time. If you and Nancy reject either one, we will accept your decision and go back to the lists to select our second choice. We have considered their mission critical requirements as well as the personal possibilities, and find these two qualified for the first and possibly qualified for the second."

"Okay, I will pass on your selections and represent you with Nancy, Charlie, Ray, and Samantha. Leave it to me," said Niels.

Chapter 28

Nancy stood as Charlie brought Irina and Ivan into the conference room.

Charlie said, "I would like to introduce Irina and Ivan Karpov to you, Nancy." Turning to Irina and Ivan, he said, "This is Nancy Borgue."

Irina reached out to shake Nancy's hand, and Irina started to cry as Nancy hugged her. Nancy shook hands with Ivan and noticed how much he looked like a young Niels.

"Hello, Ivan. I am happy to meet you and hope that we can spend time together soon, but for now I would like to spend some time with your mother. We can all get together for lunch later. Why don't you talk with your father for a while?"

Nancy and Irina went and sat at a small table to have coffee and a chance to get to know one another. While Ivan and Niels talked about university in the US and what Ivan should expect, Niels kept glancing over at the women, wondering what they were talking about. An hour later, the four met in front of the conference room glass for lunch, and they talked comfortably with each other. This went on for quite a long time, until Niels was concerned that Irina would tire. He called Charlie in to see that Irina and Ivan had a ride home while Nancy and Niels continued.

After a round of goodbye hugs, Irina and Ivan left, leaving Niels and Nancy to talk in private.

"I recognize that he is a special young man, even though he looks like a boy. He has a very high intellect. It is hard to realize that he is one year older than Alan," mentioned Nancy. "To answer your unasked question, I would be proud to be Ivan's second mother and have him join our family as a full member. I assume that is your wish?"

"You are a wonderful and very perceptive person. Yes, that would be my wish, but we will only have two years with him before we leave for Mars," commented Niels.

"Two years is a short time to be with him, but he will mature in front of our eyes. And it would be good if he would work with Alan. I think that Ivan and Alan could be in charge of all of the colony's needs here on Earth. Our future will be good having them together and on our side as they stay here on Earth and continue their education," she replied.

Chapter 29

The following day, Nancy, Charlie, and Ray sat in the conference room with Niels on the other side of the window. "Should we bring in Scott and Bill and question them about their decision to include only one name on each list?" asked Ray.

"It is up to you, but I already asked the same question of them. They said that it is their life and if it were not for mission success, and respecting our input for mission success, they would make the decision themselves that these two young ladies would be their choice, pending a final personal interview," emphasized Niels.

Nancy commented, "In my view, the personal side is more important than anything else, and I think we should respect the wishes of these two men. Unless the technical aspects of these two resumes are lacking, I recommend that we take this to Samantha for her approval, prior to the final interviews."

"Charlie, what do the two young ladies know up to now?" asked Ray.

"I have interviewed all ten applicants for potential employment at the space agency, but nothing has yet been said to them about their real assignment," replied Charlie.

"Do you believe Ronda and Linda to have the technical skills required for this mission?" asked Niels.

"I do, with one comment concerning Linda. The collapse of the underwater dome that killed twenty-two people weighs heavily on her. I checked on the details of the event and found that not only was she not responsible in any way, but she predicted the collapse and suggested ways to prevent it. She was low on the totem pole and the only woman on the team, and her suggestions would have sent the budget way over. Her ideas were rejected, and she feels that she was not forceful enough to ensure the changes were approved."

Charlie continued, "Ronda's skills are perfect for this mission, and she is a very stable person. She is a dedicated doctor and thorough researcher. I approve of both," replied Charlie.

Ray spoke up. "Prior to the final interviews, Samantha would like to meet with these two women so that she and Nancy together can revealing the actual mission and the reason that Scott and Bill will do the final interview. That way they will go into the interview with Scott and Bill knowing what is expected of them."

"I think that that is a great idea," sighed Niels, relieved that he did not have to have that conversation with the two young ladies.

Chapter 30

The lounge chairs in the hallway outside the Oval Office were very comfortable, but Ronda and Linda were not comfortable. "This is the strangest job interview I have ever had," said Ronda. On the trip from Houston to Washington, DC, Ronda and Linda had been joined by Charlie. When they asked how the trip was part of the interview process, Charlie avoided the question by telling them that all of their questions would be answered soon.

"What are we doing at the White House?" replied a very nervous Linda. "I thought I was having a job interview with the space agency. Have we done something wrong?"

"I don't think so, but here we go," answered Ronda as Lori stepped out of the door to the Oval Office.

"You two women are in for something special. Enjoy your time here, and don't be nervous. Come with me," said the presidential secretary with a smile.

When the two candidates entered, no one was sitting behind the large desk, but two ladies stood from the couch to greet them. One of them was the president of the United States.

"Welcome to the Oval Office and my home away from home," greeted Samantha. "Please sit and make yourselves comfortable. May I offer you some coffee or tea?"

"Madam President, I cannot imagine what we are doing here, but we both thank you for the honor of meeting you. Like all women around the world, we respect you and appreciate your accomplishments. And yes, I would like a cup of tea please," said Ronda.

"So would I," said Linda in awe. "I am honored to meet you, Madam President."

Lori hurried out to prepare tea for the ladies.

"First of all, let me introduce you to Mrs. Nancy Borgue, wife of Commander Niels Borgue, leader of the recent Ceres mission," said Samantha.

Keeping up with the news, Ronda knew the situation that Nancy was in and expressed her sympathies. Linda nodded in agreement, dumbfounded at where she was and with whom.

After Lori served tea and returned to her desk, the president got down to business. "This conversation will be between us four ladies and will not be official in any way. As such, please call me Samantha."

Nervous, Ronda and Linda both nodded.

"The information I am about to give you is classified and must remain in this room, and with Dr. Gonzales for now," began Samantha. "As you have probably heard, the three-man crew in quarantine now cannot leave without contaminating the whole world with the ARC1 that is in their bodies. They have come up with what they call 'the final solution,' which could involve you two."

Ronda and Linda looked at each other with questions in their eyes.

"About two years from now, they will form the first crew to travel to Mars, where they will start a colony. This will be a one-way trip with no possibility of returning to Earth because of the threat of ARC1," continued Samantha.

Both ladies looked at Nancy with sympathy in their eyes, but they were shocked when Nancy said, "I will be joining my husband on the trip to Mars to ensure a solid representative government there, including freedom of religion and the philosophy of a true colony, like that formed by the members of Mayflower."

"You have been selected for your skills and, to be perfectly honest, because you are both young and female," continued Samantha. "Pending final interviews with the crew, you will be offered a job with the American Space Agency to help prepare for the mission to Mars and to lift off with the crew to complete the colony there.

"Again, to be completely honest, Scott Nettles has specifically chosen you, Ronda, from many resumes to be the medical officer for the Mars colony. Bill Lee has selected you, Linda, to assist him in the environmental engineering for the colony," said Samantha. "These men are hopeful that you will also be agreeable to a long-term relationship with them."

The meaning was clear to Ronda, but Linda still looked confused.

"I have heard about arranged marriages before, but I never thought it would happen to me. There is so much to consider, and I'm sure Linda feels the same way, that we need time to think things through. Although I cannot accept the 'job' today, I am honored at the opportunity and agree to go through the interview process. Who knows, Scott and I may hit it off," said a very confident Ronda.

You could see the light bulb go off in Linda's eyes as Ronda spoke. She said, "I feel the same."

"Of course, the decision is not to be taken lightly, and we encourage you to talk this over with each other and your families after you are cleared to. A lot is at stake, and though we want to give you time, I hope you understand the urgency behind the decision-making process. Dr. Gonzales can help you with mission questions as well," finished Samantha.

♓

A few hours later, on the plane back to Houston with Charlie, Ronda, and Linda, Nancy said, "Charlie found my two sons and I a large six-bedroom home about two blocks from him and his wife. We have already moved in, and you two young ladies are welcome to join us in this home, should you decide to join the mission."

"Thank you, but we will stay in the provided motel until after our interviews with the crew," stated Ronda. "We would also like to have bios on Mr. Nettles and Mr. Lee prior to the interview, Mr. Gonzales."

Charlie and Nancy both noted the rather formal speech by Ronda and how quiet Linda was. They were both deep in thought, wondering about a future on Mars with men that they had never met.

"I anticipated that request and have the bios with me for you to read on the plane," Charlie said. "I will remind you that this is top secret for now. I will tell you when we can go public with the Mars colony mission."

When they landed in Houston, Linda and Ronda asked to take a separate car from Charlie and Nancy so they had privacy to discuss the latest revelations in their lives. Although they had just met, it seemed that their lot was about to be thrown together.

Chapter 31

The next day, Nancy escorted Ronda into the conference room next to the quarantine facilities while Linda waited in the outer office. "Dr. Ronda Polanski, this is my husband, Niels Borgue. Niels, this is Ronda. If you don't mind, Ronda, I will sit in on this portion of the interview. You will have complete privacy in your interview with Scott Nettles," commented Nancy.

"How do you do, Commander Borgue? I am honored to meet you, and I am sympathetic to your situation. I congratulate you on the very brave decision that your final solution represents," said a very humble Ronda.

"Thank you, Ronda, and please call me Niels. The president has relieved all three of us from our military duties so that we can concentrate on what is ahead of us. I wanted to meet with you and Linda to discuss your technical merits for the launch and life on Mars, before you two meet with Scott and Bill. I will not talk about any other aspects of your interview with them," he explained. Then he commented, "Ronda, your credentials as a medical doctor are clear, but I notice only a small amount of clinical experience so far. Will you be able to handle a wide range of medical problems on Mars?"

"While it is true that I have limited clinical experience, I have experienced a wide range of medical problems while doing my internship rotations. Plus, I understand that I will have about two years of intense training prior to entering the facilities to join you and your team. I am also sure that we will have good communications with Earth, and I will see to it that we have a large medical database in our servers on Mars," answered Ronda.

Thinking about Ivan and one of Ronda's past research projects, Niels asked, "Do you believe in the zodiac and the stated influence in astrology on the personalities of people on Earth?"

This man is a deep thinker and has gone to the heart of my research, thought Ronda. Aloud, she said, "I believe that there are cyclic and repeating genetic mutations that occur at the moment of conception. These are caused by cyclic cosmic forces on Earth that astrologists call the twelve signs of the Zodiac, only they cite the birthdate. I think that the conception date is when these influences could be in effect. I am not sure that I will be able to carry on this research if I join this mission. In any case, the research was very controversial and I would have difficulty finding funding to continue here on Earth anyway. That was why I took my position at Monsanto," she explained.

Ronda knew that with only three couples on Mars, the gene pool would not be large enough to naturally sustain a viable population. She assumed that she would be responsible for ensuring that they had sufficient genetic material and equipment on Mars to be able to supplement artificially the deficiency in natural genetic material. Niels and Nancy would have to come to grips with that concept and also plan for additional couples to follow them to Mars, though she did not know why Niels was asking about that particular research project.

"Thank you, Ronda, for your openness. I look forward to more conversations concerning your research and your progress in the medical world. Your decision is a serious one for you and for all of us on the mission to Mars. I will meet with Scott and Bill and relay to them that I give full, enthusiastic support of you as our medical officer, if you chose to accept this assignment. Of course, I realize that there are other aspects of this 'job' that are personal and only you and Scott can work out, but I wish you the best in that endeavor. I am here to help and give advice if you need," said a rather paternal Niels.

"Thank you, Niels. This is a rather unique job interview, but I realize that history shows that arranged marriages are sometimes the most successful. And when one marries an individual, they also marry the family—in this case, you and Bill. I am a big girl, and I will go into this interview with Scott with eyes open, looking forward to it," said a very serious Ronda.

Before she could leave, Niels said, "By the way, Scott had a note left for you under your saucer." He grinned as she pulled it out.

To Miss Ronda Polanski:

You are invited to a dinner date this evening. It will be just you and I in the not-so-intimate surroundings that you now find yourself. I will do my best to make you as comfortable as possible. Although there will be a glass pane between us, I hope that our meeting will be open and fulfilling for both of us.

Regards, Scott Nettles

Ronda smiled, appreciating Scott's sincerity and looking forward to the meeting with him. I think we're off to a good start, she thought as she left. She passed Linda as the other woman was escorted into the conference room by Nancy to meet with Niels.

"Hello, Miss White. Thank you for coming here," welcomed Niels. "As you can see, it is difficult for me to leave this confinement."

"Dr. Gonzales told us of your situation," replied Linda with a small nod. "There were twenty-two people in the Ocean Dome, and a lot of time was spent discussing close confinement and how to get along in those situations. Unfortunately, the confinement issue did not have time to be a problem."

"That situation is one of the things I wanted to talk to you about. I understand that the Ocean Dome collapsed about one year ago on the initial commissioning mission, with all hands lost. Why were you not part of the commissioning crew?" asked Niels.

"That whole event is very sad for me, and I still have nightmares about it. I understand why you might need to talk about it. I was not part of the commissioning crew because I was part of the design team, which was well into the design of the second dome. When I presented my findings about the flaws that my work revealed, the team felt that I was being overly critical of their work and did not take me seriously. I was the youngest person on an all-male team, and therefore they did not listen to me or really take me seriously. My suggestions were going to delay the project and cause a large overrun on the budget. I was forced to be on the outside from that point on. I had to stand by while my fiancé and twenty-one other people I had worked closely with were killed in the collapse of the dome two days after they settled on the ocean floor," said a very animated Linda.

Nancy held her hand to help calm her. "We did not know that one of the victims lost in the tragedy was your fiancé. We are so sorry for your loss. Please, tell us about him," said Nancy.

"His name was Renaldo Garcia, and we had been engaged for only a few weeks. To be honest, I don't think that our relationship would have lasted. There was a girl on the commissioning crew that was definitely interested in him, and they were going to be down there for six months. I'm sure Renaldo could not withstand that onslaught for six months. In hindsight, I should have found a way to become part of the commissioning crew, but something held me back," said Linda.

"For this mission you would be part of the crew and have final responsibility for the design, location, and implementation of the habitat we will use on Mars. This is a large responsibility, and of course all of us would help you in your effort to make that habitat the safest that science can possibly make it. Are you up to this challenge, and can you complete this project in two years?" asked Niels.

"That is a tall order, and I cannot answer you today. A lot depends on the outcome of my meeting with Bill Lee, but I will say this—I feel that I want to try, and that with the help of the space agency, we can succeed," she answered. Turning to Nancy, Linda added, "There is another aspect of my involvement in this mission concerning Bill Lee and my relationship with him. I am a rather excitable and emotional person, likely to be impetuous and not necessarily calm, cool, and collected. I will need your advice and stabilizing influence for the next two years. I understand the need for me to remain outside the quarantine facility to work on the mission, but how will Bill and I progress our personal relationship?" She finished with a sigh.

"Charlie has the key to the quarantine facilities, though you will not be allowed in until he says so. That is the rule for Ronda and Scott, you and Bill, and Niels and me. We don't like it any better than you, if that is what you mean, but you must conduct yourself like the rest of the team. Of course, I will be here as often as you need me," replied Nancy.

Niels promised once again that he would only discuss with Scott and Bill the technical merits of his interview with Linda and that her meeting with Bill would remain private.

"Good luck. I like you, Linda, and I think you would be a great asset to the mission," he concluded.

"I suggest that you both change locations and move into the home where I am living. That way we can be more accessible to each other," said Nancy.

"That sounds sensible," replied Linda. "I'll talk it over with Ronda and let you know. Right now my head is spinning with all of the decisions I will have to make. It is overwhelming."

"Of course it is," said Nancy sympathetically. "No one wants to rush you into this. We realize that this will be a life-changing event for you, but at the same time, the space agency has a schedule to maintain. Hopefully in two tears you will have time enough to develop a solid foundation with Bill and the rest of the crew and to feel at peace with your decision. Just remember that you are not alone. All of us are here to help you with any questions you may have. Don't be afraid to ask."

"Thank you," said Linda. "You are very supportive and a calming influence. I need that."

Before she left, Niels mentioned that Linda would find a note addressed to herself from Bill. When she read it on her way out of the building, she discovered her own invitation to a special dinner.

Chapter 32

"Okay, guys, this is very important to me, and you have to use your creativity and whatever resources the Navy has to make this evening the best date ever." Scott was giving directions to the setup crew, and his palms were sweating as he nervously looked on.

"I want us both to have the same meal and wine, candle lights, a round table as close to the glass as you can get it. I'm going to put my table close to the glass, just across from hers. All of this formal office furniture must be removed, and I want pictures of flowers and nature on the wall and a large bouquet of roses on the table. I want you to find and mix some old songs by Alicia Keys, Mariah Carey, Adele, and Lady Gaga to use as background music, which I would like to control from in here. Thanks for your help," he said through the glass. "Now get to work. She will be here at nineteen hundred hours."

♈

Right on the dot of seven o'clock, Ronda opened the door and entered. She stood there in amazement. What had been a plain conference room yesterday was now a very pleasant, cozy dining room with subdued lighting, flowers, and some of her favorite music playing. How did he know? At the end of the room was a small table with a candle and a vase of roses. Beautiful. When she looked up, Scott was standing a little back from the window, dressed in a lightweight summer suit with a small flower in his lapel. It was an old-fashioned look to go with the old-fashioned music.

Scott was standing back from the window so that he

could see out; he thought that he was not visible from her side, and it was just as well—he had his mouth open in awe. She was beautiful, dressed in a white sheath dress that contrasted with her naturally dark skin. Her dark hair fell casually to her shoulders. Her high heels emphasized her long, shapely legs. She was slim but rounded out in all the right places.

Scott stepped forward. "Hello, Miss Polanski. Welcome to my little world. Thank you for accepting my invitation," he greeted.

"Well, the pleasure is mine. I am overwhelmed with your planning and thoughtfulness in preparing for this unusual first date. The limo, champagne, and chocolates were a nice touch on the ride over, and Chavez was the perfect escort," responded Ronda. "Call me Ronda please. You are a national hero, and I am a little in awe at the moment. Thank you for your service, though I understand you are not in the military anymore and not currently free to leave your confinement as I'm sure you would like." She was touring the room, looking at pictures. "Wow, these roses are beautiful."

"After we announced our final solution, we thought it best if we were not members of the military any longer. We thought that the rest of the world would feel uncomfortable with three US military members on Mars. We were all discharged with special dispensation," Scott explained, watching her.

After hearing her talk freely, he was a little more at ease and started to relax. Opening up to her, he went on. "I'm glad to hear that Chavez was the perfect escort for you. Being confined in these rooms is difficult, and I hope that you will keep an open mind to our situation. I'm sure that it is just as difficult for you, but let's make the best of it as we get to know each other. Shall we have some wine before dinner?" he asked.

Ronda thought, This man is handsome, sincere, intelligent, and considerate of others. How could she encourage him to feel as comfortable with her as she was with him now?

"Chavez, please show Miss Polanski to her table and decant and pour the wine for her," said Scott over the intercom to the kitchen.

"Scott, I am curious about one thing. How did you find out about the kind of music I like?" asked Ronda. "I'm sure that I did not include it in my bio."

"I didn't know. This happens to be the kind of music that I like. That appears to be one thing we have in common already," said Scott.

Gradually, during a long and leisurely dinner, the couple found it easy to talk to each other, and the conversation was lively, amusing, and at times serious as they delved into each other's backgrounds. They discussed their likes and dislikes and were happy to find that they had many things in common. They did not dwell on the upcoming mission, although it was prevalent in their minds, but they knew that there would be many more meetings like this one. They both realized that a decision must come early to ensure sufficient time to find replacements if the answer was no. As they got to know each other better it would be easier to discuss that final commitment at a later date.

Glancing at his watch, Scott was surprised to discover that three hours had passed.

"Well," he said to Ronda, "I think our first date went very well, don't you?"

"Yes," replied Ronda, "I do."

"Good," smiled Scott. "Let's meet again for lunch tomorrow."

Chapter 33

Linda met Ronda at the door of their new home with Nancy and the boys; they had been there for a few days and had met the boys when they moved in.

"Tell me everything. Did you like him? Was he as handsome as his pictures?" asked a very excited Linda as they ran up the stairs to Ronda's room.

In the living room, Nancy just smiled and an ever-observant Jon said, "What's going on, Mom? Who did Dr. Ronda just see?"

"In due time," said Nancy. "Adult secrets." She wondered when they could tell the boys about the mission. They were getting suspicious; Nancy thought it was time for them to tell the boys about Irina and Ivan, and she decided to place a call to Niels.

He was in his comfortable attire when he answered the video phone. "Hi, honey. What's up?" answered Niels.

"I think it is time to tell the boys about Irina and Ivan. It will help Ivan get a good start here in America with someone his own age."

"I agree. Why don't you bring the boys over tomorrow and we'll tell them together. They are both smart and mature for their age, so I don't think it will be a problem," decided Niels.

♉

The next day in the conference room, Nancy, Alan, and Jon met with Niels.

"Boys, I have asked you to come today because I have something special to tell you. I hope you can have an open mind about all that I am going to reveal to you. I have told your mother this, and she agrees with me that you should know the whole story."

Alan and Jon sat and listened enthralled as Niels told them about Irina and Ivan and the fact that they had a new brother.

After some silence, Jon and Alan started speaking at once.

"When can we meet them?" asked Jon. "I can't wait to see them."

"Me too," said Alan. "I have another brother! Wow, this is awesome."

Niels and Nancy smiled at each other, knowing that they had done a fine job raising their sons.

"I'll call Irina tomorrow and ask her and Ivan to come over to the house for lunch," said Nancy.

The next day, Ivan was anxious to meet his brothers as Nancy opened the door. "Come in, come in. Welcome to our home. The boys are waiting for you in Alan's room. Let's go up now," Nancy said to Ivan as Irina went into the living room.

Both boys jumped to their feet as their mother walked in with Ivan. Nancy made the introductions and told the boys that she would be downstairs with Irina and would call them when lunch was ready, giving them plenty of time to get acquainted. As she left the room, she could already hear

Alan and Jon firing questions at Ivan.

"Do you speak English?"

"How old are you?"

"Tell us about Russia."

She heard Ivan reply, "I speak English as well as four other languages, I have just turned nineteen, and Siberia is a very unfriendly place. I never want to go there again. If you are wondering why I look so young, well, I have a story to tell you."

Nancy smiled as she went to sit with Irina. "I think they are going to be just fine," said Nancy, patting Irina's hand.

A few hours later, Nancy called the boys down to lunch. "Irina, I would like to introduce you to my sons, Alan and Jon. Boys, this is Ivan's mother, Irina Karpov."

Both boys were very formal as they acknowledged the introduction, and Alan said, "We are both very pleased to meet you and welcome you to our home. Please feel comfortable here, and we hope that Ivan can come and visit more often."

Chapter 34

Later that day, Niels and Nancy were talking on the video phone.

"Niels, when can we tell the boys and my parents about our decision? It's killing me to have to put them off. Plus, we have to make a lot of decisions about their future," cried Nancy as she wiped tears from her eyes.

"I know it is not easy for you, but we have promised Samantha that we will keep this secret until Ronda and Scott and Linda and Bill make their intentions known. There can be no colony on Mars without you three women there with us. So until they make up their minds, there is nothing to announce. Help the girls along with a decision as soon as possible, and then we can make more positive plans for the colony. It has only been three month since our return from Ceres, but it seems like forever. I can't wait for you to join me in here, but that will have to wait until just before liftoff.

"By the way, there is something I want you and Charlie to do for us. I would like to expand this facility so that Scott and Bill have their own private conference room. Perhaps it could be decorated by Ronda and Linda with your help. I feel that they will need a lot of private time to speed up a decision, and I will need this room with all the meetings that will happen when we start the engineering projects in earnest. Plus, we need this room to be together as much as possible. Did you get any feedback from Ronda concerning her first meeting with Scott last night? Scott has been on cloud nine all day, and he and Bill have been holed up in Scott's room most of the day," commented Niels.

"Well, according to Ronda, she and Linda were up late last night talking about Ronda's date with Scott, and today they went shopping together for a dress for Linda for her dinner with Bill tonight. They act like sisters and are getting along just fine. I like Ronda a lot. She is very mature and comes from a good family. Do you know that her father came from England as a young man and his father came from Poland just before the Second World War? His mother was English but from India, hence Ronda's beautiful complexion. Ronda's father is now an Ohio congressman, and her mother died three years ago from a climbing accident. I haven't talked with Linda about her parents yet, but I have the impression that they did not approve of her fiancé or her decision to work on the Ocean Dome project. She hasn't had much contact since then. By the way, I like what you have done to the conference room. It has a nice women's touch," commented Nancy.

"That was Scott and Chavez's doing for these dinners. It will be back to business tomorrow after Linda's and Bill's date."

Chapter 35

Linda and Ronda were having lunch in a small diner after a very enjoyable morning shopping for the perfect dress for tonight's date with Bill.

"Well, have you decided about marrying Scott and going to Mars?" asked Linda.

"We had a wonderful evening together, and he is very gallant. I believe he likes me and we could make a good couple and have beautiful babies. First impressions are important, and my first impressions are very favorable, but this decision about the one-way trip to Mars to start a life in a small colony with only ourselves to create a reasonable existence together is a serious one.

"So far, I like all of the people involved. I believe you and Nancy and I could get along well together. I think Niels will be a good leader, with Nancy as a stabilizing presence. I don't know Bill yet, but I'm sure the space agency uses the highest standards when selecting their astronauts.

"One of the interesting possibilities for me is to be able to continue my research in genetic improvements for the human race based on weightlessness and low gravity environments. This will weigh heavily on my decision. I realize that we have to make a quick decision because it would not be fair to Scott and Bill to linger too long, but right now, if Scott were to ask, I would say yes," said a rather emotional Ronda.

Linda held Ronda's hand and said, "Thank you for being so honest with me. We have only recently become acquainted, but I feel you are the sister that I never had. Nancy is mature and has raised a family of her own, and she has decided to spend the rest of her life separated from her sons to be with and support her husband. That takes a lot of courage and love and real values, and I would follow her leadership. Your decision will influence my decision, but that is unfair to you. So I propose that we meet after my date with Bill and find a way to make this decision together."

Her eyes shiny and bright, Ronda nodded in agreement.

Chapter 36

To Miss Linda White,

Please attend a quiet evening with me tomorrow evening for dinner. I am looking forward to meeting you and getting to know each other. A limo will pick you up at 18:30.

Regards, Bill Lee

Linda reread her invitation as she turned to Chavez and asked, "Am I presentable?"

"You are a knockout. I envy that young man. If he isn't impressed, let me know and I will knock some sense into him," replied Chavez.

"What is he like? What does he like? What should we talk about?" asked Linda nervously.

"He is a fly boy, a jet jockey, a Top Gun like Tom Cruise. Those guys are all arrogant, headstrong, and a little bit reckless, but Bill Lee is different. He is all of those things, but he keeps them to himself. They would not have selected him into the astronaut program if he was not stable and reliable. I respect him, and now, after meeting you, I am envious. If it doesn't work out, give me a call," said Chavez with a wink. "Here we are. I will see you in and be on standby if you need anything."

♋

"Hello, Linda," greeted Bill as Linda walked in. Wow, she is beautiful, thought Bill; I hope she will like me and we will get along. His future might not be so bleak after all.

"Hello, Bill," said Linda, giving him a quick look over and liking what she saw. "This has to be the most awkward first meeting ever. Thanks for this beautifully decorated room. I see that you are taking this courtship thing seriously. I have never had a blind date before, but we both have a head start having read each other's bios. We should be reasonably comfortable with each other," said Linda as she sauntered slowly across the room to stop in front of the window.

"I agree," replied Bill. "Come and sit down and we will get started."

Linda's sexy black dress and a little black lace showed her long legs as she walked closer in high-heeled sandals, mesmerizing Bill.

Finally he said, "Linda, you are more beautiful than I expected. Your picture does not come close to doing you justice." A moment later, he asked, "Chavez, please bring in the wine and appetizers."

"Why thank you, Bill. Speaking of pictures, yours looks like a Chinese version of Tom Cruise. Who were you trying to impress?" asked Linda.

Bill laughed and looked a little embarrassed. "When you are in with a bunch of flyboys, you must be the most arrogant and toughest to intimidate them and attract more women than them. I tried, but it just wasn't in me. I am confined to these quarters now, but I would love to be able to get out of here and fly you wherever you want to go, even to Mars," said Bill.

They had a slow and casual meal and talked freely, showing no hesitation in response to any subject that came up. A few hours and a few drinks later, Linda said, "Since our meeting with President Atwood, and she was pretty clear about the assignments, I know we will have a couple of years to get to know each other better. Ronda and I have agreed to meet after this dinner with you and discuss our future possibilities, but we realize that a decision must not be a long, drawn-out affair. So as far as you and I are concerned, I'm definitely interested in pursuing a relationship."

"Me too. I think this meeting went very well," said Bill. "Let's meet tomorrow so that we can get to know each other better." He was already looking forward to it.

Chapter 37

Several weeks later, Linda and Ronda were sitting at a small table in a local establishment near the Houston facilities, having a drink and lunch.

"Well, we have to consider two things, these men and whether we want to spend the rest of our lives with them on Mars, never to return to Earth," said Ronda. "That is a very heavy thought. Well, maybe not so bad about the men, but Mars!"

"You're right. Just think, we couldn't go to our local bar like we are today. On the other hand, we won't have to worry if the boys are down at the local pub with their friends, ignoring us," said Linda with a slight slur.

"Just think of Scott, Bill, and Niels sneaking out back for a quick drink behind our backs. No secrets up there!" giggled Ronda.

"We should have invited Nancy today. Maybe next time. We girls will have to stick together. Oh look, another drink. Where did that come from?" asked Linda as she looked around. She saw some men looking in their direction with intentions that were clear.

"Well, we won't have to endure unwanted attention when we are up there," said Ronda. "Let's get out of here while we can."

They went over to Nancy's and spent the rest of the afternoon opening up to her about their feelings about Scott and Bill and their pending decision.

"I don't have any problem with Scott. We have met many times in the last few weeks, and we are drawing closer each time. He is very thoughtful, but he's slow to open up and show his real feelings. I think he just doesn't want to push me too fast. It is very difficult when we cannot make physical contact. If I could just put my arms around him, I know things would progress much faster. Maybe too fast," said Ronda.

"Well, Scott will pop the question soon enough, and you will have to make your decision. But have you really considered and made your personal decision to go to Mars and spend the rest of your life with the five of us in isolation from the rest of the human race?" asked Nancy.

"I like and trust all of you, and I could enjoy being with you as a small family. I do have my work in genetics, but I do not know how to judge your feelings for me. I am not a very religious person, and I'm worried that you will resent my neutral position on science and religion, and my work in genetics, and the future gene pool on Mars," said Ronda.

"I have the same concerns as Ronda," said Linda. "I am neutral where religion is concerned and worried that you might have a conflict with that."

"You both forget that I am married to a scientist and engineer who is not a very religious person. I have had a lot of experience showing and practicing tolerance and understanding. You do not have to worry about our relationship on that matter, but I may try to move you to a more comfortable feeling with God, especially when we are nearer to God on Mars," said Nancy with a warm smile.

Nancy continued, "I understand your work and our need for security in the near-term viability of the human population growth on Mars. I am hopeful that your work will not be necessary and that there will be a long line of young people coming to Mars to naturally grow the population." Turning to Linda, she asked, "How are you and Bill getting along?"

"Great. If Bill was outside now and he asked me to marry him, I would say yes right away. A girl could not ask for a more exciting romance with a sexy man to call her own. We have talked about babies and family, and he was a little surprised at the subject. We will talk again, but Bill is young in many ways and needs my influence in matters of true love and family planning. I'm not worried on that account. I think I am in love again, and for real this time," said Linda.

"I'm happy for you, but Bill is not outside. If he asked you today and his proposal included going to Mars, what would you say?" asked Nancy very pointedly.

Linda looked to Ronda for help and finally said, "I would say yes. Love is a funny thing, and I love all of you as well as Bill." She started crying.

Nancy put her arms around Linda and said, "Thank you both for your openness and honesty. I have given a lot of thought about my decision to join Niels, and I'm sure that you two will seriously consider what the future on Mars holds for you."

Chapter 38

A few days later, Ronda was sitting with Scott in their private corner, and Linda and Bill were in their private corner, the glass separating them. Each couple could see each other, but they could not hear what the other pair was saying.

"What do you think about families? I would like to have many babies," said Linda.

Bill sat back and hesitated before answering. "You mean having little green Martian babies, with large eyes and long skinny fingers?" chuckled Bill, not knowing whether to be serious or not.

"Well, I hope that the result of our love would produce something more normal than that, but I believe our responsibility to the colony would be to have many children, and I for one would not mind that."

"Only with you," said Bill.

"Linda, I want you to close your eyes and picture you and me on a secluded beach, with palm trees hanging over the water and the sound of the waves in the background. See me on one knee as I say, 'Linda, will you marry me and let me take you to the stars?'"

Linda opened her eyes to find Bill on one knee with hope in his eyes.

"Yes, yes, yes! Let's go to Mars and live our lives together forever."

"Should we tell them?" Bill asked as he looked over to see Scott on one knee. "I wonder what they are doing."

Then Linda got up and ran over to Ronda, giving her a big hug. "I hope you said yes, because I did!"

"We did agree that this was the time and that we would both say yes. I just didn't think that the boys would get the hint at the same time," said Ronda so that Scott and Bill couldn't hear. They were too busy back slapping and high-fiving and making a lot of noise anyway.

Scott said, "Bill, get Niels. I'll get Chavez with you-know-what."

Niels and Chavez entered at the same time. "Okay, Chavez, do your thing," said Scott.

Chavez sat both women next to each other and presented them each with beautiful diamond rings that Scott and Bill had picked out on the internet. Then he stood them up and gave each one a large, lingering kiss, one from Bill and one from Scott.

Ronda and Linda were both embarrassed and looked at Chavez with renewed interest.

"Thanks, Chavez, your duties are done. I think you enjoyed that way too much. Now bring out the champagne," chuckled Scott.

"I need to call Nancy and Charlie and Samantha. We all need something to celebrate. It is four now, so let's have a party starting at seven tonight," said Niels, already giving Chavez his orders while the couples went back to their private corners.

Chapter 39

"Hello, boys. I hope you and Jon are getting along with Ivan," said Niels when Nancy escorted all three of them into the conference room for their meeting with Niels.

"Yes, Father, we have enjoyed Ivan's company and his unique stories and his very unique features. I now have a little brother who is also my older brother," commented Jon. All laughed at his openness and honesty.

"Boys, your mother and I have something to tell you, and I hope that you can be open minded and mature about this. The scientists are not going to find a way to eradicate this bacteria without killing us, and neither Scott, Bill, nor I want to be a worry, a burden, and a target for the whole world. Instead, we are going to form the first mission to Mars. We will form a colony there in preparation for others to follow. Because this mission is to form a colony, your mother, Ronda, and Linda have decided to join us. Because of ARC1, you must understand that when they join us, they also cannot come out of quarantine. When we lift off for Mars, we cannot come back. This will be a one-way mission for all of us," said Niels.

There was silence in the room as the enormity of this sunk in.

"Boys, you know we love you, but we also know how mature you are. You will soon enter into a phase of your life where you develop your independence and follow your own path. As much as your father and I would like to influence this path, we will have to do so from a distance. All it takes is twenty minutes for a message to travel from Earth to Mars," said Nancy as she hugged her boys.

Ivan said, "I promise to you both to be there and support

you and Alan and Jon as long as you need me. You have been very kind to me and my mother, and I will tell you now that I will be first in line to be part of the second wave to travel to Mars."

Jon had tears in his eyes when he said, "I will miss you, and I understand why this must be, but I also hope to be able to be with you on Mars once we are older and have gotten the education and training required."

"Dad, we thought we were going to lose you to this bacteria. Your solution is very brave, and I am very happy that we will not lose you, but I am also sad that you and Mom are going to Mars without us. Mom, we understand your need and desire to be with Dad forever, and I feel much better to have you with him. The colony will be more stable with your guidance, and we know Dad will be happier," said an animated Alan.

"It will take about two more years to finalize all the requirements for this mission, and Mom, Ronda, and Linda will remain outside the quarantine facilities until the last moment to help with all the preparations prior to liftoff. I will have assignments for all of you over the next two years also. Thank you all for your love, support, and understanding," said Niels.

Over the next hour they discussed and made plans until everyone felt comfortable with the situation. Nancy and Niels were proud of the way their sons had handled all of the details and accepted the huge change that was coming into their lives.

Chapter 40

"Charlie, bring in Ronda and Linda, and I will get Scott and Bill," called Niels over the intercom.

As Scott and Bill came into the room to join Niels, they all started to laugh. Charlie stood back, clearly trying to contain his own laughter. "What is with the getup?" Scott asked the women.

"Linda and I thought that it would not be appropriate to tease you two for the next two years with sexy and seductive clothing, so we chose bib overalls and plaid shirts to dress down. Like it?" asked Ronda.

"Ronda, you look sexy in anything you wear, but I have to admit the affect does work. My blood pressure is more under control since the last time we met," said Scott. Ronda blushed, and Linda smiled knowingly, giving her a wink.

"I was born and raised on a farm in Minnesota, but I will not wear OshKosh B'gosh. Niels, you will just have to suffer for the next two years," said Nancy with a chuckle.

Alan, Ivan, and Jon entered the conference room then, and Niels addressed everyone.

"Thank you all for coming. You will be the core team for the Mars colony mission, and yes, I have included you boys as an integral part of our planning and execution. I have recommendations and assignments for all of you. You all will report to Charlie, and we will meet here at least weekly to review progress on all of your assignments. The reason I am including you three boys is that Nancy and I feel that this mission and colony will be for your future generation and we trust that you will have our best interest here on Earth," commented Niels.

"Excuse me, Niels," interrupted Bill. "I would like to recommend a new member to the core team. My sister Joy will graduate from high school with high honors next month, and she is now alone with no family. She would like to attend the University of Arizona and major in nutritional science. It seems to me that having to grow our own food is a very important element of our mission. She worries about me and my future, and I would like to invite her to our inner circle as soon as possible," said Bill.

Charlie responded, "Having something to eat and being able to grow it on Mars is certainly within our purview, and I have to admit that the space agency is better at designing and building things rather than growing things. The University of Arizona is the leading resource for automatically deployable greenhouses, and having someone with your interest foremost working with that team makes a lot of sense. I can assure you, Bill, that I can smooth the way for Joy to join the University of Arizona for next September's classes."

"This is a democracy, so let's vote," said Niels. "All in favor of inviting Joy to join us on this mission, raise your hand." All hands were raised, and Bill was authorized to call Joy and invite her to Houston.

"We have an extra room at the house where Linda, Ronda, and I stay. Joy can stay with us if she likes," said Nancy.

"I will also see that she has a salaried internship with the space agency, and she can be a consultant until she graduates from university," said Charlie.

"Wow, I can't believe the reception and support. Thank you all! I can't wait to talk to her!" said Bill.

"Okay, we took care of food. By the way, Charlie, when

does the pizza arrive?" asked Niels just as Chavez walked in with pizza for lunch.

"Charlie, this next conversation is for the crew only and must remain within this room until I have full understanding from Samantha. I must present it to her myself, so if this is a problem for you, excuse yourself and we will call you back after," directed Niels.

"I am here to support you in all decisions that you make. This is your life and future. I will respect your need for privacy and would like to stay with you for all planning. I will not call Samantha until you give me the go ahead," replied Charlie.

"Ivan, you may wonder why you are here as part of this team, but you have one of the more important jobs to ensure our secure future. Working with Nancy, we would like you to create the outline and detailed documentation for a new sovereign nation called the Federation of Mars. We will vote on this after you and Nancy have time to work out the details. It is our intention to be independent of any nation on Earth and to be able to conduct business as any nation can. This new nation would take effect after liftoff, and you would be the representative of the Federation here on Earth and our ambassador to the United Nations. Knowing you as I do now, I know that over the next two years, while at the University of Houston, you can accomplish this task. But please remember, the official language of the Federation of Mars will be English, not Russian," smiled Niels.

"Perhaps I should explain our thinking. Ivan, I have to relate some of your background, but I think that all should be out in the open. I'm sure by now that you all know that Ivan is my son. His mother, Irina, and I met on the International Space Station nineteen years ago. Our romance was short lived before Irina had to leave the space station and return to Russia. She was sent to Siberia after they found out she was pregnant. Ivan is the first person to be conceived in weightlessness. His genetic makeup is different than those conceived on Earth. Ivan ages at about one-half the rate that we do. He really is nineteen years old. His testing shows that he has a very high IQ, and his intellect is about that of a thirty-two-year-old person. For some unknown reason, his aura is visible as a light blue image around him, especially when he is emotional. Ivan speaks five languages fluently and has shown an interest in the formation and failures of past governments, hence the reason that Nancy and I feel that he is the right man for the job," concluded Niels.

Everyone looked at Ivan again with a new understanding and sympathy; this young man had had a very difficult young life.

"Look, Ivan, you are our brother, and no matter your differences, you will always be our brother and part of our family. We like you and hope that you will accept us as your family," said Alan as a very proud Nancy looked on.

"Thank you all. I accept the challenge you have given me, Father. I only hope that I can do you justice and complete this task to your satisfaction," said Ivan.

"Ronda, I think that you and Ivan should spend some time together to research the results of his conception in space. This research could be instrumental in the ongoing success of the colony on Mars," instructed Niels.

"Ivan, I hope you don't mind my poking and prodding. You represent the very heart of my research, and this knowledge will definitely help in my planning for the future generations on Mars," said a very surprised and excited Ronda.

"No problem, let's do it," said Ivan. He was very aware of how beautiful she was and looked forward to spending more time with her.

"Ronda, your assignments are very clear. You will work with Joy on the needs for nutrition while on Mars. You will be our doctor, and not only our general practitioner. You will represent all aspects of medicine, including surgery. Ensure that our resident servers have a complete medical database, which you can work on with Bill. You will plan the needs for genetic viability of the colony and bring the necessary equipment and materials in case the future growth of the colony cannot come from Earth," concluded Niels.

"Bill, as before, you will be our pilot. You must understand all of the design, engineering, and operational aspects of the Earth-to-Mars craft and the Mars lander as well. I will assist you in this activity. You will help Linda with the equipment and spare parts we will need on Mars. You will also be responsible for communications on Mars, as well as Mars to Earth. You will be responsible for the computer servers we will need and ensure that we can maintain them. You and Linda will be responsible for all surface transportation equipment and operation," instructed Niels.

"Linda, you will be responsible for the location of the colony, the human habitat, and all other equipment needed for our survival on Mars. You will back up Bill on his assignments and also Scott on securing water on Mars. The equipment will include surface transportation as well as possible airborne transportation. Make sure that you and Bill know how to operate and maintain these vehicles," instructed Niels.

"Nancy will work with Ivan on the design of the government, assist Ronda on securing future generations and medical needs, cross train on medical practices with her, and make sure that we have a religious plan for our colony. Nancy will also be our PR representative to the media once

Samantha releases the plan to the world," informed Niels.

"Scott, you have one of the most important tasks. You must be assured that we will have a fresh, drinkable water source before we lift off. Work with Linda on site selection with water as your primary requirement. You will be responsible for any valuable geological resources that the Mars colony may send back to Earth to help balance the deficit. Help Ronda and Joy on the equipment aspects and water requirements needed to feed and sustain us. Understand the equipment required for human sanitation and recycling. Work with Linda and Bill for all manufacturing requirements. We will not always be able to get what we want from Earth," instructed Niels.

"I will be responsible for navigation, mission communication with Earth, backup pilot, and backup all of you where needed. I realize that all of these assignments will be thoroughly covered by Charlie and his team and that you can only observe and ask for clarity. Remember that you are the ones going to Mars, not them. Do not let them take shortcuts that could possibly cost you your lives," said Niels, looking directly at Linda, who acknowledged him with a nod.

"I have left Jon and Alan for last. Along with Ivan and Joy, you boys represent the future of the Mars colony. I want you to work as a team, and when we lift off and the Federation of Mars becomes a reality, you will become citizens of Mars here on Earth. Jon, for now you must finish high school with honors and go to the school that you, Ivan, Alan, and Joy feel best fits their requirements here on Earth. Alan, your mother and I would like you to go to law school to specialize in international business law. You will represent the Federation of Mars in business here on Earth," said Niels. "Are you okay with that?"

"Yes, Dad," replied Alan enthusiastically. "You know

that I was leaning in that direction anyway so that I could follow in Grandpa's footsteps. He has been a big influence on me."

"I have one last order of business, and this is a personal request. When I was a little boy, I read the stories about Tarzan, and later I read Edgar Rice Burroughs's *John Carter*. That was when I had visions of Mars. In honor of Edgar Rice Burroughs, I would like to name the first city on Mars Helium. As you know, helium is the lightest element in the universe and the fuel that makes fusion in the sun. Do I have your support on this?" asked Niels.

In unison, they all said, "Yes!"

Chapter 41

Irina was as excited as Ivan as they boarded the plane for Orlando.

"I always dreamed of taking you to Disney World when you were a child, but our circumstances wouldn't allow it. You have missed out on so much that a child should experience, and I am so sorry for that. Now it is time for us to have some fun!" exclaimed Irina.

Ivan took her hand and said, "Mama, you always gave me so much love that I never yearned for anything else or felt like I was missing out on fun things, but we will certainly make up for it now. I have read up on Disney World, and this promises to be a truly magical experience for us. I can't wait!" said Ivan.

They took a Disney shuttlebus from the airport to their Disney hotel right at Disney World and had a late lunch before going to the pool area to sunbathe for the rest of the day. Ivan had to be careful that they didn't try to do too much at once to make sure that Irina didn't get too tired.

The next two days Ivan rode most of the wild rides, but the only thing that Irina wanted to do was visit "It's A Small World"; they rode it four times that first day.

A special limousine showed up to pick them up from the hotel. After getting in, Irina said, "This place truly is a magic kingdom."

The limo had been arranged by Charlie to drive them to the Kennedy Space Center in Cape Canaveral. After entering the gate at the Kennedy Space Center, Ivan saw a fairly large group of people, and when they stopped in front of this group, they all started to applaud when Irina stepped out of the limo. A man stepped forward and offered his hand to Irina. "Welcome to Kennedy Space Center, Cosmonaut Karpov. Like all astronauts and cosmonauts, you are special to our family here, and we want to have you here as a VIP. If there is anything you would like to see or do, please ask," said Al Winslow, astronaut and director of Kennedy Space Center.

Irina was taken aback; she did not expect any special treatment, much less to be recognized.

"Why, thank you for welcoming me and my son. This is a very pleasant surprise, and I'm sure that Ivan will have a wonderful time seeing all the things that I was so involved in twenty years ago," said Irina.

"Well, Ivan is certainly welcome. This small group of people also served the space industry and was instrumental in building and manning the International Space Station, and they are here to see you. We have planned a luncheon, and you can see and meet some of your fellow astronauts that were with you on the ISS," said Winslow.

A wonderful day followed as Ivan went with his mother throughout the center, watching her revel in the attention and friendship shown to her by all of the people they met. Ivan suspected that Charlie and Niels had a hand in all of this and placed a call to Niels when he was alone.

"Hi, Father. You should see all the attention that Mother is getting. What a wonderful surprise. I think that you have had a hand in arranging all of this, and if so, I can't thank you enough. I'm going to have a hard time bringing her down from this high. I'm sure she will want to come and see you to tell you about all of the friends that you have in common that she has met here. I have to go. They are whisking her away again. I must catch up with them or get left behind. See you soon."

Chapter 42

In a stark conference room, the North Korean leader met with his most trusted advisers. These five men were responsible for all of the atrocities meted out on the North Korean people.

The supreme leader continued, "I am not happy with our position in the world. No one is taking me seriously. My hands are tied by the restrictions placed on us by nearly every country in the world. Even our former ally China has fallen under the evil influence of the almighty American government, and we cannot expect any sympathy from them. We are alone, and I have come up with an idea that will bring not only the American government to its knees but all others as well. We will be the world leader, and all countries will come to us and beg for help.

"The nuclear option has not worked, and we are too closely watched for any other weapon of mass destruction to work. However, it has come to my attention that a solution is easily achieved. Commissioner Wong, have you secured the food stocks that I requested?" he asked.

"Yes, Supreme Leader, we have sufficient supplies to last the core team and their families for three years," replied Commissioner Wong.

"Then here is my plan. You will activate the deep sleeper cell in America and give them the following instructions. They are to locate the three American astronauts being held in quarantine and destroy them in a way that the ARC1 bacteria will be released upon the world," he said in a very smug, aloof tone.

The science minister spoke up in alarm. "You realize that when ARC1 is released it will destroy all of the grain plants in the world in a very short time. Our own people will be without rice or wheat and will slowly starve."

"This is true. Can you imagine the chaos in the world? Everyone will be fighting for the existing grain stocks, and the world's population will decrease. In the meantime, we will protect ourselves and our stocks until we are the only viable leadership in the world," he said.

The science minister was in turmoil, seeing all of the flaws in the plan. For over thirty years, the supreme leader had become more and more obsessed with becoming a world leader, but now he thought that his leader was totally mad. The science minister was going to have to stop him the only way he know how before the supreme leader went any further. He started to lean over to remove his pistol, but before he had a chance to draw his weapon, a loud gunshot was heard in the room. The other three looked over to see the science minister on the floor with his brains on the table.

The remaining three ministers were shocked and feared for their own safety as they looked at the leader.

"Does anyone else want to question my authority?" said the leader with a smoking gun in his hand and a demonic gleam in his eyes. No one dared move.

"I thought not. Now get out of here and carry out my orders. And get someone in here to clean up this mess," he screamed at the remaining men, who were visibly shaken at what had just happened.

The minister of intelligence had been a staunch supporter of the leader until now. As he left the room, he decided he was going to defy the supreme leader. He would still issue the order, but he would do so electronically in hopes that the NSA would intercept and act to prevent this catastrophic plan.

♌

In Dallas, Texas, an email arrived at the home of Korean sleeper agents Mike and Sue Park with code words that would activate them for the first time since they were inserted in the US. They had come from North Korea twenty years before after intense training as covert sleeper agents and had been living in America as normal citizens. The message also came with an attachment encrypted in a onetime code that gave them detailed instructions for their mission.

"We must contact the others and activate them. Then we must all disappear to plan and execute this mission," said Mike.

Chapter 43

Niels, with Scott and Bill by his side, had arranged for an interview with President Atwood.

"Madam President, I have good news and an announcement for you. Miss Polanski and Miss White have agreed to join the mission, and Mr. Nettles and Mr. Lee will join them in marriage just before the liftoff date. Our crew is complete, and you can now release the news of the mission to the world. I have met with the crew and given assignments that also include all three of my sons as well as Joy, who will join us soon. These youngsters will be our representatives here on Earth.

"This leads me to our announcement—the crew has voted, and we all want to create the Federation of Mars. The Federation of Mars will be a sovereign entity just like any other country here on Earth and will have representation in the United Nations. It will be treated like any other sovereign nation and will be able to conduct business with the countries of Earth. The official language of Mars will be English, and the currency will be linked with the US dollar.

"Ivan is to write a constitution and bill of rights for the Federation of Mars, and he will be our representation at the United Nations, as well as our ambassador to the rest of the world. Like the Mars colony members, these four kids will also be citizens of Mars. All future people coming to Mars will do so just like any other emigrant to the United States. They will have to have immigration permission and be issued a green card for citizenship."

Samantha responded, "Well, I am very happy that the crew is complete, and also for Scott and Bill. I will prepare an announcement to the press and also have the US ambassador to the United Nations give a prepared statement with this announcement. As far as the request to create the Federation of Mars, this is something of a surprise to me. I must think about it and the effect on the United States. By the way, who are Ivan and Joy? This is the first that I have heard of them."

"I am sorry, Madam President, things have been moving pretty fast for us. Ivan is my son. He and his mother have been living in Russia the last nineteen years, unbeknownst to me. I met Irina aboard the International Space Station, and Ivan was conceived the last night that Irina was there. The Russian Space Federation sent Irina to Siberia because she was pregnant upon landing and was an embarrassment to them. I could not find them after returning from space. Irina is dying of cancer, and she wanted me to meet Ivan. Ivan is my son, but he has special attributes, and Nancy and I have welcomed him into our family. Alan and Jon now have another brother. I am sure you will be surprised when you meet him, and I also hope you will understand.

"Joy is Bill's younger sister. She is just now graduating from high school and wants to spend as much time with her brother as possible before final separation. She will go to the University of Arizona and study nutrition and the concept of automatically deployable greenhouses. We expect her here next week.

"The announcement for the recognition of the Federation of Mars was not a request. This is a condition of the crew to continue to the final solution. I have thought about this a lot, and I can't imagine any one country having a base on Mars. Even having an international agreement such as we have for Antarctica wouldn't work because people would be living on Mars and have a vested interest in all of the decisions affecting the planet," said a serious and animated Niels.

"Niels, I do not take well to ultimatums. As you know, the world looks to me to solve the problem that you represent. You three are considered a weapon of mass destruction far worse than the nuclear bomb. Like you, I also have a final solution that is very distasteful to me, but I will use it if necessary. That button can only be pushed by one of two events happening—you have a breach in containment, or I give the order. The men behind the button report directly to me. Do you understand?" said Samantha with a stern leader's voice and the look she put on for all difficult discussions.

"I do fully understand and apologize for my abruptness, but please consider this carefully. It is very important to us," said a more subdued Niels.

Samantha acknowledged Niels with a nod and continued.

"I look forward to meeting Ivan and Joy. It sounds like you and Nancy have been doing a lot of thinking about your future. At first thought, I felt that you did not have the best interest of the US in mind. We are, after all, funding most of the cost for this mission to Mars, and we might want to make a claim to it. However, as soon as that thought came to me, I realized that the US does not want to own Mars and that it is not acceptable to leave you on your own without representation. I can imagine the fear of all of the other countries of the world if the US owned a base on Mars. Your solution is much better for all involved, and therefore I support your decision.

"I have a suggestion that will let you continue with this thought and take me out of the direct line of conversation. It will not be possible for you to confront each country in the world, so I think you should take your argument directly to the Security Council of the United Nations. I will have Ambassador Hemmingway contact you and go over the protocol of requesting membership to the United Nations. The Federation of Mars will start to exist the moment of liftoff. I will inform the chief justice of the Supreme Court that he is to give Nancy and Ivan all the help they need to make your constitution and bill of rights the best documents possible for the ongoing support of the Federation of Mars," said Samantha.

"Thank you for your understanding and support. Of course, the interest of the US will have the first priority in our everyday transactions. I will have Nancy coordinate with Justice Oliver's office for a trip to DC for her and Ivan, and I will also try to set up a meeting with you while they are in DC," replied Niels.

"Now for some very serious news," continued Samantha.

"It has come to my attention that there may be a threat to the homeland. I do not have details about the target yet, but the possible threat comes from North Korea, and there's no telling what that maniac may be up to this time. I know that this doesn't affect you directly and that you could not do anything about it anyway, but I want to keep you up to date as much as possible," said Samantha.

Chapter 44

Mike and Sue Park and three other agents were driving down the highway from Dallas to Houston in a van loaded with automatic weapons and charges.

Now that the time had come, Sue Park was having second thoughts about their mission. She and Mike had settled into their new lifestyle very well; her neighbors had warmly welcomed them, and she had hated deceiving them. She had discussed her feelings with Mike, who reminded her that they had no choice. They had been warned if they failed to complete their mission when the time came, their families back in Korea would be killed.

"The intelligence data shows that the three people that we are to eliminate are located in Houston at the American Space Agency facilities," reported Mike to the others. "They are in a small suite inside one of the large assembly plants. The security there is weak. They have never been threatened and, therefore, we believe, are not very alert. There is only small arms protection at this facility, which we should be able to easily overcome. Our mission is to blow up the small facility with the three men inside. I have been assured that they stay in this facility full time and that what they are working on is a threat to our homeland."

Sue said, "Drive the speed limit. We do not want to be stopped with this stuff in the van."

"It is one p.m. now, and we will be in Houston in two more hours. We will rest in the safe house and then carry out the mission at four a.m., when security is weakest," continued Mike.

♍

Niels was sound asleep when he heard the claxons go off. The intercom brought him fully awake. "We have an intrusion! All hands on deck!" He was out of bed and immediately went to the communication console to verify that the green light was on.

Bill and Scott joined Niels. Scott asked, "What is going on?"

Just then, the door to the conference room burst open, and two men and a woman dressed in black and carrying automatic weapons momentarily stood there. The door to Chavez's room flew open, and he emerged with his AR15 in hand and opened fire toward the conference room door. The men in black opened fire on Chavez, hitting him twice. One of the men in black went down, and a second one stepped forward, throwing a satchel charge toward the main window that Niels, Scott, and Bill were behind.

Like the good center fielder he was in school, Chavez leaped up, catching the satchel charge in midflight with his left hand. He charged the conference room door, still firing with the rifle in his right hand while bullets racked his body; he was dead before the charge went off. When the charge exploded, Niels, Scott, and Bill were witness to the carnage in front of them.

Niels immediately went to the console and verified that the green light was still on. He said, "We have a green light. There is no breach. Repeat, green light, no breach. Do not execute protocol, do not execute protocol."

"Confirm, no breach, green light," came the welcome voice over the intercom.

The conference room door filled with security men, and the chief of security entered. He came to the window and spoke into the communication console. "Are you men okay?"

"Yes. We are shook up, but otherwise not harmed. We have a green light, Chavez?" asked Niels.

"I am afraid we have lost Chief Petty Officer Chavez. He managed to take the remaining intruders out with the satchel charge, and he saved the day for all of us. I have contacted Dr. Gonzales, and he will be here soon. We do not know who the intruders were, but we think they were Korean," replied the security chief.

Niels, Scott, and Bill went into Niels room, and Scott said, "I never did understand what Samantha was talking about. What was that green light protocol all about?"

"I am sorry that I didn't tell you, but I thought I would spare you the ongoing worry. As you may have realized, we are a weapon of mass destruction because we carry the ARC1 bacteria inside of us. The protocol is there to ensure that nothing in this facility ever escapes. If there is a breach of this facility, a dozen thermite bombs will be exploded and intense heat will destroy everything, including us. The execution of this protocol can only be initiated by a human. There are no automatic firing systems, and the monitoring systems are redundant so no system mistakes are possible," replied Niels.

"Holy shit. This is too much," said Bill as he left for his room, trembling all over.

"Thanks for protecting us, but from now on, be completely open with us. We are grown men and can take it. Plus, you need to share with us to help relieve yourself of these kinds of burdens. Does Nancy know of this protocol?"

asked Scott.

"No, I saw no reason to tell her and have her be more worried about our safety then she already is. And I would like to keep it that way. Thanks for your support. I will not keep anything from you or Bill in the future, but you should go talk to Bill now. He is shook up. Try to calm him down. Losing Chavez is a hard blow to us all. He was a good man."

♎

As Charlie walked in, the security team was finishing cleaning up the mess. "The damage was not bad," he told Niels. "The charge was only big enough to break the integrity of the containment and release the bacteria. I have informed the president, and she is on the phone for you now." informed Charlie.

"Scott, get Bill and come listen to what the president has to say," yelled Niels.

Samantha approached the screen, looking disheveled and shocked.

"I am so sorry we could not protect you better. I swear we will do better in the future. When we go public with the mission plans, this kind of attack should not happen again. This attack was not just on you. Their intention was to blow up your containment center to release the bacteria on the world and then take over during the ensuing mass confusion and resulting starvation. We will make the plan announcement this afternoon after I have talked to the major leaders of the world. You should make your presentation to the UN as soon as possible. I will be talking to the premier of China next. That conversation should be interesting. I will call you again with the contents of the announcement.

"I am so sorry about Chief Petty Officer Chavez. I have

viewed the security video of the attack, and be assured that he will be given the Medal of Honor. I'm not sure you knew that Chief Petty Officer Chavez was a Navy Seal and his assignment with you was to allow him time to heal from previous wounds. I will personally notify his family. Are you men all right?"

"We are okay here, just recovering from the shock. We will look forward to your next call," replied Niels.

♏

In the Oval Office, Samantha took the call from China. "Madam President, we have just heard about the attack in Houston and send our concerns. What happened?" asked the premier.

"First of all, let me tell you of the importance of the facilities that were attacked and the people in it," replied Samantha. "The containment facilities there house the three astronauts that have just returned from Ceres with the ARC1 bacteria. As you know, if that organism is released in the world, all of the grain crops will fail. This failure would greatly affect China, India, Southeast Asia, and Japan, because of the dependence on rice as a major crop, more than any other region of the world.

"The agents sent to release this bacteria were North Korean. We have proof of this, and you are welcome to examine this proof. We have intercepted communications directly from the minister of intelligence's office to the agent cell in Dallas. We suspect that he sent the communication in such a way so that we could easily intercept it and act. The target was not revealed in the communication, and we thought that the target was a sporting event in Dallas. We are sure that the order for this attack came directly from the chairman himself. Please verify this if you can, and do something about this madman before he destroys world peace."

"Madam President, I understand the importance of your comments and will call my contact in North Korea for verification. I will call you right back after my discussions," replied the Chinese premier.

♐

During his phone call, the premier listened to the minister of intelligence, his clandestine contact in North Korea.

"Yes, it is true. He is a madman and desperate for attention, and he operates without concern for anyone but himself. Please help us do something. He killed my friend, Secretary Wong, right at the conference table in front of all of his senior staff. I am afraid for my life and that of my family now that Secretary Wong's attack on the chairman has failed," pleaded Secretary Park.

"Keep your head down and protect your family," advised the Chinese premier. "Your warning to the US was received, and the attack was unsuccessful. Do not confront the chairman. Stay away from him. Call me in a few hours, and I will give you further instructions."

♑

Several hours later, the Chinese premier called President Atwood.

"Madam President, the Chinese army is now amassing on the Yalu River and will invade North Korea," said the premier. "We do not intend to acquire North Korea. In fact, our intention is to free North Korea from the current regime and see to it that North and South Korea are reunited. It is in everyone's interest in seeing that we have one Korea and peace in the area. Even the North Korean people are tired of being crushed underfoot by this lunatic. We are ready for a takeover, and we will support the new government. Please inform Japan and South Korea of our intention, and I will inform Russia. Please convey your support of our actions."

"I wish you the best, Mr. Premier. I will support you and inform South Korea and Japan of this action. I suspect that the North Korean army will surrender rather quickly as they have no heart in supporting this madman any longer," said Samantha.

"I hope you are right. We would like to have a one-shot war, with that shot at the hand of the chairman, but I don't think that he is brave enough to do that," said the premier.

"One additional thing," said President Atwood. "I will make an announcement this afternoon concerning the final solution of the three men in quarantine. They will travel to Mars on a one-way trip and will form a colony there, becoming the first citizens of the Federation of Mars. There will be three men and three women to start this new sovereign nation on Mars. We expect them to lift off within two years. We would like to have your moral and financial support for this ongoing sacrifice these people are making."

"I will give serious thought to this Federation of Mars proposal. I'm glad they have come up with a final solution. This situation cannot go on forever," replied the Chinese premier.

Back in the containment facilities' hastily remodeled conference room, Charlie, Nancy, Ronda, Linda, Alan, Ivan,

Jon, and the three astronauts awaited the call from President Samantha Atwood.

"Here is a copy of the announcement that the president's office has prepared," said Charlie. "It looks like I will have to be the front man for the time being." He passed around copies to everyone in the conference room. Inside the quarantine, Niels, Scott, and Bill printed out copies of their own and read—

> The American Space Agency has announced its plan to resolve the dilemma presented by the presence of the ARC1 bacteria. The crew of the Ceres mission will form the first mission to Mars. This mission will be a one-way trip, and the crew will be joined by Commander Borgue's wife, Nancy, as well as Dr. Ronda Polanski, mission medical specialist, and Linda White, mission habitat engineer. They will settle and form a colony called Helium, the first city under the Federation of Mars' government.
>
> Commander Borgue will make a formal presentation to the UN Security Council to request membership to the United Nations. This government will be a sovereign entity with, hopefully, a seat at the United Nations, and it will have diplomatic and business interests on Earth. The mission is already underway and will lift off within two years, at which time the Federation of Mars will become a reality.
>
> Dr. Charles Gonzales, director of the American Space Agency, will schedule a press conference with the crew present. This press conference will be open to news pool transmission and a small number of reporters.

Niels said, "Ivan, it looks like the news of the Federation of Mars will be out in the open soon. You have a lot of work to do. I understand that you will meet the chief justice of the Supreme Court and have dinner with the president of the United States in two weeks. What do you think of that?"

"Wow, I am overwhelmed. When I came here I never imagined that I would be involved in a project of this size and importance or see so many exciting things. I can't tell you all how much I appreciate your trust in me, and I promise to do my best for you. Should I bring a present to the president?" asked Ivan.

Niels nodded his approval and was overwhelmed with pride and love for his newfound son. He replied, "I know you are talented in this area, so I think you should write, by hand, a short poem in Russian, perhaps about your experience in America so far."

"Good idea! I know just what I will write about. Imagine the joy of meeting your father in a new land," said Ivan.

Before Niels could respond, the big screen in the conference room came alive, and President Atwood said, "Hello. I see that you are all present, but there is someone at the table that I don't know. What is your name, young man?" asked Samantha.

"This is my son Ivan. You are to have dinner together in a couple of weeks," said Niels.

"Well, I will look forward to dinner with you, young man," said Samantha. Then she moved on. "I need to make this short because a lot is happening now. I have talked with most of the leaders of the world, including the secretary of the United Nations, and all except one have given me strong thumbs-up for the concept of the Federation of Mars. The premier of China owes me a call back soon, but he is very tied up now with the invasion of North Korea.

"Some good may come from this attack on you. It seems that the premier did not like the fact that the chairman of North Korea tried to kill most of the people of China. He wants to reunite North and South Korea, and the president of South Korea is very much for this reunion. Goodbye for now, and I look forward to dinner with your son."

Chapter 45

A couple of days later, Linda sat at the private window, with Bill on the other side. She had sensed that he had been despondent since the bombing attempt.

"What is that pounding noise coming from next to my bedroom? It's driving me crazy. The bombing attack and Chavez's death have hit us all hard here. I liked Chavez a lot. I can't imagine him not being around, and we can't even go to his funeral. I can't wait to get out of here. Sorry if I'm not very good company right now," moaned Bill.

"I wish I could be in there to help distract you from your plight," said Linda sympathetically, "but I hope that what Charlie and I are doing will help take your mind off of your confinement. That noise you hear is a room being built that will connect to yours. It will house a flight simulator for you to practice on prior to the mission. As you know, the Earth-to-Mars orbit ship will fly itself automatically, but you and Niels must be able to override and fly it yourselves. Also, the Mars lander simulator will help you practice flying from Mars orbit to the surface and back again up to the orbiting station. This should help get you out of here, even though it is only a simulation."

"I would rather have you in here with me. That would not be a simulation but a stimulation," grinned Bill. "But short of that, this is the best thing that could happen. When will it be ready? I can't wait."

"The software is still being tested, and they hope that you will help them with it. My understanding is that the hardware will be installed within the week. You will be responsible for keeping the hardware running," said Linda.

"I feel much better," said Bill. "I can't thank you

enough."

"Well, I will collect my reward when they let me in to be with you, but in the meantime, you will have to do without me around. I will leave for the Jet Propulsion Lab tomorrow to work with them to find our new home on Mars. I have some ideas that may help them," said Linda.

"Hurry back," said Bill. "I'll miss you."

Chapter 46

It was raining on the day that Chief Petty Officer Chavez was laid to rest in Arlington National Cemetery. It was as if Mother Nature was commiserating with those gathered at the gravesite. Nancy, Ronda, Linda, and Charlie represented the crew and friends back in Houston, who watched on closed-circuit video; they listened as the secretary of defense gave the eulogy. Chief Petty Officer Chavez was an amicable man and was greatly admired by his fellow Navy Seals for his courage above and beyond the call of duty. There were over two hundred people that came to pay their respects.

Ronda and Linda cried softly as "Taps" was played, followed by a twenty-one-gun salute fired by a special team of fellow Navy Seals. Chavez had endeared himself to Ronda and Linda during their courtships with Scott and Bill, and they would miss him dreadfully.

The American flag was folded and presented to Chavez's parents, each of them leaning on one another for support during this difficult time. As sad as they were, they were very proud of their son and would draw comfort knowing what a fine young man they had raised.

Chapter 47

Nancy and Ivan were sitting in the antechamber to the office of the chief justice of the Supreme Court. Ivan looked small and lost, and Nancy patted his hand, saying, "Don't worry, you will do fine. I realize that a young man that has spent all of his life in Siberia may be a little intimidated by these surroundings. Even I am a little in awe about what we are trying to do," said Nancy.

"I had a great trip to Disney World and Kennedy Space Center with Mother, but while I was there it was difficult not to think about our assignment. Why don't we just copy the United States Constitution and Bill of Rights and change the words 'United States' to 'Federation of Mars'?" asked Ivan.

"It is very likely that the weaknesses in the United States Constitution and Bill of Rights could be changed and improved upon. There is no better advice we could seek than from Chief Justice Oliver and his staff," replied Nancy as they were escorted into Justice Oliver's office.

After introductions and greetings were completed, Chief Justice Oliver said, "I have been wanting to rewrite the US Constitution all of my life. Of course, that will never happen, but you have asked me to help you modify the US Constitution for your government on Mars. Mrs. Borgue, this is a large responsibility for you and this young man." He looked at Ivan curiously.

"Ivan will have full responsibility for this project and will be the Mars ambassador to the United Nations after we take off. Ivan is nineteen years old and is my husband's natural son, and you will find him more than capable for the task," said Nancy.

"Nineteen!" exclaimed Justice Oliver. "This world is

full of surprises! I have assigned a small group to help you with this task. They are all clerks in my office, and all are experts on the Constitution. You will have office facilities here and access to any records we have. These clerks are all law students and will have to perform their regular duties assigned, but in their spare time they help you on your assignment. I will expect an update on your progress weekly and will review your final work. I expect this project to take about one month, and the clerks have offered to put Ivan up for the duration in a small apartment complex they maintain near here.

"Although there are three clerks assigned, you will report to Penelope Winthrop, and she will see to all of your needs. Penelope is my chief clerk and the best person to advise you on this project. Any questions?" asked Justice Oliver.

A few minutes of conversation later, Penelope Winthrop met them outside of Chief Justice Oliver's office. "Hello, my name is Penelope. There is a call for you, Mrs. Borgue, from the White House. You may take it here at my desk, and I will show Ivan his new workspace," said Penelope as she handed Nancy the phone.

She saw Ivan as a boy, but Ivan saw Penelope in a different light. He had a sparkle in his eye.

Nancy sat at Penelope's desk while Penelope and Ivan went to the next cubicle.

"Hello, Nancy Borgue speaking."

"Mrs. Borgue, this is Lori, the president's secretary. The president sends her regrets for dinner tonight, but she is very involved with the Korean crisis right now. She would like to send Tony and Susan to have dinner with you and Ivan. They can arrive at your hotel at seven, and reservations have been made at the restaurant there. Is this acceptable to you?" asked Lori.

"Yes, of course. I will meet Tony and Susan, but I think I will leave the three youngsters to themselves for dinner. Thank the president for Ivan and me," said Nancy.

Hanging up the phone, Nancy joined Ivan and Penelope at Ivan's new desk. She said, "Ivan, we will not be having dinner with the president tonight due to pressing matters. However she will send her son and daughter, Tony and Susan, to our hotel for dinner at seven. I think you will have more fun if I do not join you, so you will have dinner with Tony and Susan by yourself. I have met Tony and Susan before, and I am sure you will get along just fine."

Unsure, Ivan looked at Penelope. "Nancy, do you think it would be okay if Penelope joined us for dinner tonight. Is that okay with you, Penelope?" asked Ivan nervously.

"I would be honored to meet the president's children, and I would love to have dinner with you," Penelope replied, wondering what their connection to the White House would be. She wondered what she should wear.

"I am sure it will be okay, but let me call Lori to let her know. We will see you later," said Nancy.

♓

Back in their hotel room, Nancy said, "You seem a little nervous tonight, Ivan. What is wrong?"

"I don't mind the project, and I don't mind having dinner with the president's children without you, but... Do you think Penelope is a pretty girl? Do you think she and I will get along okay?" asked Ivan.

Nancy kept forgetting that Ivan was actually nineteen years old. He would have the normal thoughts of a nineteen-year-old. Nancy would have to trust that he would behave responsibly. How is that possible, she asked herself, when, after all, he is only nineteen.

"Ivan, you have the emotions and hormones of a grown man in the body of a ten-year-old. I cannot imagine how difficult it is for you to balance all of that, but I trust that you are responsible and will conduct yourself with the dignity your mother would expect. Yes, I think Penelope is pretty, and if you conduct yourself properly, you will get along just fine. Remember, we can talk any time you like," offered Nancy.

"Thank you. I will be a gentleman," promised Ivan as the doorbell rang.

Ivan answered the door, standing back as Penelope entered the room. He was struck without words. Penelope wore a basic black dress and a pearl necklace; her auburn hair was full length down her back, and the form-fitting dress fit her petite figure like it was made for her. She and Ivan were about the same height; she wore black flats and they stood eye to eye.

"Please call me Penny, all my friends and family do," said a demure Penny.

"Penny, you look beautiful. Don't be nervous. Like I said, I have met Tony and Susan, and they are very down to earth," said Nancy.

Ivan still had not said a word when Penny took him by the hand and led him to the door. She said to Nancy, "I will bring him back after dinner. I hope he will find his tongue before then." Penny smiled.

"I will go down with you to introduce you to Tony and

Susan, and then I leave you young people alone," said Nancy.

When Nancy, Ivan, and Penny got to the hotel's restaurant, they found Tony and Susan were sitting in a private room. Two secret service officers were at the door to escort them to the table.

"Hello, I would like you to meet my son, Ivan, and Penelope Winthrop from Chief Justice Oliver's office," greeted Nancy.

"Hi, I'm Tony, and this is my little sis, Susan. I'm seventeen, and Susan is fourteen, and we live in a little shack across town," joked Tony.

"Hello, my name is Penelope, and I am twenty-one. This is my friend Ivan, and he is... How old are you, Ivan?" asked Penny.

Ivan faltered for a moment then plunged right in, encouraged by Penny's directness.

"Well, I hope to call all of you friends, so I will tell you the truth. I am blessed with unique DNA that curtails the aging process. So I look twelve years old, but I am actually nineteen. I was born in Siberia and only recently came to America. I would like to keep this between us. I do not want to be a guinea pig because of my uniqueness. The project that Penny and I are working on will be the basis of the government of the Federation of Mars," said Ivan.

Penny looked more closely at Ivan. Instead of a young boy, she saw a very interesting young man. Working with him over the next month would be exciting, she thought.

"Our mom told us some of your background and your mother's situation. We are sorry about her illness," said Susan.

"Thank you for your concern," replied Ivan, "but please, let's have dinner. You can tell Penny and me all about living in the 'little shack,' as you call it." As the group laughed, Nancy slipped away to let them enjoy their dinner together.

Conversation flowed easily amongst the four youngsters, and Penny felt at ease even though she was a few years older. They were all extremely intelligent teenagers and could cover many topics. Penny kept glancing at Ivan and was pleased that she would be working closely with him over the next few weeks.

"I have a small present for President Atwood. It is a poem I have written about a very special event in my life. I hope she likes it," said Ivan as he handed a large envelope to Tony after dinner. "She will need a Russian translator as it is written in my native language."

After everyone said goodnight, Penny took Ivan back to his room and left him at the door, telling him how much she was looking forward to working with him and getting to know him better. Encouraged, Ivan nodded in agreement before entering his room with Nancy.

"Well, how did it go?" enquired Nancy, noticing Ivan's flushed face.

"Tony and Susan are very nice people, and we got along well. They were sympathetic to our situation. Something is bothering me, though. I'm looking forward to working with Penny, but I don't like the idea of leaving my mother for a month. Our time together is short enough as it is," said Ivan, anxiety showing on his face.

"Your mother will be with Martha and me, and we will make sure that she has company and is well taken care off. You can talk with her any time and for as long as you want over the video phone while you are here. I don't think that you can accomplish this job without being here, where the resources are."

"Okay," he relented. "I'm really looking forward to working with Penny. I'm sure we will get along just fine. I'm going to call my mother tomorrow morning and tell her all about this beautiful evening."

Chapter 48

Every day for two weeks Ivan and Penny had been working closely with no time to enjoy each other's company. Penny had to keep up with her normal work as well as oversee Ivan's research. They went to the Congressional Library quite often to research constitutional amendments and other aspects of the founding documents of the United States of America. When their workload lightened a little bit, Ivan decided it was time to get together on a social basis.

That Saturday, Penny answered the knock at her door. "Hi, what a nice surprise," she said as Ivan came in with a bag in his hand. Penny had not expected him and was caught in comfortable shorts, T-shirt, and no makeup. "What have you got there?"

"Just some Chinese takeout for dinner. I thought you might want something to eat and I was hungry, but I forgot to buy something to drink."

"No problem. I have some wine, okay?"

"I've never been allowed to drink because I look so young, but I would love to give it a try," replied Ivan.

"You pour and I will serve the food up. After our dinner with Tony and Susan and your revelations about yourself, I think you need to fill me in on who you really are," said Penny in a playful mood.

Ivan expounded on his life up until then while they ate, and as they drank the wine, his tongue got mysteriously looser. They went over to the couch as they finished the last of the wine, and Penny slid closer to Ivan, laying her head on his shoulder.

"You fascinate me, Ivan."

Ivan reached up to her cheek and kissed her on the lips.

"Ivan, this time touch the tip of your tongue to mine. Relax and enjoy."

"You will have to show me what to do. I have no experience."

"Don't worry, it kind of comes naturally if you really like someone, and you do seem to be a natural," said Penny with a sigh as his hand found her breast. Ivan was overwhelmed with desire for Penny and more than uninhibited from drinking the wine. He completely forgot what Nancy had explained to him. He was totally lost in Penny's embrace.

Chapter 49

"Ivan, you seem to be down in the dumps since you have been back. What is wrong?" asked Ronda a few weeks later.

"Oh Ronda, I am so confused," cried Ivan. "Can you help me? I need some advice."

"Okay, Ivan, out with it, and we will see what we can do."

"I think I fell in love in DC. I was so happy with Penny, and I know she liked me too. She is beautiful and just the right size. We fit together perfectly. I explained my unique situation, and she believed me when I told her that I am actually nineteen. Penny is twenty-one, so we are close in age. She is very smart, working on her doctorate in law. Ronda, the nights that we spent together were wonderful. I want to be with her, but my responsibilities are here. What am I going to do?"

"I'm so happy that you have found someone more your age. I know that you have looked at me as more than a friend in the past. You must consider me to be your good friend and nothing more. I am also your doctor, and together we are both interested in your special characteristics. You realize that you may transfer some or all of your special DNA to your offspring, when the time is right, so I would like to know some details about your nights together. Do you understand?" asked Ronda.

"Yes, I think I do," sighed Ivan. "I never thought about that in the heat of the moment. We spent two weeks together every night in bed, and we used protection every night... except the first night. Oh Ronda, what have I done? Should I call Penny now?"

"No, let me call her. I'll introduce myself and we can talk. Don't worry, there is probably nothing to worry about. Have you talked to her since you have been back?"

"Yes, we talk every night, and I think she is just as lonely as I am. Let me know what you talk about with Penny," begged Ivan. She nodded, and he said, "Ronda, from now on I will treat you like the big sister I never had, and of course as my doctor. Thank you for helping me."

Ivan left, and Ronda called Nancy first. "Nancy, I have just had a heart-to-heart with Ivan. You won't believe what we talked about."

"I can imagine," said Nancy with a smile. "He has had a crush on you for some time."

"Well, there is that, but I don't think we have to worry about that now. Tell me about Penny in DC. It seems that she has made quite an impression on Ivan, and he has been moping around since he has been back."

"Penny seemed like a very sensible young lady. I'm sure that you don't become clerk to the chief justice of the Supreme Court on good looks alone. She is very intelligent. She is small, just about Ivan's height actually, and they seemed to hit it off immediately. Ivan was smitten from the time he laid eyes on her."

"Okay, thanks. I want you to keep this to yourself for now, but it sounds like Ivan and Penny have fallen in love and were intimate more than once. I'm not sure how she feels, but I know that Ivan is in love with her. I must be professional in the science involving any offspring of Ivan's. He and I talked about this, and of course he did not consider this in the heat of the moment. They had protection for every time except the first. I am going to call Penny to introduce myself and to find out if their lovemaking resulted in a pregnancy."

"Oh dear, young Ivan. It is so easy to forget that he is actually nineteen. I will keep this between you and me, but we must consider what to say to Irina soon, especially if you find that there is a baby in the future."

"I'll let you know what I find out," Ronda assured her. "Bye."

The next day, Ronda placed a call to Penny.

"Hello, this is Penny."

"Hello, Penny, this is Dr. Ronda Polanski. I am a personal friend of Ivan's, as well as his doctor, and I have some concerns about your relationship with him. Ivan confided in me his feelings for you, and he said that you sounded depressed the last time that you spoke on the phone. Ivan is also down in the dumps, so I thought I would call and see if I can help."

"I appreciate your concern," said Penny. "I need a woman to talk to, and you are Ivan's doctor as well. Is he all right? Is he ill?"

"He is okay, just a little lovesick. I am actually more than Ivan's medical doctor. I don't know how much Ivan told you about his special conditions and the circumstances of his conception, but he has ask me to clarify his physical makeup to you. Ivan was conceived in the space station nineteen years ago, and his conception in a weightless environment resulted in unique combinations of his DNA. I work with Ivan to help him understand these differences. So far, the variations we have seen in Ivan have only been positive. He ages at half the rate of you and I, his IQ is off the charts, and you may have noticed a certain glow of his aura when he is emotional."

"Oh! That glow, when we made love the first time, I thought it was my orgasm that caused me to see strange things. When I looked at him just as he, well, you know, the glow is beautiful and lights up the whole room. I love Ivan and want to be with him. I miss him so much," cried Penny.

"Did you wear protection?" asked Ronda. "I ask because it is crucial as his doctor I should be aware of any special characteristics passed on to Ivan's children."

"Oh doctor," sighed Penny, "I am now two weeks overdue, and I am normally very regular. We did wear protection, except the first time. I haven't gone to the drugstore to get a test kit yet. I guess I am in denial."

"Well, here is what I recommend. Go get the test. If it is positive, we will send you a ticket for you to visit me here in Houston, and we can discuss the future. I will not say anything to Ivan. You two can have as much time as you need after you and I meet. Can you get some time off from your responsibilities for at least a one-week visit? If you like, I can be your doctor as well, no charge of course," offered Ronda.

"I will go get the test today and call you back with the results as soon as I know," promised Penny. "I would love for you to be my doctor. Thank you. Bye."

♈

Several hours later, a very emotional Penny called Ronda back.

"Hello, doctor. I took the test, and it is positive. I don't know if I am happy or sad, but I am definitely pregnant."

"Well, congratulations," said Ronda. "From now on call me Ronda. I think we will be good friends. You met Nancy

Borgue when she was in DC with Ivan. I am going to tell Nancy the situation, and she will make arrangements for your visit. We will first meet in my office, where I will need a full medical history and any medications you are taking. I will do a full medical exam, and then we can talk about your choices."

Chapter 50

Bill was pacing in his room, the noise of construction still getting on his nerves. The door to the conference room opened, and he smiled and relaxed. His sister always had that effect on him. Joy entered and smiled, but a worried look spread across her face.

"Hi, little sis. Why the long face? Aren't you happy to see me?" asked Bill.

"Hi, Bill. I am very happy to see you again, it's just that I can't give you a hug and comfort you. I am going to learn to hate this glass between us."

"I know. I already hate it, but it has kept me alive for now and that is a good thing."

"Are you ill from this bacteria? Are you feeling okay?"

"That's the strange thing. We do not have any physical effects from ARC1, and evidently it will only affect grain crops, not humans. Of course, destroying all of the grain crops would let millions of people starve and die, and we can't allow that. This bacteria is easily destroyed with heat or radiation, so this problem will not happen in the future. But while it is in our bodies, the heat or radiation that would destroy it would also kill us, and that is not an option! Enough of me. What's up with you? Are you happy? Do you want to join our team and throw your lot in with us?"

"Well, I graduated high school with high honors and as valedictorian of my class. You should have heard my speech. Most of the rest of my senior class can barely spell their names. It is so sad. I had to tone down my speech so they could understand my message. Even then I don't think most of the teachers or any of the students understood what I was talking about. I'm not sure getting high honors means much from that school. I have received a full academic scholarship from the University of Arizona and will start in a few weeks at their school of nutritional sciences. I will specialize in growing food in remote and harsh environments. This will include automatic deployment and autonomous operation of greenhouses. I want very much to be part of your team and help where I can with your mission, but understand one thing—we cannot be separated forever. I will be on the second rocket ship to Mars. No argument. You do not have anything to say about this, so just count on a visit from your little sis on Mars."

Bill reached out to the glass separating them, cursing the obstruction; he just wanted to hug her.

"I am very proud of you, and I'm sure you will excel at anything you do. Forget high school and focus on university. You will meet a very different class of people there, and you will thrive in the learning environment. I'm glad you would like to join our team here, though I'm not sure that I like you coming to Mars. But that is a long ways off and a lot of things must fall into place before that decision. Where are you staying? Have you met any of the other team members? How is your love life? Will your boyfriend be coming here?"

"My love life is none of your business. I don't have a boyfriend—yet! Linda met me at the airport, and I will stay with her in her room until my room is ready, but I understand she will be leaving for the JPL soon. I will meet Nancy, Ronda, Ivan, Alan, and Jon for dinner tonight, and I have an interview with Dr. Gonzales tomorrow morning. I would like to meet Mr. Borgue and Scott today, if you don't mind."

Bill left his room to get Niels and Scott.

"Joy, let me introduce Commander Niels Borgue, leader of the Ceres mission and leader of the colony on Mars, and

Captain Scott Nettles, my friend and reluctant roommate. Gentlemen, this is my sister, Joy Lee."

"Hello, Joy. Welcome to Houston," Niels greeted her. "We have heard quite a lot about you. When Bill is not talking about Linda, he is talking about you. Nancy told us that you are having dinner with the rest of the team tonight. Please be relaxed. They are all nice people, and I'm sure you will like them. I know that I do," he said.

"Thank you, Commander Borgue. I am a little nervous. Scott, Bill never told me how handsome you are. I can't wait to meet Ronda, the lucky girl."

"I am the lucky one," said Scott. "Bill, your sister got all of the good sense in your family, and I can tell she has good taste. Joy, you are much prettier than I imagined from Bill's description, but then again, he hasn't seen you in a while."

"Joy, after your interview with Charlie, I would like to have a conversation at your convenience," said Niels.

"That can be easily arranged," replied Joy. "I look forward to our talk."

Niels and Scott left the room, and Joy and Bill continued.

"Bill, those two are very nice. I hope you all get along okay."

"Our relationship is good. It is necessary for us to have our own responsibilities and enough time alone. This is a small facility, and it would be very easy to get into each other's space. When all of this construction is done, they will install flight simulators so that Niels and I can practice flying the ships that will get us from Earth to Mars. I can't wait. I'm a flyboy and not designed for confinement. Linda being here helps, and now that you are here, that will help also."

"I'll be here for you, but now I have to go have dinner with the rest of the team. By the way, I like Linda. She is beautiful and seems to be very smart, but then she did agree to marry you. You always seem to land the most beautiful girls. Do right by her, you heartbreaker."

Joy waved goodbye and blew him a kiss as she left.

Chapter 51

The restaurant in the hotel was quiet, and Nancy and Ivan had a table in the back where they could see the door.

"It's nice of you to invite me out for dinner. Is there a special occasion that I don't know about?" asked Ivan.

"I just want you to know that even after Niels and I are on Mars, we will think of you as our son. I know that Irina is your mother, but you can also count on me to be there for you when you need help. I hope you like our little surprise," said Nancy just as Ronda and Penny walked up to the table.

The look on Ivan's face was one of pure joy as he rose and gave Penny a big hug.

"What a wonderful surprise! I thought I was going to have to go to DC to get you. I was seriously thinking of going tomorrow if I could get Charlie to get me a ticket."

"Penny has checked in to this hotel, and Nancy and I have a previous appointment, so we will leave you two to get caught up. Enjoy yourselves and call Nancy if you need anything," said Ronda.

As they were walking out, Nancy asked, "Is she okay?"

"She is more than okay," replied Ronda. "She is very healthy and definitely pregnant, and I hope this goes well for them."

Back at the table, Ivan just sat there and looked at Penny. "I can't believe you are here. I'm so happy."

The waiter came up for their order, and Penny said, "I'm not hungry. Let's go up to our room. We have lots to talk about."

Ivan gave their apologies to the waiter, and they left for Penny's room.

♉

The next morning in bed, Ivan said, "I thought you said we had something to talk about. We did not have much time for a conversation last night."

Penny sighed and said, "Ivan, I am pregnant. We are going to be parents in eight months. I love you, and I want you to love me and our baby." And then she burst into tears.

Ivan looked at Penny in shock, and then his expression turned quickly to joy as Penny's words sunk in.

"Penny, I love you so much. This is quite a surprise, but I love the idea of us having a baby. Don't cry," Ivan said, protectively putting his arms around her. "Everything will work out, you'll see. I assume you have told Nancy and Ronda, and we must tell my mother together and start planning our wedding. You will marry me, won't you?"

"Of course I will marry you," smiled Penny. "You have made me the luckiest girl in the world, and now we are to have a baby. It is just an added blessing. We should plan a wedding as soon as possible while your mother is still able to attend. I wonder what she will think."

"I know my mother will love you, and I know she will be thrilled at our announcement. Who knows, with her spirit this might be the incentive she needs to keep on fighting. If I know her she will be determined to meet her grandchild."

"I wonder if the baby is a boy or girl," said Penny. "Do you have a preference?"

"No," replied Ivan. "As long as the baby is healthy and

you are fine, that is all I care about."

"Me too," sighed Penny contentedly, and she snuggled up to Ivan and curled under his arm with her head on his shoulder.

Later that day, they went to Charlie and Martha's home to meet Irina.

"Mother, I would like you to meet Penelope Winthrop. Penny, this is my mother, Irina Karpov," said a very nervous Ivan. They had arrived at noon after calling Martha to let her know that they would like to see Irina. It gave Martha the time to help Irina make herself presentable even though she could not get out of bed; she was weak from the therapy.

"Mama, I know this is sudden, but having worked with Penny for a month I have gotten to know her so well and have fallen in love with her. We want to get married very soon, and it will mean everything to us for you to be there."

Irina looked surprised and then smiled warmly at the young couple.

"Ivan, this is wonderful news. I have been worried about leaving you, even though you will have your father and all of your new friends. But knowing you will have a loving wife beside you will make wonderful difference. I can take what comes knowing you will be happy." Irina wiped the tears from her eyes and continued, "I know that with Martha's help I can muster up some strength to attend your wedding. Now go, you have lots of plans to make. Have you told your father yet? Penny, please come and see me again. We have much to talk about."

"I will be moving from Washington, DC, next week, and then we can spend as much time together as you like. I am looking forward to our time together," said Penny.

"Father is next on my list. I hope he will be as happy for me as you are. Rest now, Mama." And Penny and Ivan tiptoed out of the room.

♊

The following day, Nancy joined Ivan and Penny in the conference room. Niels sat on the other side of the glass.

"Father, I would like you to meet Penelope Winthrop, my fiancée. We will be married soon while my mother is still able to participate. Penny, this is my father and Nancy's husband, Commander Niels Borgue."

"Wow, you sure are full of surprises! It is hard to remember that you are very mature for your age. Hello, Penny. I guess that you and Ivan have been closer than just working on your project," said Niels. "Welcome to the extended family, and congratulations to you both. I can tell by the confused look on your face that Ivan has not told you the whole story. Sit down and Ivan and Nancy will tell you why I am in this glass prison and the history of Niels and Irina."

After an hour of explanation, lunch was served and Penny said, "That is quite a story. I have always wanted to write a book, and this looks like a much more interesting saga than any I could think of. Of course, this is a personal story, and I would have to have all of your permissions."

"If you are going to join our family, then you will also become a member of the Federation of Mars. I will have to find you a task that will aid our mission," said Niels.

"I would love that. I have two more years of law school before I apply for the bar. I will complete those two years at the University of Houston while Ivan completes his degree there too. What do you think you would have me do, keeping in mind that I may be somewhat limited in physical activity about eight months from now?" asked Penny with a mischievous look in her eye.

"Penny and Ivan are expecting their first baby in about eight months. Ronda is Penny's doctor, and we are all looking forward to the birth. Ronda will be ready to help Penny and Ivan understand if the baby has any of Ivan's special characteristics. Are you ready to be a grandpa?" asked Nancy.

"This is just one surprise after another! I'm too young to be a grandpa, but I'm sure that Nancy will make a great grandma," joked Niels.

Nancy said, "Ivan and Penny have met with Irina, and she is very happy for both of them, but they have not yet told her about the baby."

"Here's what I have in mind," said Niels. "I have been thinking about this for a while. Stuck in here, all I can do is think and play chess with Scott. There will be a need for the Federation of Mars to raise a large amount of money to fund the ongoing needs of the colony. One of the ways will be to sell goods made on Mars back to Earth, such as heavy water. That is in short supply here on Earth but plentiful on Mars. Heavy water will be used on Earth for the first fusion reactors to make electricity. However, prior to that, I think that you, Ivan, and Alan can contract with a major media network and sell our story as a series of ongoing pictures into our mission—the planning and implementation, of the people, hardware and life on the way to Mars, as well as life on Mars. You get the picture.

"There is a significant amount of law and business. Therefore I want Alan involved in this enterprise. It would ensure a revenue stream into the Federation of Mars coffers and hopefully cover the costs of running it. Think about this assignment and discuss it with Ivan and Alan, and let me know if this is of interest to you," concluded Niels.

Penny replied quickly, immediately excited about the future role she would play. "You really are commander and the leader that everyone would like to follow. You have a unique way to welcome a lady into your family, but I love it. I'm sure that we will get along just fine. Your idea is wonderful, and I'm sure it will succeed. I will discuss this with Ivan and Alan and Nancy and report back to you with our recommendations. This would be a large responsibility, and I'm not sure that I can handle it, but as a three-man team I hope that we can come up with a satisfactory plan."

Ivan turned toward Nancy. "Nancy, Penny and I have discussed this, and we would like to ask you to perform the wedding ceremony for us. We would like a small wedding that will include my mother as well as Niels, Scott, and Bill. Penny will invite her mother and stepfather, and we will of course invite the rest of the crew and immediate team. I hope that we can fit them all into this conference room for the ceremony," said Ivan.

"I would love to preside over your wedding," said a delighted Nancy. "I suggest that you let Martha plan the details. The new support crew here can provide the necessary facilities and food you will need. Chief Petty Officer Yolanda Black and her team seem very capable of handling this event," said Nancy.

Yolanda had been promoted to take Chavez's place after his untimely passing and was proving to be a valuable asset.

"I will tell Charlie that we will want this room, and Yolanda and her crew," said Niels. "This will be a happy event. We have all been too serious, and we need a diversion to liven up this place."

Chapter 52

The pre-wedding dinner was held at Charlie and Martha's home, with Niels present via video teleconferencing. Penny had invited her mother and stepfather up from Florida for the wedding and dinner. Penny's two brothers and two sisters said hello and congratulations over the videophone prior to dinner. Irina was weak but wanted to walk in on her own. Martha and Irina had gone shopping the day before, and Irina had on a new dress. She also had a special dress for the wedding the next day. She felt wonderful, and it showed.

It had taken only a week for Yolanda and her team to transform the conference room into a small chapel, with chairs on either side of the aisle and an archway of red roses under which Ivan and Penny would stand while making their vows. Music had been piped in, and flowers were everywhere.

The day of the wedding, Irina was sitting comfortably in the front and looked well. She was still beautiful in spite of the disease that ravaged her body and the therapy that left her weak. She looked content as she quietly chatted with Martha, who was sitting beside her. Niels, Scott, and Bill were in their dress uniforms, looking very smart and very handsome; they were also very frustrated that they could not be fully part of the ceremony, but they were resigned to the situation. Charlie was Ivan's best man, and Ronda and Linda were Penny's bridesmaids. Joy volunteered to throw the flower petals into the aisle as Penny walked down.

Charlie was trying to keep Ivan calm, but when the wedding march was played and Penny walked down the aisle on her stepfather's arm, Ivan gasped in amazement. He stared at her in awe. She was so beautiful, and he beamed at her as she joined him under the archway of roses. Nancy took their hands as she spoke of their commitment to each other and their future together, pronouncing them man and wife. As Ivan kissed Penny, Irina noticed a very light blue glow surrounding Ivan and encompassing Penny as well, as if Ivan wanted to wrap Penny in his special kind of embrace. It was beautiful, and those that were aware of Ivan's special aura chuckled knowingly.

Chief Petty Officer Black quickly rearranged the chairs around tables that were laden with food and drink. A beautiful wedding cake sat in the center. Duplicate food and drink were already in the room with Niels, Scott, and Bill. The happy couple was toasted many times, and considering the circumstances, the wedding was a huge success.

An hour into the celebration, a call came in on the video screen from Chief Justice Oliver. "It looks like I have lost the best clerk that I have ever had. Congratulation to both of you. I wish you the best. You know you can call anytime and depend on my ongoing support. By the way, I have approved of your work, and the final Federation of Mars documents are being drawn up for you now. Both of you must come visit this old man again."

After the chief justice hung up, the video phone rang once again, and the president of the United States came on the line. "Congratulations to both of you. Ray, Tony, and Susan send you their love, and we all hope you will be happy together. Oh, and Ivan, I enjoyed your poem very much. Ray and I will have it framed and keep it with us in remembrance of you and the subject of the poem, your father," said Samantha.

"Thank you, Madam President," acknowledged Ivan respectfully. "Please say hi to Tony and Susan and tell them that we hope to see them for dinner again. We both enjoyed their company."

After the reception, Charlie had arranged for a limousine to take the happy couple to a fancy hotel downtown, where they spent their first night together as man and wife.

Chapter 53

A few days later, after Penny and Ivan had left for their honeymoon, the crew and Charlie were in the conference room having their weekly technical meeting when the video phone rang. Charlie answered, "Hello? We are in the middle of a meeting, and I have asked that all calls be held until after."

"I know," said an animated Linda, "but I must talk to you because I have new and exciting information for the team!"

"What is it? What's up?" asked Charlie, noticing she was with the west coast team.

"Miss White is much too excited to be able to calmly tell you our findings, so I will take over for her," said Carl Young, director of the Jet Propulsion Lab.

"First of all," he continued, "you should all be proud of Miss White. She is very hard working, and a little pushy." He smiled. "She is very much focused on what she wants. She had a vision for the right environment for the habitat, and even though we felt that that vision was not possible, she has been proven right. We have found what we were looking for.

"As you know, most of the plans for a habitat on Mars have been a dome inflated to Earth pressure and then covered with a durable material, such as a plastic, that would protect the dome from radiation, dust storms, and physical damage. Miss White's concept eliminates the need for the plastic dome over the habitat."

"We found it!" interrupted Linda. "My idea is for the citizens of Helium to be cavemen!"

Carl continued, "The idea of inflating a dome inside a cave was never under consideration, but by doing this, the cave protects the habitat from the elements and physical damage and greatly reduces the cost of the mission. Scott has instructed us that apart from the habitat itself, water and energy are the primary needs of the colony. With those things in mind—habitat, water, and energy—here is what we found."

On the screen, the team could see a view of the surface of Mars.

"You see Crater Sharonov at fifty-nine degrees west and twenty-eight degrees north. If you look just south of the crater, you will see an outflow channel, and just on the southern portion of the outflow channel are the cliffs of Helium. This location is just north of the equator and holds the best promise for mild year-round weather and for water near the surface. These images were just taken by us using the Mars Global Survey Satellite, which we can position and view the area of interest from many angles. This angle best shows the Caves of Helium.

"Scott, you will notice the small crater just in front of the caves located in the lowest point of the outflow stream. We feel that the bottom of that crater will be the best location to drill a well in hopes of finding not just water, but very hot water due to the nearby mountains and previous volcanic activity. This hot water could be used for geothermal energy production," explained Carl.

The team looked at the Caves of Helium, trying to take in the scope and magnitude of what they were about to undertake.

"Can you zoom in on the caves some more? Have you estimated their size?" asked Niels.

As he zoomed in, Carl answered, "We think the largest cave is about eighty feet wide and twenty feet tall. We cannot tell how deep it is. The second cave is about half the size of the first, and the third is about one third of the first, but all of the caves are about twenty feet tall at the opening. The floors of the caves are about twenty feet above the floor of the valley, and the floor of Crater Lake is about thirty feet below the floor of the valley. The rim of Crater Lake is forty feet above the valley floor, giving a depth of Crater Lake a max of seventy feet," said Carl.

"What is the valley floor like? Can we have a reasonable spaceport there?" asked Bill.

"Yes, the valley floor is an old seabed. It is flat and strung with small rocks, mostly hematite, which is a good indicator that water once covered the whole area, but we do not see any large artifacts that would hinder a spaceport. The real challenge will be landing a cargo ship into Crater Lake to deploy the drilling platform. We could never get the drilling platform over the rim of the crater."

Carl went on, "When we sent the Mars Global Survey Satellite to Mars three years ago, we dropped off communication satellites at strategic locations between Earth and Mars so that there would always be a path for communications between the planets. Even though there will always be a twenty-minute delay due to the distance between Earth and Mars, there will never be a blackout due to positioning. We also positioned four global positioning satellites in stable orbit around Mars, and we can now pinpoint Helium precisely.

"Charlie," said Carl, "we would like to proceed with the implementation of the drilling mission. I will get back to you tomorrow with detailed plans after I contact our civilian contractors."

"Okay, Carl. We will be here for your call tomorrow afternoon. Good work. You have given us a lot to think about, not to mention a few surprises. Could you put Linda on for a private chat?" asked Charlie.

"Hi, I am so excited! Bill, I can't wait to get back to you to share everything that has happened," said Linda, barely waiting for her teammates to leave.

"Linda, I can't tell you how proud we are of you and your creativity. Hurry back!" said Bill.

"Your concept of the cave dwellers of Mars is new and a bit of a surprise to us, but it has a lot of merit. Please gather all of your notes and JPL input, get a red-eye back tonight, and we will meet here first thing tomorrow morning," said Charlie.

"I will be there! But JPL is providing their private jet to fly me back this afternoon," said Linda. "Bye! I miss you all."

♋

The next morning, the crew and Charlie were sitting in the conference room when Ronda and Linda walked in. Linda went directly to Bill's private window while the others made coffee. Following the women was Carl, who sat down with Charlie.

"Hi, Bill," said Linda. "I missed you. How are you doing?"

"Much better now that you are back. I can't believe what you have done for us. It gives me a lot of hope that we can pull this thing off. We have a great team. They have finished the installation of the flight simulators and software, and I am allowed in for the first time today. They have rigged a signal button out there so that you can ring me when you are here and I will come out. I may spend a lot of time in there, but for you I will forgo my love of flying anytime to see your pretty face. I will also ask them to connect a remote monitor for Niels and one for you in the conference room so that you can see my progress and share in the excitement of flying."

When they were done talking, Linda came back to join the meeting and Bill went over to Niels and Scott.

"Hi, Carl. I'm surprised to see you here. Thanks for taking care of Linda and allowing her to voice her ideas," said Bill.

"It is our pleasure to work with Linda and be of service to you. We all sympathize with you and your situation, and we will do anything to get this heroic endeavor on the way," said Carl.

Once everyone had their cups of coffee and was settled into seats, Carl began. "The first flight to Mars will leave directly from the Kennedy Space Center aboard a Saturn Five rocket. It will carry the drilling platform and the large solar power plant needed to power the drilling platform. The power plant will convert the power into microwave energy and beam the energy to an antenna on the drilling platform. They will land separately. The drilling platform will land in Crater Lake, and the power unit will land on top of the cliffs above the Caves of Helium.

"If we do strike water and the crater starts to fill," continued Carl, "we will never be able to get the drilling platform out of the crater. Hence the reason for a remote power supply. There is some talk about having floats on the bottom of the drilling platform and trying to recover it while floating in Crater Lake. Later, this same power supply will be able to beam energy to wherever you need it, provided there is a receiving antenna and conversion from microwave to AC at the receiving end, or you will be able to wire it directly to the habitat.

"The REOCs, the return to Earth orbit container rockets, will refuel themselves on the surface of Mars from the carbon dioxide in the Martian atmosphere and the extra hydrogen that they carried from Earth, and then they will take off to return to Earth orbit to receive another load. We think that about six of these REOC ships can keep a continuous supply to Helium at a reasonable cost, and they can carry a large load because the ships will refuel themselves while landed on Mars and do not have to carry the return oxygen fuel to Mars. The ships are autonomous and do not have accommodations or life support for humans. They will also get to Mars faster because they can accelerate faster without humans on board.

"The REOC ships will dock up to the new near-Earth orbit supply depot that will load and unload the cargo containers and refuel the REOCs. The four cargo containers for each REOC will fit into four clamshell pods on the outside of the REOC. After landing on Mars, the pods will open and the containers will be lowered to the surface. The orbiting supply depot will be stocked by a fleet of high lift–high altitude planes with the cargo containers inside of high-altitude-to-orbit rocket planes. Both high lift and rocket planes will return to Earth's surface for reuse."

After taking a sip of coffee, Carl went on. "A few years ago, we contracted the European Space Agency to supply the Near Earth Orbit Depot. The American Space Agency is building the REOC ships, which were started five years ago and will be modified for the Mars leg of the trip. China will supply the fleet of high-lift planes and rocket plane cargo carriers based on the early models started twenty years ago. That leaves the *Mayflower II* ship to be developed between the USA and Russia. This ship will be assembled in near-Earth orbit at the ISS and will be designed such that it will never enter Earth's atmosphere or Mars' atmosphere, similar to the *Ceres Cruiser*.

"After you arrive in Mars orbit, you will leave *Mayflower II* by *Orion*-like entry capsules that were tested in 2016, three crew members at a time. Bill, Linda, and Scott will be first, and Niels, Nancy, and Ronda will be in the second, after the first team has secured Helium.

"This is the hardware and sequences that we envision for your trip to Mars. Fortunately, a lot of work has gone on before, and we have a big head start. Two years seems to be a schedule we can work with. Any questions?" asked Carl.

"Thanks, Carl," said Niels. "I'm sure there are about a thousand questions. First, though, I would like to talk about the Cavemen of Mars. I'm having trouble seeing the whole Helium complex."

"Since we talked yesterday, the JPL team has come up with preliminary drawings of the Helium complex. I will put them up on the screen. It looks like we will have to supply a lift up from the valley floor to the cave floor. It is about twenty feet but rather steep, and the soil may be rather loose. I recommend that we make it wide enough for cargo containers and have it powered similarly to an elevator.

"There has been talk of making the drilling platform waterproof and using it as the pumping station for water to the Helium complex. If, in fact, we strike the water we expect to, we would like to plan a cap over the whole crater that will act as a lens to focus the sun's energy to heat the whole environment inside the crater, keeping the water as hot as possible. This capping of Crater Lake would come later, after the crew is available to support the cap's installation."

Carl continued, "After all six of you are successfully on the surface and in your temporary habitat, we will send the inflatable dome and erector set's internal structure to you and you will assemble and inflate it in place in the cave for your final habitat. After it is inflated, you will assemble the internal structure using an erector set scheme made from eighty-twenty extruded aluminum material, which you will help design prior to your leaving. We will build the material for this design after you have landed and made complete measurements of the caves. This internal structure will support all permanent living facilities and all working facilities."

"The next four rockets will take off from Earth containing the four temporary habitats that will be able to house all six of you for at least ten years. These will be modified Saturn rockets. The second stage will be hollow and contain the living quarters, and there will be four rockets surrounding the main structure. The upper stage will house the fuel regeneration unit and will remain with the rocket after landing. The temporary habitats' full lifespans will not be necessary, but these units could be used in case of an emergency and the whole unit can lift off of Mars with you in the habitat. They will also include food—yes MREs—and basic supplies, also sufficient for ten years.

"Some time prior to your landing, we will land and deploy eight greenhouses. These units will have crawlers on them, and we will be able to position two of them next to each temporary habitat, which you will be able to connect via a tunnel. Then the environment inside the greenhouses will be able to supplement the life support in the temporary habitats. As you know, plants love carbon dioxide and give off oxygen. These will be self-contained and have all the plants, water, fertilizer, and power needed to grow vegetables and crops you will need after you land," said Carl, and he took another sip of coffee.

"We will also land and offload all of the technical equipment and spares needed for communication, computer, science, entertainment, and power requirements. All of these elements except the greenhouses will remain in their containers, and you will have to assemble the powered ramp, construct the inflatable habitat in the cave, erect the internal structure, and unload each of the containers and assemble the various components.

"This will be made easier by the low gravity of Mars," explained Carl, "but this low gravity is an unknown relative to the effects on your bodies, so one of the temporary habitats will be a spa that contains exercise equipment, special body conditioning devices, and medical equipment that Ronda can use to monitor your conditioning and health. This spa will also be connected to the temporary habitats via tunnels. This fourth habitat will also function as the center for meetings, communications, and entrainment. These are the broad-stroke elements we have in mind so far, and we all must work on the details together. Any questions so far?" asked Carl.

"There sounds like a lot of work that needs to be done while outside of any life support systems. What kind of, and how many, environmental suits will we have?" asked Scott.

"Good question. When you land from the *Mayflower II* on the surface of Mars, you will have on a flight suit that will have full life support. The oxygen can be resupplied from the *Orion* landing craft, if need be. Once inside your temporary habitat, you will find three more suits made to fit each of you and provide full protection and life support while outside of the protected habitat. These suits will have their own storage cabinets that will protect them and supply any depleted material," answered Carl.

"What will supply electrical power to the city of Helium?" asked Niels.

"There will be the solar power unit up on the cliffs of Helium that can beam microwave energy down to devices or later be wired directly. We will deploy an array of solar cells also for power to the greenhouses and temporary habitats. If we are successful with sourcing hot water, we will use the temperature differential between the water and the naturally cold surface of Mars to create electricity using a Rankine cycle generator," replied Carl.

Very quietly, Joy spoke up. "When you said that the greenhouses would be connected to the temporary habitats, it implied that the crew would be able to work in the greenhouses without their space suits on. If my understanding is correct, the ARC1 bacteria will kill all grain plants, and we must grow grain in at least two of the greenhouses to be able to support a proper diet for the crew."

"Very well said," said Ronda, "and I don't think anyone has thought of that problem. Let me work with you on this issue, and we will report back to the team our findings."

Charlie addressed the crew. "As you might have guessed, I have assigned the JPL to be the lead group to get you to Mars and support you there. Carl has agreed to lead the support team and be your primary point of communication during this total process, which I think will take at least ten years. He will also be the focus for all contracts to outside contractors needed to complete this mission. I will be the coordinator for all international cooperation projects. If there is nothing more to discuss, Yolanda is ready for us now, so let's have lunch."

Chapter 54

The next day, Charlie escorted some gentlemen into the conference room while Niels, Scott, and Bill waited behind glass.

Charlie was saying as they came in, "As you have seen, gentlemen, this facility is very secure with a failsafe protocol in place. It may not be the most comfortable setting for these men, but it is better than the alternative. Let me introduce you to Niels Borgue, Scott Nettles, and Bill Lee. This is Mr. Igor Transvinki, chairman of the Russian Space Federation, Mr. Wu Chao, chairman of the China National Space Administration, and Mr. Nigel Thoms, chairman of the European Space Agency."

The three men went up to the window as if to shake hands and then just stood there. They did not know what to do or say.

"How do you do, gentlemen?" said Niels. "Thank you for coming and showing interest in our project, and giving us your support."

"Thank you for your contributions in the past and the future," said Nigel Thoms. "We understand that the concept of the Federation of Mars is going to be presented to the United Nations soon, but I want you to know that, in the interest of science and advancement of space exploration, we three support this concept completely."

Charlie said, "Nancy, Ronda, and Linda, the other members of the crew, will be here shortly. I would like the whole crew to hear what these gentlemen have to offer this mission. In the meantime, I have asked the staff to prepare coffee and snacks."

Nancy, Ronda, and Linda came in and helped themselves to refreshments. They were introduced as they sat down to start the conference.

Charlie began, "First, let me explain that the respective governments that support these space agencies have agreed on the following—each of the four agencies will provide twenty-five percent of the cost of the project, including ongoing support for ten years. If there is something you need on Mars, all you have to do is ask for it and it will be supplied. In return, anything returned from Mars, such as heavy water, will be shared equally by the four agencies. Do you have anything to add, Niels?"

Niels looked directly at the three chairmen. "That is a very generous and comforting offer," he said, "but I would like to point out that the Federation of Mars will operate as a separate entity. All business will go through the Federation of Mars representative here on Earth. Also, the Federation of Mars will contract with a major media outlet that will tell our story as an on-going video event starting soon. The revenue from this contract will go to supporting the staff of the Federation of Mars located here on Earth. This revenue will not be shared with our space agency partners. It should also be understood that when we refer to the Federation of Mars, we include the two moons of Mars."

"We understand that all of these contractual details will be refined and signed before takeoff. This conference is to cover the broad strokes and come to an understanding of who is responsible for what and when," said Charlie.

He continued, explaining, "According to Carl Young at JPL, the drilling platform rocket has been completed and will be delivered to the Kennedy Space Center next week. The Saturn 5 rocket will be used as the launch vehicle. The flight plan will be installed in the rocket by the JPL. We hope to send this rocket on its way to Mars in about two weeks. The flight to Mars orbit will take four months. The landing, commissioning, and drilling will take another four months, which means in about eight months, assuming we find water, we could have a go for the mission. The crew cannot leave for Mars until we have discovered a sufficient supply of water for them. If we do not strike water at the Helium location, we will try again at different locations until we find the best one. In the meantime, progress on all other aspects of the mission should continue.

"Mr. Thoms, what are your responsibilities and progress to date?" asked Charlie.

"The European Space Agency has been tasked to provide the near earth orbit depot where the REOCs, return earth orbit crafts, will be resupplied and sent on their way back to Mars. This NEOD is being assembled in orbit similar to the way that the ISS was assembled. The NEOD is much simpler and smaller than the ISS and will support a crew of four that will be rotated every six months. The NEOD will not have gravity and will be in a stable orbit. The NEOD will have ports that will automatically receive the rocket plane that has been developed in coordination with the China National Space Administration and the REOCs that have been developed at the American Space Agency. The transfer of cargo containers to the REOCs will be external and accomplished by moveable arms designed by our Canadian friends. The NEOD will be the refueling station for the REOCs and will also use the high lift plane and rocket planes to transfer fuel up to the NEOD. This fuel will be stored in external tanks for safety reasons. The refueling process will be manually operated by the crew on the NEOD.

"The design of the NEOD is complete, and in-orbit fabrication was started a few years ago. We have had twenty flights to date to transfer the material to orbit. An assembly crew has been up there for six months, and it will take them four more months to complete the assembly. A commissioning crew will then take over and will receive the first rocket plane from China. We expect the first cargo to be supplies for the NEOD and a load of fuel to test the fuel-transfer process. We hope to have the first REOC ready to leave for Mars in eight months," said Dr. Thoms as he sat down.

"Thank you, Dr. Thoms. That is a very ambitious schedule. Niels, do you have any questions?" asked Charlie.

"Yes," Niels said. "It is my understanding that after water is discovered on Mars, the next cargo to be sent to Helium will be the temporary habitats. While it is important to have water, this crew cannot leave for Mars without the temporary habitats in place and operational. Will these rockets that carry the habitats be sent direct to Mars from Earth's surface or via the NEOD? It seems that the schedule dictates that they go directly from Earth's surface to Mars."

"The drilling platform has already left from Earth, and the temporary habitat rockets will leave from Earth's surface also. The first REOC that will leave from the NEOD will carry eight automatically deployable greenhouses, and the next REOC will carry other supplies. From then on all REOCs will leave from and return to the NEOD," answered Charlie.

When Niels nodded, Charlie asked, "Mr. Wu, what is the status in China?"

Mr. Wu, speaking perfect English, said, "Thank you, Dr. Gonzales. The concept of the high lift–high altitude plane has been around since the early 2000s and has been described by professionals as well as by private citizens. Commercial ventures were started then to take tourists into sub-orbit trips. The very high prices of these trips have since stopped this commercial operation, but much was learned. The load-carrying capabilities and the top altitude have been increased by developments in new jet and rocket technologies. This high lift plane combined with the rocket plane development shows that this is a practical low cost and safe method to take cargo into low Earth orbit. The latest ablative shielding means that the rocket plane will be able to be flown back just like the old shuttle and reused. It will not require any special runway for landing and can land at just about any large commercial airport. We have just finished the prototype of both crafts and will begin flight testing next week. It is possible that we can help supply some of the material needed to supply the NEOD. I will work with Dr. Thoms concerning this schedule."

"Thank you, Mr. Wu. Any questions?" asked Charlie.

Bill spoke up. "The design of the cargo containers must be for the rocket plane and the REOCs, as well as handling here on Earth. It also occurs to me that we will also have to handle these containers on Mars. Who is responsible for the design of these containers?"

"Good question," said Charlie. "Bill, JPL has already issued the final design of the containers. The NEOD, REOC, and rocket plane have been designed with the handling of these containers in mind. The transfer of these from rocket plane to REOC will be handled by the crew on the NEOD. All container handling on the surface of Mars will be anticipated by JPL and will be different for the varying different contents of the containers. These containers will be eventually reloaded back on to the REOCs after refueling on Mars and returned to the NEOD, where they will be transferred to the empty rocket plane returning to Earth. That is when material sourced on Mars can be sent back to Earth. Mars' gravity is one-third that of Earth, making it easier to handle these containers, but don't worry. JPL is making the container handling automated with the use of crawlers that will drive themselves to the storage area.

"By the way," added Charlie, "the three of you will not be able to practice driving the crawlers except through the simulators, but we will see to it that the three ladies also will have plenty of practical hands-on experience in the simulators prior to liftoff. Reloading these containers back into the REOC will be automatic.

"Well, Igor, what have you been up to in Russia?" asked Charlie.

"We at the Russian Space Federation have the important task of designing and building the Earth-to-Mars-orbit craft that will carry the most important cargo, the six members of the new colony on Mars," said a rather pompous and self-important Igor. "I believe that the crew has named this craft the *Mayflower II*. The design of this craft has been accomplished by cooperation between my team, the JPL, and the crew here. Fabrication has started next to the ISS, with the final and most important section being delivered in three weeks. This is my surprise for you—for many years we have been developing a nuclear-powered ion drive for use in long-distance space travel. This development is complete, and members of the American Space Agency have reviewed testing of this drive. These tests have been very successful, but the Russian Space Federation does not have a planned near-term mission for this drive. It will be attached to the *Mayflower II* by a long boom. The *Mayflower II* will remain in Mars orbit until it is needed back in Earth orbit. When additional colony members are needed on Mars, they will also travel by the *Mayflower II*."

"Thank you, Igor. That drive is a very worthy addition to this mission. Any questions?" asked Charlie.

"Yes. Will the use of this drive change what we know

about the duration of the trip to Mars?" asked Scott.

"JPL has recalculated the various trip plans to Mars orbit depending on the position of Earth and Mars at the time of departure. This drive has a much higher escape velocity potential, and generally speaking, if you start quickly, you get there sooner. We think it will take at least three months off of the trip," said Charlie. "Any other questions?"

"Yes," said Nancy. She asked, "Will the design of the *Mayflower II* include our social needs? Even though the trip will be faster, it will take many months to get to Mars."

Charlie answered, "The *Mayflower II* will rotate while in flight and create gravity equal to Mars gravity at the extremities of the four habitat arms. There is a private habitat for each family and a communal space at the end of the fourth arm that will include kitchen, meeting, communication, and entertainment facilities, as well as medical facilities for Ronda to use if necessary. There will of course be a video intercom between the private habitats. The center of *Mayflower II* will not have any gravity, and we have planned a large space that will be empty for you to use for weightless entertainment. We have envisioned a kind of eight-cornered basketball. This should be good fun and good exercise.

"This space can also be used near the end of the trip to assemble equipment needed in Helium. This equipment will be sent to the surface in reentry rockets carried in *Mayflower II* just like the *Orion* capsules will be. Your trip to the surface will be in these *Orion* capsules. They will be slowed by parachutes and have a soft landing on inflated balloons. In the front center of the *Mayflower II* will be a command center where you all will sit strapped in during the initial launch and where all of the flight controls will be located.

"If there are no other questions," finished Charlie, "I would like to bring this meeting to a close and invite these three distinguished gentlemen to dinner."

Bill whispered to Scott, "This is the first time I'm glad that we are in here and don't have to go to dinner with those self-important windbags!"

Chapter 55

Ronda had established a medical office on the space agency's Houston campus, and she spent one morning the next week on the office's phone with Dr. Cuttle at the CDC in Atlanta, requesting his help in understanding the ARC1 bacteria in great detail. She made plans to meet him in his labs to continue her comprehensive study of the organism.

Later that afternoon, she and Ivan discussed the tests she had planned to find out about his special characteristics. Ivan was very relaxed after returning from his honeymoon with Penny.

"Ivan, the standard testing of your blood sample shows that you are very normal, chemically speaking, and that you have a very healthy profile. The genetic testing, however, shows that you are different than 'normal' humans. These differences show up in quite a few areas. The anti-aging process is probably due to an enlarged pituitary gland that shows up on the MRI scans of your brain. This gland controls growth and sexual functions, and your enlarged pituitary gland increases blood flow and oxygen to the hypothalamus area of your brain. The increase of your intelligence can possibly be explained by the very large blood flow to and within your brain and the fact that your brain is about ten percent larger than normal brains."

Ronda continued, "The colorful aura that we partly see is a genetic mystery. The radiation technician told me that he had to stop the first full body MRI scan and recalibrate the machine because the return signal from your cells was so strong that the machine became saturated. The results were swamped out. He had to detune the return signal by two hundred percent to be able to get a usable signal. He said that he had never seen these phenomena before.

It seems that your cells emit a very large energy field that affected the MRI machine, and this increased cellular excitement could explain the blue glowing aura field that surrounds you. Combined with your increased pituitary gland function, they may explain why that energy is more visible during sexual activity.

"The aura around you is visible, and therefore I should be able to photograph it and record these phenomena for science. I would like to start the video while you are in a normal state and then record the increase in aural intensity as you increase your emotional involvement, and by that I mean your sexual involvement. Will you let me do that?" asked Ronda.

"You mean you want to film me while Penny and I make love? No way!"

"Well, there are other ways to raise your sexual emotion and be discrete about it. For sure I would not show your face. Do you know what VR goggles are? They would cover most of your face and still display the visuals needed for you to drive your emotions to climax. If you like, you can have Penny in there with you. Off camera, of course."

"You mean watch porno while you film me?" asked Ivan.

"It is not really necessary for you to do this, but it would be the only chance for the scientific world to see the aura. I really would like to record these phenomena."

"Okay, I'll do it, but only with Penny in the room with me, and I get final approval before you release the video."

Ronda hired a videographer the next day and had her sign a nondisclosure agreement. Together, they set up the small room adjacent to Ronda's office. When Penny and Ivan arrived, Ivan took Ronda aside and asked, nodding to the videographer, "What is she doing here? I don't want anyone watching."

"Don't worry, I won't introduce you. She is a professional videographer, and I have explained to her your sensitivity. But I wanted to do this only once, so we must record this successfully the first time. We will not have a microphone in the room, so you and Penny can talk," Ronda explained. When he didn't object, she went on, "Now go in with Penny and get ready. You must be completely naked so that we can see the whole aura."

When they went in, Penny turned the lights out to give Ivan a little confidence. He took off his clothes and lay down on the examining table, which was covered with sheets. He put on the VR glasses and waved to the camera to let them know he was ready. When the VR video came on, the first thing Ivan saw was Ronda on the beach in her bikini. In his ears he heard Ronda say, "I wanted to start you off with something friendly, but don't worry. The rest of the video is by professionals, not images of me. Thank you for this."

As the video continued, Ivan started to respond, beginning to glow faintly. Penny sat at the foot of the bed and stroked his leg lightly. Brighter and brighter Ivan glowed, until the photographer had to reduce the iris on the camera. Penny reached further up his leg and then started to stroke Ivan to speed the process along.

"I hope that is you, Penny," Ivan said with a husky voice. "I like that. You should see what these people are doing."

All of a sudden, the room lit up very brightly and it was all over.

"Did you get that?" Ronda asked the videographer.

"Wow, that was something! Did all of that light come

from him?" asked the video technician. Ronda didn't answer. "Yes, we recorded it all. I will play it back for you."

Ivan and Penny came out and left quickly, both of them more than a little embarrassed.

Chapter 56

A few weeks earlier, Ronda had asked Charlie to call Monsanto to secure Dr. Eileen Ortiz to assist Ronda and Joy on a special project. Eileen flew to Atlanta and met Ronda and Joy at Dr. Cuttle's lab at the CDC.

After introductions were made, Ronda got down to the point.

"We must create a genetically modified strain of corn that will resist the ARC1 bacteria. Then we must do the proper tests and field trials and produce enough seeds for the Mars mission's greenhouses. If we can succeed with corn, we can then move on to other grains. It is too risky to trust that the crew will not accidently contaminate the water used in the greenhouses."

"This should not be too difficult. This bacteria is much simpler than most others we have addressed. The hard part will be designing double-blind tests and executing them. Dr. Cuttle, do you have any suggestions?" asked Eileen.

"We do not have the facilities here to do those kinds of tests, and we have a very limited supply of ARC1 bacteria, which you will not be allowed to remove from this facility," said Dr. Cuttle.

"Might I remind you that we have an unlimited supply of ARC1 and a perfect test environment?" Joy asked. "We could prepare a grow bed with the test planned out and hand it into the quarantine facility. The ARC1 in the facility should be enough to ensure contamination, and Bill and Scott can run the test."

"Great idea, Joy," said Ronda. She asked Eileen, "What do you need to get started, and can you schedule this project such that we can have seeds ready for launch in eighteen months?"

"Thanks to Dr. Cuttle I have the profile of the bacteria at a genetic level, and I can start work right away. Monsanto has given me top priority in the lab for this project. I think the first tests can be started in about six months, because it will take this long to grow the test plants. Joy, I will call you when I am ready, and you can fly up and hand carry the test back to Houston," said Eileen.

Chapter 57

It was not long after that the whole crew was in the conference room, including Ivan, Alan, Joy, and Jon for the day's technical meeting when a call came in from the JPL.

"Hello," said Carl, "I thought that you all would like to watch the landing of the drilling platform and its power supply. The crew here has made final firing sequence commands, and it is now up to the automatic systems to land the platform in the center of Crater Lake. The drilling platform and the power supply have been sent to the surface of Mars separately, and the landing locations have been programed using GPS coordinates to make the final adjustments. They will both be slowed by retrorockets, and when slow enough, parachutes will deploy. Airbags will soften the final landing."

The crew watched the image of Crater Lake, seeing the parachutes of the drilling platform deploy. A few minutes later, the drilling platform dropped free of the parachutes and fell directly into Crater Lake, bouncing three times before coming to a rest. The platform was upright and looked ready to start drilling.

The whole crew cheered, and they could hear the team at JPL cheering with them.

"You couldn't see, but we have images of the power supply landing on the cliffs above Helium," said Carl. "It looks like we have hit the bull's eye this time."

He went on, "The next step will be to deploy the antenna on the drilling platform and the power supply, align them, and turn on the power to the drilling platform. The drilling platform has enough ten-inch diameter pipe to achieve a depth of five hundred feet if necessary. It will take about two weeks before we can start drilling. I will set this up with you so you can watch."

"Thank you, Carl, and your team as well. Congratulation on a successful mission," said Charlie.

Two weeks later, the Houston team was assembled once more in front of the screen in the conference room, looking at a close-up of the drilling platform in Crater Lake while they listened to Carl narrate. "The platform carries twenty-five twenty-foot sections of pipe, two of which have already sunk. The third is now being threaded on, and then drilling will commence. If we hit water, the platform will automatically cap the well, but we will have enough time for the testing systems to test the water. We will test for purity, salinity, temperature, and any organic material."

They watched while the platform added the third pipe and started drilling again.

"How long before all of the pipes have been used and we know what to expect in the future?" asked Niels.

"We have had soft drilling so far, but we expect to hit harder rock soon. If we are going to find water, we expect it will be under a layer of rock that would act like a cap and allow pressure to build up below the rock cap. Do you agree, Scott?" asked Carl.

"Well, I hope so," the old Ceres science officer replied. "All you can do is keep drilling. Do you expect igneous rock or softer sand stone?"

"We don't know what to expect, but the drill can handle any type of rock and there is an extra drill bit if necessary," said Carl.

As they were watching, a fourth pipe was added and drilling was restarted. The image was excellent, and they saw what looked like mud at the base of the drill. They could tell that the drilling rate had slowed down. It looked like it was straining.

They watched for another two hours and were about to discontinue the video feed when the fourth pipe dropped very quickly. The platform was about to add the fifth pipe when a large jet of water shot out of the top of the platform. The platform continued to add the fifth pipe and then started the capping procedure. The geyser shot what looked like fifty feet above the platform and continued flowing while testing took place prior to final capping.

The team in Houston cheered, jumping up and down and thumping each other on the back.

"How long before we get the first test reports?" asked Scott.

"The testing is very quick, and the telemetry should transfer the data to us in another twenty minutes. I will call you back when we get the results," said a very happy Carl.

Twenty-one minutes later, the call came in from Carl; he was happy and excited.

"Well, we have found pure water on Mars. No salt content, and a very small amount of organic material. The temperature is one hundred eighty-three degrees and should be very useful for geothermal energy. We have everything we could possibly want, and I recommend that we finalize this site for the new colony on Mars."

"I agree," said Niels. "Let us start final preparations for this trip. It looks like this idea of the Cavemen of Mars will become a reality."

Chapter 58

Seven months later, Niels, Scott, and Bill were standing around the small table that housed the grow pots. Each pot was numbered, but they did not know which pots carried the modified corn. The grow lights were on, and they saw small plants poking through the soil. They had put their hands into a tray of water that was used to water the plants to ensure that the introduction of ARC1. This had been verified by a special dye that Ronda and Dr. Cuttle had developed to detect the presence of the bacteria. The small plants were about three inches tall; the crew had to take pictures every two days to monitor the progress of growth.

"Look, some of the plants are starting to wilt. I hope that those are the untreated ones," said Scott.

"Just a minute, I'll be right back," said Niels, and he went to his room. When he came back, he had a small notebook in hand. "That is great," sighed Niels, reading over the study's key Joy had slipped to him. "All of the wilted plants are from original seeds and were not modified. The modified seeds are still growing."

"I'll call Ronda now and tell her the good news," said Scott.

Chapter 59

The next day, Penny was filling in the team on the revenue-generation plan to have a contract with a media outlet to tell the story of Helium. She sat at the conference table and was a little uncomfortable; she had a hard time sitting for long periods of time during this late stage of her pregnancy. Since she had gotten up that morning, she had experienced some cramps, but since then they had begun to feel more like labor pains. She probably should have stayed home, she thought, but Penny knew this meeting was important. She wanted to get it over with before she was tied up with the baby. Besides, Ivan was going to be at this meeting, and she didn't want to be far from him at this time.

"Ivan, Alan, and I have decided to create a new media network called MBS, the Mars Broadcasting System. The MBS will create all of the programming and sell it out to other media outlets on a weekly basis. All video collected will belong to MBS, and we will have control of all of the content. We have hired Betty Carter to perform the video editing and create the program content for each week's episode. Alan will be the program manager for now and contract with each outlet to set up the business. Alan and I will jointly control the flow of money for the business. When Ivan becomes more known to the public via his function as ambassador to the United Nations, we will put him in front of the camera as the host," said Penny, wincing when she felt another pain coming on.

"Are you all right?" asked Ivan, anxiously looking at Penny.

"I think the baby is calling a halt to this meeting," she said. "You and Ronda had better take me to the hospital, now!"

♌

After an overnight vigil at the hospital with Nancy and Linda, Ivan came out of the birthing room with a smile on his face. "We have a beautiful baby boy, and mother and baby are doing fine," said Ivan as he gave both women a big hug.

After giving the nurses time to clean up Penny and the new baby, Ivan went back into the room and saw Penny in the bed holding little Joey; she was beaming, and she looked beautiful. They had agreed on the name a few weeks ago, Joseph Winthrop Karpov, after Penny's grandfather Joseph Winthrop, the founder of the family fortune.

"He is beautiful," said Ivan as he held little Joey and stroked Penny's cheek. "Are you okay?"

"Yes, he came quickly and easily. If I thought it would be so easy, I would have done this sooner," lied Penny with a happy smile.

"I wish my mother could have been here," said Ivan sadly. "It's a miracle that she has lasted as long as she has. I think that she has been waiting for little Joey before she lets go. I think we should take Joey to her as soon as you feel up to it. I would like to present her grandson to her while we still can."

"Of course," replied Penny, taking Ivan's hand to comfort him. "I'm feeling fine, and if Ronda gives us both the go ahead, then we should go tomorrow."

That is just what they did. The next morning, Ivan, Penny, and the baby left the hospital to go to the hospice where the members of the staff were doing all they could to make Irina's last days as comfortable as possible.

Charlie and Martha were in the room, and Irina was sleeping as the young family walked in. Martha and Charlie fussed over the baby while Penny and Ivan slowly awoke Irina.

"My dear children," Irina said. "What a nice surprise." Her eyes swept over the group, and she realized that Penny had had the baby.

"Mama," started Ivan, beaming with pride, "meet Joseph Winthrop Karpov. Little Joey, your grandson."

Ivan held Joey for Irina, as she was too weak to hold him herself.

"Why, he is just beautiful," exclaimed Irina, tears of happiness filling her eyes. "I can't believe God has allowed me to live long enough to see my precious grandson and to know that you are both well and happy."

Ivan and Penny stayed, talking quietly to Irina until she slipped peacefully to her final sleep. She had a smile on her face.

"Don't be sad," said Penny, holding Ivan in her arms as a doctor told them it was all over. "She died a happy woman, and that is all we can ask for. Come, let us take Joey home and get him acquainted with his nursery." Penny was very tired and wanted to be in her own bed.

Three days later, Irina was remembered in a simple ceremony in the conference room so that Niels could say his farewell privately before the rest of them arrived. There were many flowers, and, to Ivan's surprise, the Russian ambassador to the United States was there to honor Irina for her service. The graveside ceremony was attended by Irina's new friends, and Ivan was proud to see her so honored.

Chapter 60

A few days later, Charlie addressed the team in Houston with Carl looking on via video.

"We have sent eight container ships to the Mars surface, and all have landed successfully, dislodged their cargo, and refueled. All eight of them have returned without mishap. They have left four rockets on the surface that will be used as the temporary habitats. There are now four temporary habitats ready for your occupancy, and eight greenhouses will soon be attached to the habitats. The next REOC, which will land next week, will have the escalator for the rise up to the Helium caves that you will have to assemble when you get there. We will not send your final dome habitat until you are there and can measure the caves properly. It will take about six months to fabricate and ship this final habitat and internal structure. This membrane will be too heavy, even on Mars, where things are much lighter, for you to move it up to the cave. It will be shipped to you in sections, and you will have to assemble and glue these sections together in place.

"The NEOD is completed and manned and has functioned perfectly in sending the REOCs to Mars. We can depend on this station to function as long as we need it. The high lift plane and rocket have also functioned as expected, and the transfer of cargo containers is now fully automated. China is building another set of high lift and rocket planes to act as back up and possible use if need be. This technology has shown that the cost of getting goods to near-Earth orbit is no more than getting goods from China to America, which has been a pleasant surprise for us.

"The *Mayflower II* is nearing completion and will start final loading and testing next month. Building the *Mayflower*

II next to the ISS has been shown to be a good decision. Using the ISS as a staging station for both material and the construction staff has made the planning and logistics much easier and faster. All of this means that the mission could lift off in about two months. What still needs to be done is for Nancy, Ronda, and Linda to go through basic astronaut training. Once that happens, the three of you can join Niels, Scott, and Bill for a very happy and joyous event."

"What is involved in astronaut training?" asked Linda. "I didn't know we had to go through that stuff."

"This training is not the full training that normally happens here. It has been modified to your special situation. For example, you need to learn how to put on your spacesuit rather quickly in case of emergency, also where your spacesuits will be located at all times. You will go through a shortened version of weightless training in the pool and experience the feeling of acceleration and G-forces in the centrifuge. You are all in good condition with the use of the exercise room we have provided, but you will all go through final physicals and have remote telemetry transmitters implanted. Ronda, we will expect you to update the remote telemetry transmitters that Niels, Scott, and Bill already have implanted after you enter the quarantine facilities. Our team will of course teach you how to do this, and we will test all of them after implantation," said Charlie. "Nancy, have you planned any special events for after you enter the quarantine facilities?" asked Charlie.

"Oh, Martha, Yolanda, Ronda, Linda, and I have something in the works, but I would not like to discuss it now," she replied, smiling secretively.

Chapter 61

It was afternoon at Martha and Charlie's home, and Penny was in their room breastfeeding Joey when Ivan walked in. The blinds were closed, and the room was a little dark. Ivan stood back and took it all in, amazed when he saw little Joey glow very slightly.

"What is wrong? You have a funny look on your face," said Penny.

"I do believe that little Joey is very content, because I see a small blue glow coming from him." Ivan smiled as he came and sat down next to Penny.

When he went to stroke the top of Joey's head, the infant glowed even brighter.

"I can see him glow now," breathed Penny. "That is beautiful, just like his father."

"Is he finished feeding? I want to hold him."

Penny handed Joey over and watched as the two auras touched. A happy look settled over both of them, and Penny could swear that they were communicating.

"When is the next feeding?" asked Ivan. "I want to invite Ronda to see this wonderful phenomena."

"Invite her over about nine tonight."

When Ronda showed up that evening, Penny and Ivan moved into the living room. Martha and Charlie were also there to see this "special" event, which had not been explained to them yet.

"Hi, Ronda. We have something to show you. Would you like a glass of wine?" offered Penny.

When the doctor shook her head, Ivan dimmed the lights. Penny put little Joey up to her breast and started feeding him. After about five minutes, Joey started to glow, and both Penny and Ivan smiled proudly.

"That is beautiful, to see such contentment. Oh, Charlie, I am so happy for them," said Martha.

"I am a scientist and an engineer, but this is a miracle. I would not be able to explain it, but I can enjoy it and share in your happiness," he replied.

"But wait, there is more," said Ivan, and he reached for Joey. As he touched Joey, he stopped nursing and reached for Ivan. He picked up Joey, and the two auras touched and glowed as one.

Penny said, "I think they are communicating in some way that we do not normally understand. Tell us what you feel, Ivan."

"I feel completely relaxed and contented and happy. I'm not sure if that is me or Joey. He and I are going to have to practice this more often. As he grows older perhaps this feeling will grow into something more," said Ivan with a dreamy look on his face.

"For sure some of Ivan's unique genes have been transferred to Joey," said Ronda. "With your permission, I will test Joey's blood and map his genetic makeup in comparison to yours. This is very good news. As far as the new phenomena of Ivan and Joey sharing something as their auras come together, well, that is new and unexpected and wonderful. Ivan, I have one observation for you—do not pick up Joey when you are angry, overly excited, or very emotional. We do not know how much Joey will learn from you when being held. Hold him when you are relaxed and happy, perhaps when you are listening to music or playing a word game on the computer, something like that. This is only a precaution. We do not know what is actually happening here. As you progress, I would like you to keep notes on these feelings with Joey, but by all means, be his father and be as normal as possible."

"Okay, Ronda. Penny and I will observe and feel and note for you everything that happens. I will be careful as to when Joey and I share auras together. So far, this is very relaxing and seems to be very natural," said Ivan.

"A mother, especially when breastfeeding, has a very close bond with her baby. I'm sure she experiences something like you and Joey experience when you share auras. But think of most fathers. They tickle the baby, throw them up in the air, make funny faces at them—very different than what you are experiencing with Joey. I'm sure your time sharing auras with Joey is much better than poking and making faces," smiled Ronda.

They spent the rest of the evening together while Penny finished feeding Joey, and the three women put Joey to bed.

Chapter 62

Niels was sitting in his room when the video phone rang. He quickly put on his sport coat and answered, "Hello, this is Niels Borgue."

"Hello, this is Ambassador Hemmingway. President Atwood has asked me to call you and walk you through the process of application for membership to the United Nations. Most applications are made by personal appearance. However, in your case, an exception can and will be made. Your appeal and formal application can be made via telecom, and any question-and-answer period will occur at that time. The Federation of Mars foundational documents should be presented to the Security Council prior to your call. I will see to it that the Council considers your application while you are on the phone. You may have to go on hold for a while as we debate and vote. Understand that the Security Council will only vote to recommend membership to the General Assembly, which will then vote yes or no. This is just a formality as the General Assembly always follows the recommendation of the Security Council. I have sent you separately a recommendation for your speech to the Security Council that was written by the staff at the White House with input from me. The president and I want this application to succeed, and I will work on your behalf to see that it does."

"Thank you, Ambassador Hemmingway. I have not been looking forward to writing this speech. I am an engineer and an astronaut, not a diplomat. I highly respect your skills, and it looks like I will have to develop some of those skills in my new role," said Niels. "I will work on this and get back to you concerning timing when I am ready."

Chapter 63

The next day, Niels was telling Charlie about his call from Ambassador Hemmingway.

"Charlie, I need coaching, and we will need some kind of prop for this speech to the United Nations. I am not very good at this," said Niels.

"Well," began Charlie, "Nancy and I have already talked about this. First of all, I believe that Nancy is the best one to coach you. She has been in the pulpit for many years and knows how to convince an audience. As far as what the scene should look like, you should be seated with Scott and Bill behind you. In the foreground, outside of the glass, should be Nancy, Ronda, and Linda, and you all should be in your Federation of Mars uniforms."

"I didn't know that we had uniforms. Have they been designed? What do they look like?"

Nancy, Ronda, and Linda walked into the conference room just then, wearing the new uniforms.

"Scott, Bill, come here! You have to see this!" exclaimed Niels.

The ladies were wearing form-fitting, one-piece uniforms similar to the costumes worn by the actors in *Star Trek*. The ladies' uniforms were red, and the ones for the men were blue. There was a logo above the left breast, and the uniforms had built-in booties with rubber soles and proper internal foot support.

"That is very attractive and looks very functional and comfortable," commented Niels. "Come a little closer. I want to see the logo."

As Nancy stepped closer, Ronda and Linda could not resist showing off, walking around the room and posing for all angles with seductive smiles on their faces.

"Those uniforms are very form fitting, and you all look great," said Bill.

The logo was simple but effective. It showed the familiar picture of Mars with the canals and other features of its surface. Overlaying that was an image of the *Mayflower II*.

"That logo is perfect. I wouldn't change a thing. Do you thing we could open the presentation to the United Nations with it full screen?" asked Niels.

"Great idea. I will get Penny working on that right away. She actually is the one who designed the logo. She has many talents and is perfect for the job of media coordinator," mentioned Nancy. She went on, "Ronda, Linda, and I have had fun designing the uniforms. We didn't ask you boys because this was a women's prerogative. We will wear normal cotton underwear and then a one-piece white jumpsuit that acts as an insulator to both heat and cold. This jumpsuit has a zipper all the way down for obvious reasons. This fabric breaths and is washable, and it moves with the skin and the outer fabric. You hardly know you have it on. The outer fabric is weatherproof. There is no rain on Mars, but the wind can be very bad. Of course, we will be wearing the spacesuits when we go outside. This outer fabric is very tough and will help protect us from bumps and bruises. There is a hat that goes with the uniform that covers the ears and attaches under the chin, but we didn't wear it today because it is ugly. We hope you boys like it, and we want you to put yours on now and model for us."

Charlie put the three uniforms into the airlock, and the boys went to their respective rooms.

Three handsome men emerged, completely transformed into a cohesive unit ready to take on the universe.

"From today on we will all wear this uniform whenever we can be seen by the public, which is almost all the time now seeing as Penny and her team are constantly recording for the weekly shows. Charlie, can you have more made?" asked Niels.

"Yes, I think ten sets for each will be enough," said Charlie.

Chapter 64

Chief Justice Oliver had prepared a beautiful set of leather-bound documents presenting the Federation of Mars Constitution and Bill of Rights as a present to the new government of Mars. There were also ten copies of these documents for use by the crew, one of which had been sent to the Security Council of the United Nations.

The screen in front of the Security Council showed the logo of the Federation of Mars, and then the scene changed to show Niels sitting with Scott and Bill behind him. Nancy, Ronda, and Linda sat in front of the glass just below Niels.

"Thank you for taking the time to hear our story and application. I would like to introduce to you the members of the new colony on Mars." As Niels introduced the team, the camera showed a close-up of each of them, and they gave a small wave to the camera.

Niels gave the application speech, concluding, "This is the end of our life on Earth and the start of a new life on Mars. We welcome you to visit in the future, and by all means send us your children. We will welcome them."

"Thank you, Mr. Borgue," said Ambassador Hemmingway. "We will go offline now for discussion and the vote. Please wait and we will get back to you soon."

"You did a great job," said Nancy. "I think you will make a great spokesman for Mars."

A little while later, Ambassador Hemmingway came back onscreen. "You have one hundred percent approval from the Security Council. We will present our recommendation to the General Assembly tomorrow and expect their approval that afternoon. We all wish you

Godspeed and look forward to reports of your success."

Chapter 65

Dr. Ray Atwood had a surprise for the three astronauts; a few months ago he had sent a form to the Nobel Committee to nominate Niels Borgue, Scott Nettles, and Bill Lee for the Nobel Prize in Biology, citing the discovery of life outside of Earth, in the form of the ARC1 bacteria they found on the asteroid Ceres, proving that we on Earth are not the only living things in the universe. In doing so, he also asked the committee to create a new category called Exobiology, the study of extraterrestrial lifeforms.

The vote came in in favor of the nomination, and the astronauts were awarded the Nobel Prize in Biology. They were notified and invited to attend the ceremonies at the Stockholm Concert Hall in Sweden on December tenth. Ray came went himself to give the crew the good news.

"Ray, this is a great honor and a very big surprise to the three of us. What are we going to do?" asked Niels. "We cannot leave here to travel to Sweden, and I understand that we have to give a lecture a week prior to the presentation."

"I have requested a special dispensation that you be represented by proxy, for both your lecture and to receive your prize. I received that dispensation earlier today. They only ask that you be live on video to receive acknowledgement of your achievement from the king of Sweden," explained Ray.

Niels turned to Scott and Bill and asked, "What do you think? Should we accept? It wasn't really a scientific discovery. It was really a pain-in-the-ass accident that just happened to us."

"It is my understanding that upwards of a million dollars is awarded," observed Scott. "We could put that money to good use in the account here on Earth for support of the Federation of Mars. Yes, I think we should accept."

Bill said, "I would like to recommend that Nancy represent us in Stockholm when the time comes."

"How about it, Nancy? Do you want a VIP trip to Sweden?" asked Niels. "All you have to do is give a speech and collect a check and a medal for us."

They all turned and looked at Nancy. "I am so proud of all of you, and this award and recognition is so appropriate. I would love to be your spokesperson and tell the whole world how proud we all are of you," she said, beaming.

A few months later, on December tenth, Nancy found herself on the stage of the Stockholm Concert Hall. The committee had asked Nancy to give her lecture to the full audience in front of the king of Sweden because of the special nature of the category and the situation the astronauts were in. Niels, Scott, and Bill had worked with Nancy prior to her trip to make sure that she covered all of the important things that they wanted to say. This was not only a scientific finding, but a new awakening as to the future of space exploration and what humanity may find.

With Niels, Scott, and Bill in their new Mars uniforms on the large video screen behind her, Nancy started.

"I am honored to be here in front of this august body, representing three men, one of whom I am married to and love very much and two whom I have recently met and respect very much. These men not only traveled to the asteroid belt, landed on an asteroid, found water, and traveled back. They also brought back life. This life is in the form of a bacterium named ARC1, and it permeates their bodies and cannot be removed or destroyed without killing them. You see behind me the three gentlemen I am talking about. Let me introduce to you Astronauts Niels Borgue, Scott Nettles, and William Lee.

"This bacteria that they carry grows in and thrives in water but is easily destroyed. If you had a glass of water with the bacteria in it, you would just have to put it in a microwave oven for thirty seconds to kill it. I'm sure that you have heard that, if released, this bacteria would destroy all of the grain crops in the world and we would never be able to grow grain again. Therefore, you see these three gentlemen in quarantine. They can never come out without risking starvation around the world.

"Rather than commit suicide and have their bodies destroyed by high heat, they have chosen to leave Earth and start a colony on Mars. This is the reason that you should honor their bravery, in addition to the confirmation that they have brought you of life outside Earth."

As Nancy approached the podium to receive the medals, there was a standing ovation that lasted for ten minutes.

Chapter 66

Construction was almost finished, and Niels, Scott, and Bill were supposed to make the final breakthrough into the chapel. Niels had doubts about containment integrity, but he had been repeatedly reassured by the construction foreman that all was okay. Tools in hand, they made the final breakthrough into the new, small chapel. It was a beautiful, narrow room with a full arch of roses at the end and flowers lining both walls. This was a onetime use room and would be destroyed with the rest of the facilities after they left for Mars. Pictures lined both walls of the lives of all six of the crew. There was a microphone for Nancy to broadcast the wedding to the whole world. Cameras were located in strategic locations to capture the occasion in its entirety for Penny and her team.

"Nancy, all is ready here as we planned. How are you and the girls doing?" asked Niels precisely twenty-four hours after the breakthrough.

"Well, they have the normal pre-wedding nerves. Linda was sick this morning but recovered. The limo is here, and Penny is hovering around with her crew filming everything. They actually walked in on Ronda partially naked," laughed Nancy. "How are Scott and Bill holding up?"

"I've kept them busy up to now, but now that there is some downtime I fear that they are too nervous to have their normal nap after lunch. But we are having a drink. Do you think we can still schedule for two o'clock?" asked Niels.

"Well, I hope so, but you have to remember that we are entering the quarantine facility and can never come out. We have to say our goodbyes and have our last hugs, as well as dress for a wedding. You will just have to be patient and control your drinking. The last thing we need is two drunken grooms and one drunken best man to contend with."

All were on hand in the conference room as the limo pulled up; Nancy in her vestments and Linda and Ronda in their white wedding dresses entered, and all gave a big sigh. After giving their mother a final hug and goodbye, Alan and Jon went to Ronda and Linda respectively and offered their arms. Ivan and Penny escorted Nancy to the airlock portal while Nancy's mother and father looked on with tears in their eyes. The three ladies stood waiting for Charlie to open the portal and allow them to enter.

In the meantime, Niels had taken the two men into the chapel and placed them on either side of the rose arch.

Charlie gave the three women a kiss on the cheek and said, "Thank you for all you have done and all you will do. It has been an honor and pleasure to both Martha and me knowing you all. Godspeed to Mars."

Charlie opened the portal with a large hiss as air was drawn in, and three women made the first steps into the rest of their lives.

After a complicated series of openings and closings of airtight doors, Niels left the two men and went to escort the brides down the aisle. Nancy went to her position under the rose arch, after giving Niels a lingering kiss.

The processional music started to play, and Scott and Bill saw Ronda and Linda in the flesh for the first time. The men were in full military uniform, including Niels, and both women felt at ease and truly in love for the first time in their lives.

The crew watched the ceremony on the large screen in the conference room, along with the whole world thanks to Penny and her filming crew. Nancy beamed throughout the ceremony, and when the two couples kissed to seal their vows, you could hear the cheer go up in the conference room and around the world.

Yolanda and her crew had prepared everything for the group in the main quarantine area, as well as the one in the conference room. When the wedding party came into the living area and looked out the large window, they saw a very happy crowd of people applauding and cheering. Champagne was poured in both rooms, and the toasts started.

After a few rounds, Ronda whispered to Linda, and she, Linda, and Nancy disappeared into Nancy's room. Following their lead, Niels, Scott, and Bill disappeared as well.

In Nancy's room, Ronda presented Linda and Nancy with a small package. "I know that this is a strange time, but I will not have a better one than now. You have been off of the pill for a couple of years now, and we do not want to have to deal with a pregnancy prior to arriving at Mars. So here they are. Use them. And Linda, I hope there are enough," laughed Ronda as she handed over a good-sized box of condoms. "But remember, no pregnancies until the Mars landing. Then more is better."

Twenty minutes later, they all emerged dressed in the Federation of Mars uniforms, with one exception—Ronda and Linda still had their veils on.

Food was served, drinks were poured, and the cakes—there were two—were devoured.

After a respectable amount of time, the two young couples thanked everyone for coming and made a hasty retreat to their respective quarters, amongst catcalls and whistles from those remaining. It wasn't long after that when Niels and Nancy also said their farewells to the guests, receiving their own chorus of cheers and handclapping.

Chapter 67

Joy and Jon were in the conference room for a special meeting that they had requested with Nancy and Niels.

"Mom and Dad, Joy and I have planned out our future and hope that our plan to support you on Mars will meet with your approval. As you know, I am continuing my education at the University of Arizona. I will follow Joy in studying nutrition and specializing in growing food in harsh environments. When I graduate, Charlie will see to it that I go into astronaut training. The reason for this is that Joy and I have a plan to grow food using Martian soil, greatly improving your capability to be self-sustaining on Mars. This plan will need testing, and the university and the space agency have agreed to support us in this endeavor."

"Jon and I have spent a lot of time together planning this, and we find that we get along very well together. We are both looking forward to seeing this through," said Joy.

Nancy thought that there might be more than this project drawing these two together, but she didn't want to say anything now. She would talk to Jon privately later on to see if her baby boy was happy.

"Jon, going through astronaut training is a surprise to us. We are proud of your accomplishments in high school, and we approve of the University of Arizona and the nutrition program there, but why do you need to be an astronaut?" asked Nancy.

"The project is still in the formative stages right now, and being an astronaut may not be necessary, but I wanted to let you know just in case," said Jon.

"One astronaut in the family is enough," said Niels,

"but I will support you in any decision you make. You are an adult now and can make your own decisions, and we both appreciate your ongoing support of our effort on Mars."

"Mom and Dad, you have heard Joy and I sing together before, but we have found a song that will always remind us of you two. We would like to sing it for you now. We think of Mars as an 'Island in the Cosmic Stream.'"

As they started the strains of "Island in the Stream" by Kenny Rogers and Dolly Pardon, tears came to Nancy's eyes. She suddenly realized that once they took off for Mars, she might never see her sons again. Nancy and Niels joined in with at the refrain of the chorus, and there wasn't a dry eye in the room by the end of the song.

"That will be our theme song, and you two sing it so beautifully. Thank you for being so caring and thoughtful," said Nancy. "We will leave in a few days, but we will carry you in our hearts and always think of you when we hear and sing this song."

Later that evening, Penny was watching the recordings from that day, and she came across the singing. It was so beautiful that she knew right then that she needed to include it in the ceremonies during lift-off.

Chapter 68

Charlie was nervous and running around checking on everything. Martha tried to calm him but to no avail. The Mars crew was about to come out of the quarantine facilities, and nothing could go wrong at this late stage. They would travel to the Kennedy Space Center, where they would board the rocket plane that would take them to the *Mayflower II*. This was the last time that the people in Houston would see the crew, and hundreds had shown up to say goodbye.

Penny and her film crew were at the Houston facilities to film their departure, and a second crew was at Kennedy to film their actual departure from Earth. Penny played the theme song, and the crew could hear it in their spacesuits; it lifted their spirits.

When they landed at Kennedy Space Center, they were still in their spacesuits, each person carrying their life support cases. They boarded a bus and were driven past a very large crowd of well-wishers waving and cheering and saying goodbye. The bus took them out to the rocket plane suspended beneath the high lift–high altitude plane that would take them into the upper atmosphere before dropping the rocket plane, which would then ignite and take them to the ISS.

After they were seated and strapped in the rocket plane, Niels said, "Say goodbye to Earth gravity. From now on, we will either be weightless or under Mars gravity. This will be trip number five to the ISS for me, but your first. Enjoy it. Many people will follow in your steps in the future."

As the theme song started to play again, the high lift plane started rolling down the long runway and lifted off with no discernable feeling inside the rocket plane. After they reached the planned altitude and location, the rocket plane dropped from the high lift plane, and the rocket fired, throwing them all back into their seats. The rocket plane vibrated and shook under extreme acceleration, and the whole crew hung on with white knuckles. Before they knew it, the rocket engine had stopped and they were in outer space.

"Look," said Linda, "there's Earth."

The large, round Earth filled the whole viewing window, and they all were so in awe of what they saw that they did not even realize that they were weightless.

Both Niels and Bill were busy at the console communicating with the crew at the ISS, getting final directions for their final approach docking.

As the ISS came into view, they could see *Mayflower II* next to it, standing about 100 yards off from the ISS. The rocket plane had automatic landing and coupling sequences with the ISS; it had landed there many times before because it was now the primary resupply craft for the ISS.

"*Mayflower II* looks smaller than I expected," commented Nancy.

"It will get larger as we get closer, but it does not have to be very big to do the job. The new drive takes a lot of bulk away. See the long boom out the back with the bulbous bulk on the end? That is the drive," said Scott.

Closer and closer they got, until the ISS and *Mayflower II* filled the whole window. Docking was gentle, and when the airlock portal opened, the crew, still in their spacesuits, unstrapped and floated across to the ISS.

The plan was to take the Mars crew over to *Mayflower*

II as soon as possible. There were already six astronauts on the ISS, and adding six more was not possible. The trip to the *Mayflower II* was to be via tethered EVA, one at a time with a member of the ISS accompanying each Mars crew member over. The tethering was something like an old bosun's chair and hand-over-hand motion to get them there. This part was very scary, especially for Nancy, who had to darken her facemask completely, and she still closed her eyes. The crew of the ISS offloaded the personal effects and also transferred them to the *Mayflower II*.

There was a large storage area extending behind the center of *Mayflower II*, located back toward the ion drive. This area was full of containers that held supplies and items that they would need after landing on Mars. One of the containers was large and contained the crawler that would help them move equipment and containers around on the surface of Mars. All of these modules were designed to enter the Mars atmosphere and find the Helium location using a beacon to guide them. The crew would launch these containers after they were stable in Mars orbit.

When all of the crew were transferred into the Tank, the large empty center of the ship, they hung on to the handrails on the side of the room and didn't move.

"See the temporary signs above those portals?" asked Niels. "Lee, Nettles, Borgue, and Conference Room. If you open those portals you will see a passageway with a pole down the middle. This is the way to your quarters out through the arms that will provide gravity when we start rotating. At the front of this tank you will see another portal that will take you forward to the deck where you will be strapped in for launch and where Bill and I will have full control of all aspects of this ship," said Niels. "Now find your quarters and take your personal effects with you, and we will meet on the deck in one hour."

Scott and Bill had also been in zero gravity but in much smaller, confined spaces, and the portals to their openings seemed like a long way away. Linda let go and floated away out of control. "Wee! I'm flying," she said as she bumped into a duffle and then into a wall. Then she turned a little green and said, "Bill, help me, let's go down now."

Bill and Scott let go at the same time and showed some control as they caught Ronda and Linda, taking them to the portals.

Once inside the arms, motion was much easier; the center pole helped stabilize them and made it easy to move hand over hand out to their quarters. At the end of each arm was another portal that opened into the ceiling of their quarters; the pole extended down to the floor. The small, apartment-like quarters were upside down, and it was hard to get orientated. They could not sit on a chair or lay in bed because there was no gravity yet. The quarters had a bedroom, bathroom, and living area, which included the kitchen area as well.

"This will look great when we have gravity, but for now it is useless," said Scott. He suggested, "Let's go up to the control deck and strap in so we can relax without worrying about bumping into something."

They met Linda and Bill in the Tank. Niels and Nancy were already there when the others arrived. They all stayed in their spacesuits for fear of contaminating the ISS crew with ARC1. The ISS crew had escorted each couple to their respective quarters, carrying their duffels, and then headed back to the Tank. The ISS crew pointed out the baskets in each of the eight corners of the Tank and handed Niels a ball slightly larger than a softball, explaining the rules that they had created for eight-corner basketball with two-man teams.

"We really enjoyed playing while waiting for you to arrive. The record score right now is four goals in one hour, made by Cosmonaut Sasha. See if you can beat that!" said Kelly. "In fact, we liked it so much, and the workout it gave us, that we will soon receive a new module to the ISS that will provide us with our own Tank!"

They said goodbye and thanks to the ISS crew, and when they departed, Niels said, "Welcome to your new home for the next six months."

Chapter 69

"Strap in and we will prepare to detach from the ISS. As soon as we detach, we can start rotation and create gravity," said Niels.

"When we blow the cables holding you to the ISS," said the ISS controller, "they will blow on both ends and then be jettisoned into outer space. JPL has planned another module for the ISS that will be a permanent port for the *Mayflower II*, and we will not have to use tethers anymore."

A small bang was heard, and the *Mayflower II* was free in space. Niels issued some commands, and the rotation jets fired; they started to slowly rotate. "It will take us about an hour to get up to full rotation, so sit back, relax, and watch the view," said Niels.

As they sat there, they saw the ISS to their right and behind that the Earth, a beautiful blue, green, and white; slowly, as they rotated around, the sun came into view, then again the ISS and Earth. Again and again they went around for an hour as the rotation gained speed; they got used to the rotation and the changing view.

"Here on the deck and in the Tank there will be essentially no gravity because we are in the center of the rotating ship. You will only feel gravity in your quarters and in the conference room due to the centrifugal force that the rotation gives us. As you climb down to your quarters you will feel increasing gravity, so be careful when you get close as you could fall if not careful," warned Niels. "Also remember that the gravity of Mars is only one-third that of Earth, so if you fall it won't be very hard, but be careful how you jump when you are on the floor of your quarters. You might hit the ceiling. Experiment and slowly get used to your surroundings."

Checking the console in front of him once more, Niels said, "We are now up to full rotation speed. Go to your quarters and get acclimatized to your new environment. Lay down, unpack your duffels, et cetera. Have fun and I will see you in the conference room in two hours."

The conference room was comfortable and well appointed; Nancy could see that they would spend a lot of their flight time in here. There was a big screen TV and a large table with six chairs that were bolted to the floor so they wouldn't float away prior to rotation. The crew could unbolt them after rotation and move them around if needed. The full kitchen promised many meals together during their flight. There were four lounge chairs and one couch. A closet was full of games and books for those old-fashioned ones that liked their entertainment real and not just on the screen. There was a medical room off the conference room, and on the other side of the conference room was a small workshop supplied with tools and materials that they might need. Ronda had personally supervised the stocking of her medical office, and only she knew what was in the small, secured room attached to her office. This small room had special coolers to store genetic material for possible future use; also stored in this area was a crate that held an artificial womb and the associated equipment needed to make it function.

After all six were together in the conference room, Niels said, "There is no turning back from now on. This is your last chance to return to the ISS, but remember—you will not be welcome back on Earth. Shall I commence with the prelaunch procedures?"

Scott and Ronda held hands, and Bill and Linda embraced. Nancy went up to Niels and said, "We want to go to Mars with you. Lead on and let God be with us all."

Chapter 70

Two hours later, they were all strapped in up on the deck, waiting for JPL to finalize uploading the flight plan needed for their time and place in space, where Mars was now, how fast it was traveling, and the location of Mars prior to their arrival.

Niels informed the crew, "The acceleration and velocity will be gradual. You will not be thrown back into your seat. The ion drive will accelerate us to four-point-five meters per second, which will get us to Mars orbit in about six months. At about halfway there we will use the small jets to turn us around, and then the ion drive will start to slow us down for the rest of the trip. Actually, Mars is currently its farthest from Earth now, but the trajectory will be the shortest route to where Mars will be in six months. We will travel beyond the sun and meet Mars on the other side. We fire the ion drive in twenty minutes."

The crew of the ISS appeared on the screen, waving and cheering. "Goodbye, and thank you for all your help. Come and visit some time!" said Nancy.

The scene on the screen changed to their old conference room in Houston, and it was filled with their friends and families, all waving and blowing kisses. Then the presidential logo came on, announcing President Atwood. Penny had set this up, and it would broadcast around the world.

"It is my understanding that you will start your trip in about five minutes," said Samantha, "so I will make this short. I have authorized a living memorial in your honor that will include a substantial endowment in your names. This endowment will be used for scholarships for students who want to possibly join you on Mars someday. Bill Lee's sister,

Joy, will be the first to receive this scholarship. Godspeed, and know that all of Earth is behind you and wishes you well."

Soon the crew felt a small push, and the view of the ISS started to move backward. They were on their way. All was quiet as they settled deep into their own thoughts.

Chapter 71

Once underway, the crew settled in for the long flight. Ronda gave each of them a full physical, and Niels officially assigned each of them the duties and chores they had agreed on before takeoff. It was clear that they were going to have a lot of free time, as almost everything was automatic. The quarters were comfortable, and soon they all settled in and made their quarters their own, hanging pictures and adding personal items. Each quarter had a small kitchen, but the crew soon started taking all of their meals in the conference room together. Once the sleep cycle was established, they settled in to a routine. The food was not great, but Nancy showed skill at making the most of what was available; she was designated chef of the *Mayflower II*.

Niels went over the emergency procedures for all possible things that could happen and made sure they all knew their assignments. He emphasized that the schedule for exercise was very important and must be followed every day.

A challenge was made, and they designed a round-robin, double-elimination tournament for eight-corner basketball. They drew lots, and Nancy and Linda were selected for the first match. Both women returned to the privacy of their own quarters to develop their strategies for the upcoming competition.

Chapter 72

Daily communication with JPL and Penny and Ivan was set up; the delay was not very pronounced as they were still close enough to Earth to be able to talk in real time.

"Penny, the tournament is set, and we will transmit the video to you for your program. Let us know if the cameras are set up in the right places," said Niels. "Nancy will challenge Linda for the first match. Each match will last one hour, and we will have two matches each day. Bill and Scott will be the second match today. You have the rules. Hopefully we will put on a good show for you. We will be wearing our white undersuits for the matches because it is quite warm and the air is dense and heavy in the Tank. Some of the crew has used this last month to practice getting used to the ball and its motion and action in weightlessness, but we have not been up against each other yet, so do not expect too much. I'm sure we will look awkward, but we will try our best."

"We are all set here," replied Penny. "We will record the whole match and edit out some of the more awkward moments prior to sending the video of the matches to the rest of the world. Carl will start the tournament with a talk as to how important exercise is while in space. Make sure that the lights are turned all the way up, though I hope your undersuits are not transparent under the bright lights. We don't want to have an X-rating for our first sports event in space."

"We didn't think of that, but we will be wearing normal underwear also, so I hope we do not reveal too much."

As Nancy and Linda entered the Tank, Ronda and the boys watched from the landing platform behind the glass door. Linda and Nancy floated up to the camera and gave a wave to Penny before going to their respective corners. Niels let the ball float into the center, and the game was on.

Nancy guarded the left four corner baskets and Linda the right four. At Niels signal, they each pushed off from the wall behind them and flew toward the center after the ball, shooting past it and rebounding off the far walls and back toward the center, out of control. The ball continued past the center, toward the adjacent wall. Nancy and Linda bumped into each other in the center with a hard impact.

"Are you two all right?" asked Bill.

"This is not as easy as it looks. Ronda, get the bandages out. This might get bloody," said Linda as they went to their respective corners to start over. The ball was still floating untouched near the wall.

Niels gave the go signal once more, and this time the push from both women was much more controlled. Linda got to the ball first, and she was ready to throw it toward one of Nancy's baskets when Nancy crashed into her and the ball came loose. Nancy gave a small shove against the wall and caught the ball, moving toward Linda's goal. She made an easy throw into one of the baskets.

"One to nothing," yelled Nancy, throwing her hands in the air. It sent her spinning.

Linda was in the center nursing a bruised shoulder, a determined look on her face.

"Wow, Nancy is tough," said Bill. "I didn't think this game was going to be so rough."

"Okay, time out. Both of you come over here. We need to discuss some new rules," said Niels.

As Nancy and Linda floated over to the platform, Nancy said, "My goal still counts. What are these new rules? We are just fine."

"Nancy, I know about your history in sports. It is only fair to tell the others how competitive you are," said Niels, giving them time to recover from the initial contact. "Nancy was the star of her school's field hockey and the lacrosse teams, and she also played for the men's ice hockey team in her senior year. Nancy, back off some. We can't afford any serious injuries."

"Okay, but how do we not have contact? We can't even control our motion enough to get to the ball, much less avoid hitting each other," said Nancy.

"Look, I can handle it. Let's get started again," said Linda aggressively.

"Well, here's what I think—to make the game more graceful and to get it under more control, use your hands to push off. Let's have fewer violent collisions and bruises," said Niels.

"I agree, but my goal still stands," insisted Nancy again as she offered Linda her hand.

They went back to their starting positions, and Niels threw in the ball. This time the game proceeded with much more control, and they learned that a small touch to their opponent just as they were going to throw toward the basket made them miss. The game ended one to nil, and Nancy was jubilant, spinning gracefully in front of the camera.

The game between Scott and Bill was very different. They both came out fighting and banging, and neither one could gain an advantage on the other. They were anything but graceful and flew around the Tank out of control, chasing the ball in frustration for one hour. The game ended zero to zero, with both of them exhausted and bruised and somewhat embarrassed.

Penny came on, laughing. "That was great! We got it all. Next time try a little harder and you might score a goal instead of just getting beat up. See you all soon! Thanks."

The matches continued for days with very few goals being scored, but Ronda showed the most skill. With her deft doctor's touch, she eluded her opponents, and she used the walls to clear herself for many shots on goal. The more shots on goal she had, the more accurate she became, until soon her shots were almost always a goal. Ronda was crowned the tournament winner and given a golden coffee cup as the prize. The reward ceremonies were broadcast around the world, and a message came in from the ISS. "You still haven't beaten cosmonaut Sasha's record! Practice more, and try harder."

The next call they received was from Penny. "The tournament was a great success. People around the world want to join you, and the Federation of Mars coffers are full. We are having no problem selling your story to many affiliates around the world. Carl has a beautiful speaking voice and a natural talent as a narrator. Plus, he has inside insight that greatly helps," she said. "As you know, Alan and Jon have started school, and both are doing very well. Ivan will address the United Nations next week, though he is still uncomfortable speaking to such an important group. With a little more practice, he will do just fine. He practices his speech on Joey when we put him down to sleep, and he usually falls to sleep very quickly. Ivan will send you a copy of his speech as soon as he is happy with it. By the way, we are pregnant again! It will be a girl this time, and the big event will be in three months."

"That is great!" said Nancy. "Congratulations to both of you. Do you have enough room at the embassy for a new baby?"

"This place is huge. We have many spare rooms.

President Atwood was very helpful in finding it for us. It seems that the previous occupants were asked to leave the country for clandestine reasons. I have to go now. Some company is coming. Keep the videos coming. Bye."

Chapter 73

About halfway into their trip to Mars, one artificial night the crew was asleep and all was very quiet aboard *Mayflower II*. Their sleep cycle lasted eight hours, and about halfway through, the claxon sounded. Everyone leaped out of bed and ran to the intercom to report in.

"Bill to the deck, ASAP! All others report to your emergency stations!" said Niels.

When Bill arrived to the deck a few minutes later, Niels explained, "The main computer is reporting a breach in the hull in sector twenty-two. I believe that we have run into a meteor shower." Speaking over the loudspeaker again so all could hear, he said, "Scott, there is a breach in the hull in sector twenty-two. Take your kit and get there ASAP. I do not know how large the breach is, but we are losing air. Make sure you are careful near the breach. Do not let it suck your skin into it. Seal it as soon as you find it."

"Roger, on my way," replied Scott.

As Scott reached sector twenty-two, which was the tube leading to the conference room, he heard the hiss before he saw it. Following the noise, he located the breach hidden behind a column, and as he looked, he saw a crease in the outer skin of the arm. The crease was about ten inches long, but the hole in the center of the crease was only about one-quarter of an inch. He mixed the epoxy compound and tried to reach behind the column, but his arm was too large to get all the way to the hole. Just then, Linda came up to see if she could help; her arm was much smaller than Scott's. She reached the hole while Scott steadied her. The suction was very strong, and she almost touched the hole with the side of her arm, but Scott pulled her back just in time. The next time she was more careful and managed to stick the epoxy into the hole. It held, and the hissing stopped.

"We have stopped the leak," announced Scott. "Check the computer to make sure there are no other leaks."

"All clear, no other leaks. This appears to be a random strike. Bill is looking ahead with radar, and we see no other material coming toward us," said Niels. "Let's meet in the deck and review."

Once everyone had left their emergency stations and met up on the deck, Niels said, "That was a close call. The hole was small, and we did not lose a significant amount of air. Thanks to you, Scott, we are safe."

"It was actually Linda that saved the day. I couldn't get my arm in far enough to reach the leak, but skinny Linda reached in and plugged the hole," said Scott.

"Just like the little boy with his finger in the dyke," laughed Linda nervously.

"Thank you both for your quick response, and you, Linda, for backing up Scott," said Niels. "Bill and I will go and examine the surrounding area and apply more epoxy if necessary."

They all went back to their quarters, but no one went back to bed. They had all been reminded just how vulnerable they were, just one tiny speck in the vastness of space.

Chapter 74

A few space days later, Penny was on a private call to Niels. "You have been traveling for four months, and the videos you are sending are getting boring. I have had many complaints from the affiliates about programming. Can you do anything to make the videos a little more interesting?" she asked.

"I don't know what we can do. We are also a little bored. There is only so much you can do in a small confined space, but I will talk to the others and see what we can come up with," said Niels.

During the next crew meeting, Niels laid out Penny's problem. "So you see what she is up against. When we get to Mars there will be plenty to send back, but in the meantime we need to help her. Go back to your rooms and see if you can come up with something we can do to liven things up."

After they got back to their quarters, Ronda said, "I have an idea, but we must try it first. It may be too difficult to pull off. Let's go try now while everyone is in bed. We will have privacy."

Scott asked, "What are we going to do?"

"Here, take this memory stick and follow me."

Ronda shot up the tube like she had been doing it all her life, and Scott followed.

When they got to the landing platform and had their feet in the securing sandals, Ronda plugged in the thumb drive. "The Blue Danube" started to play. "We are going to learn to do the no-step-hip-square waltz. Would you like to dance?" said Ronda with a smile.

Just before stepping off, Ronda made sure that the cameras were off, and she adjusted the thermostat up.

She led Scott to the middle of the Tank and instructed him to the choreography that she had in mind. After about an hour, Scott went back to the landing platform sweating profusely.

"It is so hot in there. Let's turn it down a little bit," he panted.

"No, the hot, dense air makes it easier to fly and soar. It gives us more and easier moves to make. Here, let me help." Ronda unzipped Scott's undersuit and stripped him to his waist, tying the floating arms around his middle. "There, that should help, and now I have more inspiration. What a nice hunk you are!"

"Okay, let's continue, but first let me help you get out of your suit. I need inspiration too." Scott then unzipped Ronda's undersuit and pulled it down to her waist. He quickly reached behind her and undid her bra, removing it before she could protest. "Now I am inspired and ready to dance the night away," he said with a grin.

"Scott, what are you doing? Someone might see!"

As Scott pulled her hands away from her breasts, he said, "You are beautiful, and look, you are floating."

"This is a very uplifting feeling, and it feels good," said Ronda as she pushed off and floated away.

Scott joined her and held her in his arms in the traditional dance hold. As the music played, they started small dance movements, and Scott said as he looked down, "There is more jiggle and sway to this step than before. I like it."

"Pay attention and concentrate on our dance," said

Ronda as she floated away on her back, knowing that she was alluring and teasing him.

Sometime later Scott looked over to the landing platform and saw Bill and Linda watching them practice.

"That is beautiful. We want to try," said Linda. "Can we join you? Please teach us."

Immediately Ronda's hands went up to her breasts. "Oh, we didn't mean to wake you. Of course you can join us, but first—"

"Don't bother."

Linda started to strip, and then she nudged Bill out of his staring stupor. He also stripped, and they both joined Scott and Ronda in the center.

"This is a very uplifting feeling," said Ronda to break the ice.

"You may say so because you have a lot to lift, but look at little me, with very little to lift," said Linda.

"This is going to be fun. What do you want us to do?" asked Bill.

It was easy to modify the choreography to make it a true four square dance, and Bill and Linda were naturals and joined right in.

Sometime later they heard Nancy from the platform say, "What are you doing?" Niels and Nancy had been standing there for a few minutes, enough time for Niels to get an eyeful.

"We thought that a dance would make an interesting video to send back to Penny for her weekly show, and we are practicing. As for the attire, or lack of it, it is very warm in here," said Ronda.

"The dance is a great idea. Carry on with what you were doing, and don't worry about your attire, but Niels and I will not be joining you for this dance," smiled Nancy as she grabbed Niels. "Come on, you have seen enough. We have things to do back in our quarters."

Nancy led the way, and just before Niels left the platform, he reached up and turned on the cameras that transmitted back to JPL.

That should give Penny plenty of ammunition to negotiate with the affiliates, thought Niels with a smile.

♍

The large screen came on at the JPL lab. It was five in the morning, and only a four-man crew was on, three men and one woman. There was nothing on the screen until Ronda floated by facing the camera. The three men jumped up and started cheering. A few seconds later Scott drifted by, and the woman jumped and also started cheering.

"Do you think they know that the cameras are on?"

"I don't think so. Are we recording this?"

"Yes, I think we should call Penny. It is eight o'clock her time in DC. She will want to see this live and tell us what to do. It is actually very beautiful."

Penny was preparing breakfast for her family when the call came in from JPL.

"Penny, are you getting this feed?"

"Yes. Wow, those guys have really surprised me this time."

"We did not turn on the cameras remotely," insisted the JPL crewwoman. "It is the middle of their sleep cycle. Do you want us to turn off the cameras? We think that they don't know that the cameras are on."

"What they are doing is beautiful. Leave the cameras on and I will talk to them later. Send the recording to me after they are finished, and show it to no one. And turn off your screens!" instructed Penny.

♎

At the next briefing with Penny and the crew, Penny looked a little sheepish and was uncharacteristically quiet. Nancy said, "What is the matter, Penny? Are you and the baby all right?"

"Yes, we are fine, but I have a great favor to ask of you, especially Scott, Ronda, Bill and Linda. I received a raw video of you all dancing the other night, and it was beautiful. Only I and the four technicians at JPL saw the video, and they have been sworn to silence. They swear to me that they did not turn on the cameras remotely. My editor, Janet, has also seen the raw video, which she has severely edited to make it acceptable to all ages and also to not reveal the whole dance that you are going to perform—hopefully fully clothed. I have titled this episode 'Dancing in the Dark,' and Carl will show how adaptive we can be in unique environments. He will explain that this is just a practice session and that the full presentation will come on a later show. This will keep them watching and help with the affiliates' need for more exciting programming," said Penny. "I will upload the new show for your approval. Let me know."

They all sat there and looked at Niels. "Yes, I turned on the cameras. What you were doing was beautiful, and I didn't want to miss that opportunity. I apologize. I should have asked you first," said a contrite Niels.

"Okay, let's see how Penny has taken this X-rated video and made it acceptable to all ages," said Nancy. She looked at Niels. "And from now on, no more tricks."

The program was very tastefully done; viewers would be able to tell that the dancers were partially dressed, but they were never fully revealed. They phoned Penny back with all of them approving the program.

Chapter 75

The crew was gathered in the conference room in front of the big screen a couple nights later when the presidential logo came on. Samantha appeared sitting behind the large Lincoln desk in the Oval Office.

"This is a private call because I have not talked to you in a while. I do watch your weekly episodes, and your latest one was very interesting. You all are very beautiful people, and I am sure you enjoy each other's company, but do you have to show the whole world? You really know how to put on a show. I think I will use some of your tricks for the next election. Though, on second thought, I don't think the American public would like to see me in my natural state.

"I have good news for you and all the people of the world. Tonight I will go on TV and announce that there is now a unified Korea. They have formed a democratic government representing all of the people of the Korean peninsula. China has been very supportive of this move, and all Chinese troops have pulled out and are returning to China. There has been a large movement of people between North and South as families get together after generations of being apart. It brings tears to your eyes to see the reunions.

"I understand that you are over halfway to Mars and that you have turned around and are gradually slowing down. Good luck on the rest of your trip, and I look forward to 'The Dance.' Goodbye for now."

"Well, it looks like we have to work harder on the no-step-hip-square waltz," said Ronda.

Niels and Nancy took over the production, and Ronda was the choreographer. They added some small costume bits, like trailing streamers made from old bits of fabric, to enhance the action. They got very good at control in weightlessness, and their movements became more dance-like; they flowed from one movement to the next effortlessly. Finally they were ready for the production in front of live cameras. Communications were established back to Earth, and Penny gave the go-ahead by saying, "Lights, camera, action!" Niels gave the go sign to the couples in the center. As the music started, the dancers soon forgot about the cameras and fell into the natural rhythm of the dance.

"That was great!" beamed Penny. "I will personally nominate you all for the Emmy for best dance show. I can't thank you enough. I'm sure that this will do the trick!"

Back in the conference room, Niels announced, "I have been saving this for a special occasion." Then he opened a bottle of scotch and poured drinks for all.

Chapter 76

About a month later, Bill and Linda couldn't sleep, so they went to float in the Tank. They held each other for a warm embrace, and also so that they wouldn't drift apart. Bill kissed her, and she kissed him back with a long passionate embrace. Linda said, a little bit breathlessly, "Have you ever wondered what it would be like to make love in weightlessness?"

He guided her back to the platform, where he turned out the lights and undressed her while she undressed him. They floated back to the center, both breathing hard now and in a hurry to get to the inevitable conclusion. They tried to get into position, and every time he tried to penetrate, she slipped away. "Where are you going?" he cried.

Linda laughed and said, "This is too hard! Let's go back to our quarters and finish this in our bed, where there is gravity."

The next day, Linda was secluded in the workshop all day, and Bill spent time with Niels on the deck. When they all met for dinner that evening, Ronda asked Linda, "Where have you been all day? I was looking for you for a game of Scrabble."

"We will play tomorrow. I just needed a little personal time to contemplate the next moves we will make," Linda answered cryptically.

That night, Linda said to Bill, "I want to try again, but this time we will do it differently. I am sure that it will be wonderful."

Bill couldn't wait to get to the Tank, being always ready. As Linda started to undress, she moved in a seductive way that got Bill very aroused. She then reached into the hanging bag on the platform and pulled out a harness.

"What is that for?" asked Bill.

"This is an intimate coupling harness that I made earlier today. It is to prevent the coupling couple from becoming uncoupled during coupling."

"Wow, that is a mouthful. I bet you can't say that quickly three times in a row."

Bill didn't really understand, but he couldn't wait to try it. He stepped into the leg holes, and Linda slid the harness up around his butt. Then she held on to his neck and slid her legs into the other leg holes. She locked her heels around his knees, and they pushed off. By now they were both very aroused and were gently bouncing off of the padded walls. She guided him to the point of near fulfillment, and then she tightened the straps and gave a big sigh. They stayed in that position for a short while, and she then loosened the straps a little bit, just enough so that Bill could have enough room for full penetrating motion. They then moved together in the age-old dance of ultimate pleasure. This time, the experience was more satisfying, and Ronda and Scott heard the results of the noisy climax to the experiment as they entered the Tank. They came to the platform and saw that Bill and Linda were huddled in the dark in a far corner.

"Are you two okay?" asked Scott.

"We are okay, but you two have to turn around. We will come to you there," said Bill. He and Linda slipped out of the harness and came to the platform, dressing while Scott and Ronda had their backs turned.

"We won't ask what you were doing, but we will ask how. We tried it and found it impossible. What is that thing?" said Scott, pointing to the harness floating nearby.

"Linda made this earlier today, and I can attest that it works perfectly. She calls it the intimate coupling harness," said Bill. "Tell them what it is for. I couldn't possibly repeat it."

"It is to prevent the coupling couple from becoming uncoupled during coupling," said Linda, almost purring with satisfaction. "Come on, Bill. Let's leave them to figure it out."

"I don't think they will have any problem. Good luck."

♏

A few weeks later, Linda took Ronda aside. "I have a confession to make. When Bill and I were testing the harness, we were so excited that we forgot to use protection. I have just missed my period. I am always very regular. Can you test me to make sure?"

"Come to my office. This won't take long," said Ronda.

Less than an hour later, Ronda said, "It is positive. You are definitely pregnant. Congratulations."

"Niels and Nancy will be quite upset with me, I am afraid. They specifically warned us against getting pregnant before arriving on Mars. I could use your support please," pleaded Linda.

"Of course I will stand up for you, but first you have to tell Bill."

"I will tell him tonight," promised Linda, wondering how he would react.

Later that evening, Linda led Bill to the Tank, and as they floated together embracing, she said, "Bill, I have something to tell you. Remember our first test of the harness?"

Bill nodded, a smile on his face.

"Well, we got so carried away that we forgot about using protection, and as a result I am pregnant."

"You're what! Linda, that is amazing! I'm so happy! Are you okay? We're going to have a baby! That's awesome!" he exclaimed. "Oh. Oh, I wonder what the others will say. After all, we did agree not to conceive before arriving at Helium."

"Yes, I know. Ronda confirmed my condition, and she will support us when we tell the others."

"Do you realize that our baby might be like Ivan? It will be the first baby born on Mars," said Bill in awe. "I need some time to take this all in. This is fantastic!"

Chapter 77

During the next crew meeting, the difficult topic had to be discussed and Ronda began.

"As you all know, we are a small group, much too small to create a viable population on Mars. We will need additional groups of people to be able to naturally expand to a self-sustaining population without inbreeding and the myriad of problems that brings with it. But before that will happen, we have to show the world that any birth on Mars will produce normal children. The first child to be born on Mars will be to Linda and Bill, about eight months from now."

Linda smiled, and Bill grinned sheepishly.

Nancy looked sternly toward the two of them. "There was a reason for not wanting anyone to conceive in space, as you well know." But then she broke into a smile and said, "The damage has been done and there's no going back, so congratulations. I'm happy for you both and will pray that you have a safe delivery and the baby will be healthy."

Both Linda and Bill gave a sigh of relief, and Linda said, "Thank you, Nancy. We conceived in the Tank the night I created the harness. We were so excited to try it that we forgot to use protection. We are very sorry for violating the rules and will accept any punishment you decide."

"As far as I am concerned, there is no need for that," replied Nancy, and Niels nodded agreement.

"You actually succeeded in the Tank?" asked Niels. "I didn't think that was possible. You need to show me this harness thing. You may have a patentable device there," he said, teasing Bill and Linda. "Look, this was bound to happen, and this should be a happy occasion. There will be no punishment, but I will need to consult with you and Ronda to modify your assignments. We had planned that you will be with Bill and Scott on the first Orion capsule to land on Mars, Linda, and I want to be sure that you and the baby are up to it. It is possible that we could change the order and have you and Bill stay on the *Mayflower II* with Ronda. You could have the baby here while Scott, Nancy, and I go to the surface first."

"I don't think that kind of change will be necessary," said Ronda. "I will monitor Linda and the baby for the next six weeks and report any problems, if there are any. Linda is very healthy and strong, and she will only be two to three months along, hardly even showing, before it is necessary to drop down to Helium. Women have been through much harder turmoil in the past and still managed to overpopulate Earth. We can handle it," smiled Ronda as she held Linda's hand.

"We are about a month away from orbiting Mars, at which time Bill and I will stabilize our orbit to be synchronous above Helium. We can then prepare for descent to the surface. There will be a lot of communication with Earth during this stage, and I recommend that we do not tell anyone about the upcoming happy event until we are all on the surface, unless you and Ronda declare a medical emergency and need advice from Earth," said Niels.

Later that night, Nancy and Niels were in their quarters getting ready for bed.

"Niels, I have been thinking about this for some time, and I feel that now is the time to talk about it."

"What is on your mind?"

"I hope you won't be angry with me, but this might be

exciting for you too."

"Now you really have my interest," he said.

"Well, you may or may not know that Ronda extracted some of my eggs while we were back on Earth. I am of the age that the well of sons and daughters could run dry at any time. But it has not run dry yet, and the time is now. I have only one request—I love Alan and Jon, but I would like a baby with Ivan's characteristics. It worked once for you, and it will work again. I know that we made rules about this, but Linda and Bill have already broken those and I really want to have a baby like Ivan. We will not be able to have a baby like Ivan unless the baby is conceived in weightlessness," pleaded Nancy.

"You mean the Tank?"

"Yes," she said. "Linda told me that they hang the harness in the net bag by the platform."

"Wow," breathed Niels. "If you are sure, I'm willing also. Do you want to go now?"

"Yes! The timing could not be more perfect."

Chapter 78

Mars entered their view along with its two moons. They were days from entering orbit, and this view was beautiful. The red planet filled the whole viewing window on the deck, and the crew was quite taken with their new home. Niels and Bill spent most of their time the next few days making sure that they entered and stabilized in geosynchronous orbit above Helium. The rest of the crew secured their quarters and packed for the trip to Helium.

Entering orbit was successful; the computers did all of the final maneuvering, and the crew could look down to the mountainous area near where Helium was to be located. It looked strange and desolate and gave all of them pause to consider their future. On the screen, JPL had patched the view of Helium as seen from the geological survey satellite, and the crew could see the temporary habitats waiting for them. Even though they couldn't wait to get on the surface, the comfort of the familiar *Mayflower II* was going to be hard to leave. No more eight-corner basketball, no more dancing and floating in the Tank. They would miss it all, and in place would be unknowns and hardship and adventure.

There were six containers in the large rear storage area behind the Tank. These containers were configured to be entry vehicles that would enter Mars' atmosphere and automatically land in the plains just outside of Helium. Inside four of them were last-minute food and personal effects the crew wanted with them. The fifth was the largest and most important. It contained the crawler that the crew would use on the surface to move and manage the containers in and out of the final Helium habitat in the caves, as well as for general transportation needs. The bay doors to this storage area could be opened from the deck, and the containers launched one at a time, their progress monitored by images from the geological survey satellite. All four of the smaller containers landed safely, and the crew held their breath as they watched the crawler land very near Helium. The container opened automatically, and they all cheered when they saw the crawler emerge. Ronda personally loaded the sixth container with the contents of her medical lab, making sure the cryogenic tanks were plugged in. She needed to ensure the contents remained frozen until she could move them to her final lab at Helium when she landed. This final container dropped out, and Ronda said a little prayer that they would land safely.

Chapter 79

Bill, Linda, and Scott were strapped into the *Orion* capsule. Ronda, Nancy, and Niels wished them good luck as Niels closed the hatch. The capsule was released, and Bill fired the small control jets. They slowly drifted away from *Mayflower II*. Bill then fired the retro rockets to start slowing down for entry into Mars' atmosphere. They were thrown backward as the capsule started slowing down. Soon the gravity of Mars started to take over, and they entered the atmosphere. The capsule started to glow a fiery red. The thin atmosphere of Mars was still enough to slow the capsule; small drogue parachutes could slow them even more until the large parachutes finally stopped their fall. Just before touchdown, three large airbags inflated. The parachutes detached, and the capsule fell onto the airbags, which cushioned the landing before quickly deflating.

Linda was white knuckled. She had closed her eyes for most of the trip down; all the strange noises just made her more scared, and she screamed and held on for dear life. Bill and Scott enjoyed themselves. They had experienced this kind of thing on the previous flight to Ceres.

When they looked out of the porthole, they saw that they had landed less than twenty-five yards from Crater Lake. They were upright, and all systems showed green lights. They were already in their spacesuits but had yet to put on their helmets. By prior agreement, the most senior member would be the first to walk on Mars. That was Scott.

With all of them in suits and their helmets on, Scott opened the hatch and radioed to Niels, "Leaving Capsule One now."

As Scott stepped down from the capsule, he radioed

back to Niels and Earth, "Mars, welcome us to your fold. Allow us to walk your surface and make you our new home."

He could hear cheers from the rest of the crew, and he waved up to the satellite, back to all watching on Earth.

Linda and Bill emerged from the capsule after him, and the first thing that Linda thought about was how desolate it was—no trees and everything the same dirty red. This was going to be harder than she had thought.

"Bill, look up there," she said. "See the caves of Helium? They are just what I was hoping for. The slope up seems higher and steeper than I imagined."

They were about a quarter mile from the caves, and to their back was the slope of Crater Lake. In front of them, about halfway to the caves, were the four large rockets containing the temporary habitats. These rockets had reformers in the upper sections that made the oxygen component of the fuel from the carbon dioxide in the Martian air. When mixed with the hydrogen stored in the rocket and fired, it would be enough to lift them off the surface and back to *Mayflower II*, if an emergency should come up that required them to leave. The four engines were arrayed around the outside of the rocket, and the rest of the inside was configured as their temporary home. A ladder could be lowered from the center of the rocket's bottom for access to the home. Four different colored light beacons were blinking from the top of each rocket.

The three made their way toward the rocket with the red light, the common rooms with the kitchen and shared areas where all six could meet. This conference room and spa also had all the major communications equipment.

Scott couldn't resist showing off by running with large leaps in the low gravity. Bill and Linda, hand in hand, went at a more leisurely pace.

When they got to the habitat, Scott released the lever for the ladder and climbed up to release the latch to the hatch that allowed them to enter the air isolation chamber. This chamber was large enough to hold all three of them at once and was there to allow them to go from Mars air to Earth air sealed inside the habitat.

Once all of the Mars air was purged from the chamber, breathable air was pumped in. When the indicator turned green, they could remove their helmets and enter the habitat proper.

The power was already on and the internal temperature set to seventy degrees Fahrenheit. After removing their spacesuits and storing them in the receptacles that restored the air they had used, the first thing that Scott did was fire up the radio and call Niels.

"We are in the habitat, and everything is normal, just the way we expected it from our training. We will examine the rest of the habitats next and report when finished."

"Okay, we are ready up here to join you as soon as you give the word," replied Niels.

Scott went to the green beacon light, and Bill and Linda went to the blue light.

Bill lowered the ladder, and he and Linda entered the airlock to their new home. The home was similar in size to the quarters in *Mayflower II* and had the same rooms. The home needed personalization, but Linda was pleasantly surprised. Later, Bill and Scott would use the crawler and its long arm to remove the panels over the windows from the outside.

As Linda was looking around, Bill came back from the

kitchen area with a bottle of wine.

"I asked the team on Earth to leave this for us so that we could celebrate our landing and new home." Bill opened the wine and poured them both a glass. "Pouring in one-third gravity will take some getting used to, but look how the wine comes out more slowly, and it seems thicker."

"I'm sure that there will be many things that we will have to get used to. Here's to our successful landing and to our new home." They clinked glasses.

Bill called Scott and Niels and reported, "All is well here, and Linda and I are going to bed. See you tomorrow."

It wasn't long after that that Linda lay in Bill's arms, crying.

"What's wrong?"

"It's so isolated and far from home. Earth, I mean. I hope Ronda and Nancy get here soon. I'm sorry, Bill," sobbed Linda. "It's just my hormones out of whack. Quite normal for a pregnant woman. I think reality has just set in. No matter how much training we had or how much they told us what to expect, it's quite a shock to come to terms with. We are going to be here for the rest of our lives. Our baby will be born here and won't experience the beauty of Earth." She quietly sobbed again.

"I know how you feel. I am also intimidated by what we have to do here. I am very proud of you. You are very brave, and I love you very much."

In spite of her fears, Linda slept quite well. She was almost back to her cheerful self the next morning and ready for assignments.

Chapter 80

"Hello, Scott," said Bill the next morning. "I thought that we should check out the phone system. Sounds like it is working normally." They had a cell system; cellphones worked within the total system so that they could call a habitat phone from their cell or vice versa.

"I will meet you and Linda at the conference room in twenty minutes. We can have breakfast together and then call Niels. I'll have coffee ready when you get there," said Scott.

After a lighthearted breakfast, they radioed *Mayflower II*. "We have checked out the other habitat, and everything looks okay. The power is on, and the airlock works normally. I think we are ready for you three to fly down and join us. Let us know when you leave *Mayflower II*, and maintain communications as you fall to Mars," said Scott.

"Confirm," said Niels. "You know that we will lose communication as we go through the upper atmosphere, but after the drogue chute deploys we should be able to reestablish communications."

"Good luck, and safe flight," said Linda.

♐

The *Mayflower II* was shut down to the minimum operational requirements needed, and Ronda, Nancy, and Niels were in the second capsule. Niels opened the hatch and let the capsule drop down for its trip to Mars.

When Niels fired the retro rockets to slow them down, he was not aware that the rocket took an extra three seconds to shut down. They were off course from the beginning. The fall into the atmosphere went uneventfully, if you called a fire-glowing hull and severe buffeting, uneventful. When the drogue parachute opened and slowed them down, Niels called Scott and Bill to report all was well. The main chute opened at the right altitude, and they could hear the three airbags inflate with a bang. Niels thought it didn't sound right, but he wasn't sure. The main chute was released, and the capsule fell to the surface of Mars with a large jolt, pitching forward on to its nose and plowing into the Mars dirt. Niels was sitting in the forward seat, with Ronda and Nancy on either side and above him. They were strapped in tight, but Niels had loosened his upper strap to more easily reach some of the controls. When they hit and were thrown forward, Niels was thrown into his straps and his head flopped forward into the inside of his helmet, striking his temple and knocking him out. When they came to a stop, the capsule was on its side, the hatch buried in the ground. They could not see out, and they could not get out. Nancy and Ronda were hanging from their seat harnesses.

Nancy was the first one to catch her breath and recover from the shock of the severe impact. She said over the intercom, "Is everyone all right? Niels? Ronda?"

"I'm okay," said Ronda. Then there was silence. "It looks like Niels is in trouble. I will have to remove my helmet before I can check him."

"The air is okay, and we do not have a breach," said Nancy after they both had released their seat harnesses and fallen down to the bottom of the capsule.

"He is out cold," said Ronda as she looked over Niels' still body. "It looks like he has suffered a concussion. I don't think it's serious, but it is hard to know."

Nancy got on the radio. "Nancy to Bill, come in. Hello?

Come in, Bill or Scott. We are down. We crash-landed, and the capsule is on its side. We cannot get out. Niels is unconscious. You must find us and rescue us," she said as she called for the fourth time.

"Give it up. I think our antenna broke off. They may be hearing us, but we will not be able to hear them with the antenna broken," said Ronda. "I'm sure that JPL was tracking us down and they will tell Bill and Scott where we are."

♑

Back in the habitat, Bill called one more time, trying to establish communication with Niels to no avail.

"Scott, get on to JPL and see if they tracked them, and if so what their location and condition is. Maybe they can see them with the global geology satellite. I know it will take twenty minutes for our request to get to Earth and twenty minutes for their answer to get back to us, but I don't know what else to do."

One hour later, they got an answer from JPL.

"We had to reposition the GGS, but we have found them. They are lying on their side but otherwise seem to be intact. Two of the airbags are still inflated, and the one on the bottom is deflated. That imbalance is probably what sent them into a nosedive. They are about one hundred miles from you at these coordinates. It looks like you are going to have to go to them. We do not think they can get out or see out, as the capsule is lying on the hatch.

"Here is what we recommend—the crawler can go about seventy-five miles on one charge, so you will have to rig one of the greenhouse solar panels to recharge on the way. The crawler arm is strong enough to lift the capsule upright after you deflate the other two airbags. The capsule is over the horizon, so you will not be able to see it. You will have to trust the navigation system on the crawler, and we will be able to track your progress. We recommend that you take rescue rockets with you, the ones that explode and give off light. The others may be able to hear them and it will let them know you are coming. Get to work, and good luck."

Bill, Linda, and Scott immediately went to work. Bill got the crawler out, and Scott and Linda went to the nearest greenhouse and started removing a solar panel from its ground platform. When Bill got there, he used the long crawler arm to lift the array into place on the back of the vehicle. Scott scrambled up to the array and secured it with cable and clamps while Bill rewired it into the battery system. All was set and ready to go.

"I will keep in radio contact and let you know my progress," said Bill.

"You're not going," said Scott. "I am. That is my wife out there, I know how to operate this thing, and the navigation system is automatic. I'm going, and that is final."

"Scott, you are the senior officer here, and I respect your need to go to your wife. Linda has put food and water in the crawler. Good luck. Bring them back to us."

It was awkward to hug with spacesuits on, but Linda tried anyway. Scott climbed into the crawler and set off across the desolate plain of an old seabed on Mars.

The crawler was aptly named; at max speed, it went ten miles per hour. Scott programmed the coordinates that JPL had given them and let the computer steer the crawler to its destination. The path was strewn with small rocks, but the crawler's suspension absorbed the bumps and the ride was reasonably smooth. After seven hours, Scott had to stop for five hours to recharge the crawler batteries with the rewired solar panels. He ate, and then he put on his helmet and went outside. He figured that he was about seventy miles into the trip, so he hoped that a loud explosion would be heard in the capsule. He aimed the flare gun in the general direction of the capsule and fired; a loud bang and flash, and that was all. He could barely hear it himself. The thin air of Mars did not carry sound very well. He went back inside, set the alarm, and went to sleep.

♒

Back in the capsule, Nancy and Ronda had gotten Niels into a more comfortable position and removed his helmet. Ronda used a small flashlight from her medical bag to check Niels' eyes. "No change. There is nothing to do but wait until his body says it is time to wake up."

Nancy said, "I figure that it will take somewhere from ten to twenty hours for them to get to us. I don't think we were very far off course. If Niels was awake, he could shoot the stars or whatever they do to find out where we are, but even that would be impossible to do because we can't see out. We have plenty of food and water, so we just have to keep our spirts up and have faith that they will come."

Just then, Niels started to move and wake up. "Oooh, my head. What happened? Where are we?" he moaned.

Nancy immediately went to him and started kissing him awake.

"What is happening? Am I being kissed by an angel?" said Niels. He tried to sit up and then slipped back down.

"Take it easy, Niels," said Ronda, quickly checking him over again. "We crash-landed. You banged your head and have been out for five minutes. We are okay, and the capsule is okay, but we are lying on our side and the hatch is beneath us. The antenna is broken, so we cannot communicate with Scott and Bill. Can you tell us what happened and where we are?"

"Water and a snack, and then I will clear my head and get to work. Do you have any aspirin in that magic bag of yours?" asked Niels.

"Here, but I want you to take it easy. No sudden movements and tell me if you feel nauseous," cautioned Ronda.

An hour later, after working hard on the onboard computer, Niels said, "Here's what happened. We had two problems. The first was a burn that lasted for three seconds too long, putting us about a hundred miles off course. The second was more serious. When the airbags inflated, only two of the three inflated properly, so when we dropped, we bounced forward and pitched nose first into the ground. Then, to make matters worse, the two bags that did inflate properly did not deflate, keeping us in this position. The antenna is broken or detached, and we have no ability to communicate unless we can get out and reattach the antenna."

"Do you think Bill and Scott can find us and come to our rescue?" asked Nancy.

"I'm sure that JPL can find us and that Bill or Scott can bring the crawler here and take us back to Helium. The crawler can hold four people, so we should all be able to go back together. The problem is that because of communication delays and the fact that the crawler can only go ten miles per hour, we may be in for a long wait. I suggest that two of us sleep for four hours and then the other person sleep for four hours. Get comfortable, have some water and food, and go to sleep while I wait for Scott and Bill."

♓

Scott was getting worried; he was getting close to where JPL said he should find the second capsule, but he still had not seen it.

When he was five miles away, he stopped and got out on top of the crawler. He thought he could see a small, metallic glimmer in the distance; he got out the flare gun and fired again before getting back in and continuing.

Niels was jolted awake by the bang, and Nancy and Ronda both grinned in relief.

"They will be here soon. Let's have something to eat and get ready for company," said Niels.

On the crawler, Scott radioed back to Helium. "Have them in sight. I am about two miles away. They are on their side, and the capsule looks intact. I'll call you when I know more."

The first thing Scott did when he got there was to take a wrench and tap on the hull of the capsule. He got an immediate response. He then examined the ship and found the antenna bent back and the electrical wire broken off. He bent the antenna back and reattached the electrical wire. Transmitting from his suit radio he said, "Ronda, are you there? Can you hear me?"

"Scott, is that you? Thank God that you have found us! We weren't sure that you could. We are all okay, but I can't wait to get out of this tin can. Pry us open as quick as you can," she responded.

"Niels, status please," asked Scott.

"All systems go, no problems to report. What is your plan?"

"First, I am going to report to Bill. JPL is listening to my transmission, so they also will be informed. Then I am going to try to use the crawler arm to right the capsule to its normal position. Do you see any problem with that plan?"

"No, but do it slowly and keep your ears open in case something comes up. We will have our suits and helmets on as a precaution."

After reporting in to Bill, Scott connected the crawler arm to the top of the capsule and returned to the cabin to control the arm manually. He slowly raised the arm, and its cargo, a small amount and then returned to the capsule. "I am going to deflate the two airbags, so hold on. This could bounce you around a bit."

Scott then took his knife and punctured both airbags, slowly letting out the air. The capsule settled back slowly while the crawler arm steadied it. He then returned to the crawler and raised the capsule to its upright position.

"Okay, let me recheck all of the diagnostics," said Niels. "All looks good here. What next?"

"Well, you can choose. You can ride the capsule back to Helium swinging and swaying, or you can come inside with me and ride in comfort."

"What do you think, ladies?" asked Niels.

"It is up to you. Do you feel up to transferring from the capsule to the crawler? You are the one who had the bang on the head," said Ronda.

"I say we transfer and do it now. It's a long trip to Helium," said Niels.

Ronda entered the crawler last, and when she took off her helmet, she gave Scott a big kiss. "That was from all of us for saving our asses from the cold, dark reaches of a remote planet."

The trip back to Helium was uneventful but much more enjoyable for Scott than the trip out. There was a big party when they got back, and Linda and Bill were ready with dinner and drinks.

Chapter 81

They all settled into the temporary habitats and quickly learned that it was a pain to have to put on and remove the environment suit every time they wanted to go from their habitat to the conference room, so they settled into a pattern of scheduled meetings and work excursions outside. Linda and Scott were the first work team, and their job was to climb up to the caves and precisely measure the length, width, height, depth, and curvature to the main cave. They used a laser range finder that measured and recorded automatically from the center of the cave. This data was transmitted to JPL so that they could start fabrication of the final inflatable dome for inside the cave.

The containers that were sent via the REOCs automatically crawled from the landing area to the designated storage area and were put into line in the order that they were supposed to be opened. Each container had a small electric motor driving the crawler tread wheels that was maneuvered under beacon control transmitted from the storage area. This motor control could also be controlled by the crew with handheld controllers. The first two containers held the parts for the motorized ramp that would carry containers from the ground up to the cave floor level. Niels, Nancy, and Bill were the team to unload these parts and assemble them in place.

Bill and Scott were assigned to climb up to the top of the cliff and throw down the wires connected to the large solar array before then connecting them into the master circuit panels that would be mounted in the cave.

Niels and Scott were assigned to climb up the slope of Crater Lake and connect the pumps that would pump water from Crater Lake to the distribution system. They also had to lay out and connect the distribution system with material from the third container.

All of this work was for basic infrastructure and took a long time; it was hard and challenging. The team met in the conference room first thing in the morning to have breakfast together and to lay out the work assignments for the day. No more than three at a time were to work outside, and the rest worked inside the conference room. They all met again in the evening to have dinner together and review that day's work. They sent a communication to JPL at that point of the day and reviewed any new communications received from JPL. They also watched movies and television that they received each day, and they were current with the news from Earth. They worked six days a week, and Nancy insisted that Sunday was a day of rest, contemplation, and fun.

After five months of hard work, they all agreed that Linda and Ronda would do no more work outside. Linda was eight and half months along, and Ronda wanted quick access to her when the time came. Ronda had converted one of the conference rooms into her medical office and stocked all of their medicine and equipment inside.

During one of their weekly medical reviews, Ronda asked Nancy, "How are you feeling? Your vital signs are good, and your blood work is good. You are six months into your pregnancy, so from now on you must reduce your activity. Let the boys work outside from now on. Linda and I will stay inside and prepare to deliver our precious cargos."

"Okay. Cooking, house cleaning, and having babies are what I have done all my married life, so no problem," said Nancy. Then she realized what Ronda had said. Surprised, she asked, "What do you mean? Are you having a baby too?"

"Well, I haven't told anyone but Scott yet, but we are about one month into having the first baby conceived on Mars. All three of us are pregnant. I will have to train you and Linda what to do when my time comes."

"Congratulation to both of you!" Nancy said, giving Ronda a big hug. "Can we tell the rest of the team tonight and have a small celebration?"

"Sounds like a plan. Let's tell Linda now and put something special together for tonight."

That night, they had a fine meal and drinks. They called Ivan and the boys to tell them the good news and ask them to pass it on to everyone involved in the project.

Chapter 82

Two weeks later, Linda went into labor. Bill had to come running from Crater Lake and arrived just in time to be with Linda. Lower Mars gravity did not help; there was a lot of screaming and handholding, but the birth went smoothly. Bill held a beautiful baby girl in his arms while Ronda and Nancy took care of Linda. When the baby started crying, Bill did not know what to do. He handed the baby back to Linda; she became quiet, and Linda smiled in pride and satisfaction, happy that it was all over and the baby was fine.

Later, when they were alone, Bill asked, "Have you thought of a name for our baby girl?"

"Have you noticed yet that she has an aura around her like Ivan? I thought we could name her Aura Joy Lee. What do you think?"

"That's beautiful, and my sister will be proud to have our baby named after her. I love it."

Nancy planned a special communication to Earth. She had asked Penny earlier to patch them into a live feed so they could explain the importance of this event. She also asked Penny to let all of the affiliates know about the schedule for the live feed for that week's program.

Nancy had Niels and Scott set up the camera in the cave facing out so that the two moons of Mars would show in the background. They all put on their spacesuits and helmets and went to the cave for the transmission. They left Aura in her crib, asleep for this part of the presentation. This part of the program would be recorded by Penny and combined with the live part to be sent later.

Nancy was the spokesman for the team. When all were in position, she began.

"We are talking to you from the cave where the city of Helium will soon emerge. In the background, you can see the two moons of Mars. Everything here is strange and alien to what we're used to on Earth. We have had to adjust our normal lives to accommodate the different environment here, but we are now comfortable and safe. We are learning how to enjoy this strange place. We want you to feel that you can come here and make a home for you and your future generations. This is a new frontier and needs to be settled. We will now go into our temporary habitat so you can see how we live, and also to see our surprise for you."

They moved inside and set up the camera so that all of them could be in the picture at one time. They all had on their blue outersuits with the logo of the Federation of Mars showing.

"There is hope for the future of the human race outside the confines of Earth," said Nancy, and she held up a naked baby Aura up above her head. "I present to you the first human conceived in space, Aura Joy Lee. She represents the future of the human race. God has blessed us with the first child of the stars."

Niels then turned out the lights, and the whole world could see baby Aura glow a very light blue.

Ronda caressed her belly and wondered what the first baby conceived on Mars would be like.

Epilogue

Back on Earth, Ivan and Penny were sitting on their couch. Penny had baby Julia in her arms, and Ivan had little Joey on his lap as they watched the telecast from Mars. When baby Aura was presented, little Joey reached out his hand, pointing his finger to the screen. His hand and finger radiated a light blue, with the blue aura streaking out toward the screen.

"It seems that little Joey wants to meet and play with baby Aura."

Both Penny and Ivan smiled happily, looking forward to being able to bring this special family together forever.

CPSIA information can be obtained at www.ICGtesting.com
Printed in the USA
LVOW10s1352080616

491755LV00016B/143/P

9 781945 058516